"If you carry a wand, you'll look like someone impersonating a fairy godmother. Is that what you want?"

"Don't be ridiculous."

"I'm only trying to find out what you really want for our anniversary."

"All I wanted was a wand, and I'm obviously not going to get it from you, so let's just drop the whole thing."

Kedrigern remained silent, pondering the matter. "My dear, if your heart is set on a magic wand, you shall have one. I can't promise to have it by our anniversary—it may take time."

"Of course. I understand."

"I'll have to do some hard bargaining. And I'll have to . . ." In the dark room, the noise of his swallowing was clearly audible, as was the faint gasp of pain as between clenched teeth he uttered the hated word ". . . travel."

AND SO CONTINUE THE MULTIPLE MISHAPS OF
KEDRIGERN . . .

"A pleasant, leisurely . . . series of enchantments and adventures."

—*Publishers Weekly*

JOHN MORRESSY
KEDRIGERN IN WANDERLAND

ACE BOOKS, NEW YORK

This book is an Ace
original edition, and has
never been previously published.

KEDRIGERN IN WANDERLAND

An Ace Book/published by arrangement with
the author

PRINTING HISTORY
Ace edition/August 1988

ISBN: 0-441-43264-6

Ace Books are published by The Berkley Publishing Group,
200 Madison Avenue, New York, N.Y. 10016.
The name ''Ace'' and the ''A'' logo are trademarks
belonging to Charter Communications, Inc.
PRINTED IN THE UNITED STATES OF AMERICA

10 9 8 7 6 5 4 3 2 1

For Barbara,
on behalf of all those grateful chinchillas
whose lives she has spared

"If we do not find anything pleasant, at least we shall find something new."

—VOLTAIRE

⸱⸱⸱❧ One ❧⸱⸱⸱

the road to dendorric

THE TRUE BEGINNING of the story is Hamarak's finding of the enchanted sword, the great dark blade Panstygia, Mother of Darkness, formerly known as Louise. One could, if one wished, go back to the original curse of Vorvas the Vindictive, and the long immurement within a living oak tree; but that is really background information, easily and briefly provided at the proper time.

One might also open with the conversation between Kedrigern, the wizard of Silent Thunder Mountain, and his wife Princess, on that evening in the autumn of the year following their fateful, and successful, quest for Arlebar and The Magic Fly, as they sat by their hearth, she adapting her wardrobe to allow free use of her newly acquired wings and he perusing the rare volumes bequeathed to them by Arlebar. But while the princess and the wizard are the primary figures in this story, they are second in point of time. It starts with Hamarak.

Hamarak's great strength had always been his great strength. His earliest memories were of being able to work harder and longer than all those around him. He had never been without work for more than a few days. It was usually hard, dirty work, to be sure, but it was work. He seldom lacked food and shelter, and usually had a coin or two in his purse, which he invariably spent on warm fresh bread. This was his only self-indulgence.

Hamarak was very big, very broad, and very strong, but he had a mild disposition and a quiet manner. He was neither clever nor stupid; given time, he could think his way through a knotty problem, but he preferred to leave such exercise to those who enjoyed it; he did not. He had ordinary features, serviceable without being particularly decorative, grotesque, or comical: a broad flat nose, a wise mouth more inclined to remain closed in a placid smile than to open in unnecessary speech, brown eyes that were usually focused on nothing in particular. His hair was thick and black, his hands callused, his skin browned by the sun. In all respects save size and strength, Hamarak was a perfectly ordinary man, and he expected to lead a perfectly ordinary life; in truth, he fervently desired it. His life so far, all twenty-some-odd years of it, had been an uneventful round of eat, work, eat, work some more, eat, sleep, and an occasional binge on fresh-baked bread, and he was content to go on that way.

But one bright autumn day, as he was felling trees on a patch of land newly acquired by his current master, Hamarak heard a voice. It was a woman's voice, sweet and sad, and it carried a hint of ringing metal in its resonance. At first the words were not clear, merely a muffled incantatory murmur from among the trees; but as he walked on, Hamarak heard the message in a voice soft and mournful, and now distinct:

> "Woodsman, woodsman, set me free
> From my prison in the tree!
> Free the princess in the blade,
> And your deed shall be repaid!"

Hamarak stopped in his tracks and looked about sharply. This had to be a trick. There was a kitchen wench in his master's service, a pretty little thing she was, too, but with a cruel way of mocking a man, and this was just the sort of prank she'd play on him, drawing him off into the woods with fairy voices and promises of reward. He would have none of it.

The voice called to him again. It seemed to come from an oak tree that stood alone in a little clearing, a venerable old giant, split at the fork and mortally cleft halfway to the ground, but still in full leaf. That was unusual. Hamarak came closer, and heard the voice yet again. It came unmistakably from inside the tree. This was not a trick, it was magic, and magic was worse than a kitchen wench's pranks, far worse.

> "Kindly woodsman, can it be
> You have come to set me free?"

Mournfulness had given way to hope, and that hopeful voice was addressed to Hamarak. It had to be. There were no other woodsmen near. Though he was much bewildered and a little frightened, Hamarak felt compelled to reply.

"Is someone in there?"

He waited, feeling foolish. The reply, when it came, was in a clear and exultant voice that rang like a hammer on an anvil.

> "Woodsman, fell this riven oak
> With the power of your stroke!
> Free the princess in the sword
> And enjoy a rich reward!"

Hamarak did not fully understand what was going on, but certain facts were clear: someone inside the tree wanted to get out, and he had a good sharp axe in his hands and knew how to use it. How the person had gotten in there at all was beyond him; perhaps slipped down that deep cleft; but the voice had mentioned a princess, and Hamarak had never heard of a princess climbing a tree. Of course, his knowledge of princesses and their ways was limited to hearsay. It might well be that princesses were always getting stuck in trees, and there was nothing out of the ordinary in all this, and nothing magical about it. All the same, he would have to be careful, and make sure he cut down only the tree and not its royal occupant.

"If I chop down the tree, won't I hurt you?" he asked.

"Strike away, and have no dread—
   I am high above your head.
Let the chips fall where they may,
      Only set me free today!" the voice cried eagerly.

That was clear enough, and there was no point in delaying. Hamarak stripped off his leather jerkin, spat on his palms, rubbed them together in a slow, businesslike gesture, and took up his axe. He paused after each of the first few strokes to listen for a cry of pain or warning, but none came, and he set to work in earnest. He saw that he need chop only halfway through the trunk in order to effect his rescue, since the weight of the undercut portion would split the tree at the cleft and bring it down, enabling anyone inside to escape. He worked quickly, with a smooth regular motion, and the results were exactly as he had hoped. With a cracking, rending, squealing rush, the oak split to the mark of his axe, and half the trunk went crashing to the ground.

When all was still, Hamarak stepped forward, puzzled. He had seen no one emerge. He heard a shivering metallic sigh of relief, and looked around wildly for the source. There, on the pale surface of the fallen trunk, lay a naked blade of deep velvety black. The pommel of the hilt was the finely sculpted head of a woman, and as Hamarak stared in awe, it spoke.

"Thank heaven!" it exclaimed. "Oh, what a relief to be out of that dreadful tree, and not to have to speak in rhyme anymore!"

"Was it you . . . in there?" Hamarak asked.

"It was. You must be the woodsman who chopped it down. Thank you ever so much, young man. It was decent of you. Do you have an upper garment of some kind?"

"My jerkin."

"Then put it on, please. I'm not accustomed to the sight of half-naked woodsmen. I am a princess."

Hamarak frowned. This was getting more confusing. "You're a sword," he said uneasily.

"Put your jerkin on, and I'll explain. Go on, there's a

good fellow," said the sword. Its manner was so self-assured, its voice so coolly commanding, that Hamarak obeyed without further delay. When his jerkin was laced, he presented himself before the sword, which said, "That's much better. Now, before I proceed, I must ask you a very important question: do you wish to be the greatest swordsman in all the world?"

Hamarak weighed the question for a time. "Do I have another choice?"

"Don't be difficult. Just answer the question. I'll repeat it: do you wish to be the greatest swordsman in all the world?"

"No," said Hamarak.

"Oh, good. That's really very good, young man. I can't tell you how pleased I am to hear it."

"There are other things I'd like, though," Hamarak said hopefully, recalling an earlier mention of reward.

"Yes, I'm sure there are. Now, tell me this: is there a decent sorcerer nearby, or a wizard? Any kind of enchanter will do."

Hamarak scratched his head slowly and thoughtfully. "Not around here. There used to be a witch in the cave up on the mountain, but she died."

"How stupid of her. Where is the nearest sorcerer?"

"I heard a man say that there's a wizard in Dendorric. That's somewhere off to the east, a long long way from here."

"Then we must leave at once. Take me up, and let us be on our way."

"But I don't know the way to Dendorric! I don't have any money, or food, and my boots are worn. I have work to do right here—there are trees to be cleared, and my master will be angry if I don't get them down. I can't just leave!" Hamarak protested.

"Now, listen to me. What *is* your name? You haven't told me," said the sword impatiently.

"I'm Hamarak."

"Listen very carefully, Hamarak. At present I am

Panstygia, the great black blade of the west. But I have not always been a sword, and I do not intend to remain a sword any longer than is absolutely necessary. Do you follow me so far?''

"I think so. You're a sword, but you're not really a sword. You're really a princess.''

"Very good, Hamarak. I am Princess Louise, of the Kingdom of the Singing Forest. For reasons I do not choose to go into at this time, I have been transformed into a sword by a wicked sorcerer. Only a sorcerer of equal power, but less wickedness, can undo the vile enchantment that binds me in this form. Whoever assists me in finding that sorcerer will be richly rewarded.''

"Isn't there any reward for just getting you out of the tree?'' Hamarak asked wistfully.

"Don't be selfish, Hamarak. If you're not prepared to make some sacrifices, you might as well have left me in the tree. You're involved now, and you must carry on to the end. Tell me, what is the name of this wizard in Dendorric?''

"The man called him Mergith.''

"Mergith . . . ,'' Panstygia repeated thoughtfully. "Never heard of the fellow. Well, he'll just have to do. Let us away, Hamarak.''

"Will I be rewarded if I take you to Mergith?''

"Handsomely. You need only name your reward, and my brother and sister and I will confer it with pleasure.''

Hamarak reached out his hand for the blade, but hesitated and then drew it back. "What about your brother and sister? Do I have to get them out of trees, too?'' he asked.

"They're no concern of yours, Hamarak. Get me to Mergith, and you'll have your reward.''

For the first time in his life, Hamarak saw the chance to have everything he longed for. He imagined warm fresh bread with butter melting into it; his own farm, and a house, and a sturdy wife who would bake every day, and two fine oxen, and new boots: in short, all that a man could wish for in this world. Even a new plow. He reached out and took up the black sword.

"Well done, Hamarak!" said Panstygia heartily.

"What do I do now?"

"Head east, and keep asking the way to Dendorric. Nothing to it. There's one thing—a man walking with an unsheathed sword is liable to generate undue excitement, so I'd better disguise myself while we're traveling. When you need me, I'll become a sword again."

"It doesn't matter. I'm not a swordsman."

"You will be, Hamarak. Trust me. Now—to Dendorric!"

That very afternoon, Hamarak was able to trade his axe for a much-mended but still serviceable cloak and enough money to buy ten days' food. He learned, to his chagrin, that Dendorric was at least twenty days' walk from this land, if the weather remained dry and the bridges were open. Under adverse conditions, it might require months of slogging. In either case, there was no certainty that a traveler would reach his goal. The way led through a forest said to be teeming with wild beasts and cruel brigands, where false trails misled the unwary and danger lurked at every turn of the path. Dendorric itself—if he ever reached it—was described as a cold and inhospitable city whose ruler was a man to be avoided. Hamarak took in all this information, drew his cloak around him, and trudged on.

He occupied his mind along the way in his customary fashion. He observed the shadows, and the colors of the autumn foliage, and when he could see them through the leafy canopy, the shapes of the clouds overhead. He listened for birdsong and watched for the spoor of small animals. From time to time he thought of fresh bread.

Contemplation had never been a significant activity in Hamarak's life. On the few occasions he had attempted it, the effort left him confused and upset. He was dimly aware that if he allowed himself to think for any extended period about what he was now doing, he would become more confused and upset than ever. So he confined his mental activities to the immediate vicinity and the best possible future.

The days passed, wearying and mostly uneventful. Hamarak exchanged few words with Panstygia along the way, despite his desire to know more of her story. She had disguised herself as a staff, in which form she could not speak, and when he summoned her, she always expected to be told they had arrived, and was cross and somewhat surly. She gave Hamarak repeated, but vague, assurances of success and promises of reward, but revealed very little about herself. Her manner made him feel stupid and inadequate. This was becoming a frustrating business.

Hamarak managed to make his funds last for an extra day. And then, when his last coin had been spent and his scrip was empty, he came upon a merchant, the merchant's daughter, and one elderly servant seated by the roadside, jellied with terror. One of the merchant's wagons had overturned, and he was frantic to right it and be out of the woods before dark, for fear of robbers. His other servants had already fled, and the merchant himself was torn between the urge to save himself and his daughter, and the desire to preserve his property.

At first sight of Hamarak the servant fainted, the daughter shrieked, and the merchant prostrated himself on the ground, blubbering. It took some time for Hamarak to reassure them, but when he had finished unloading the wagon, righted it, repaired the damage to the canopy, and then reloaded the goods, completing the task by midafternoon, they accepted him as a friend and benefactor and asked him to accompany them.

"Are you going to Dendorric?" he asked.

"Not while Mergith is in power," the merchant replied. "But our way will take us within two days' walk of Dendorric. Come with us. We'll all be safer, and you'll be spared much walking."

"Do you have food?"

"My good man, you will be our honored guest. But

let's leave this place before dark, or the brigands will surely find us.''

The stopped for the night at a small, very dirty inn. Hamarak wisely slept in one of the wagons; the others took accommodations at the inn, and found their beds teeming with hungry life. For the next few days they were too preoccupied with scratching themselves to take any interest in him.

For six days, Hamarak listened to the merchant lament the state of his business, the daughter recount in minute detail the plans for her forthcoming wedding, and the aged servant complain of her flea bites, her teeth, her feet, and her wind, and all three go on about the forest robbers. According to these three, ferocious brigands, formidably armed, hid behind or in every tree, under every bush, and within every shadow; but Hamarak saw no trace of them or their handiwork. The woods were peaceful and still, the track was clear, and they made good time. But on the seventh day the brigands made their appearance.

Hamarak was walking beside the lead wagon, wondering how many bakers he would find in Dendorric, and what kinds of bread they baked, and how golden the butter was, and whether anyone in the city made strawberry-rhubarb jam, when the black staff in his hand gave a little shake. He snapped out of his musings and looked around. Behind the second wagon he saw three armed men stealing up on them. One bore a sword; the other two carried short spears. As Hamarak started forward to warn the merchant, the first wagon came to an abrupt halt and the merchant's daughter gave a shrill scream. At a crossing in the trail, two men barred their way with drawn swords.

Hamarak stepped before the horses. In a slow, earnest voice, he said, ''Please let us pass. The lady is on the way to her wedding, and I must be in Dendorric soon.''

The brigands looked him over. He was bigger than either of them, but the dust of the road lay thick on his cloak and boots, and he carried no weapon, only a heavy staff of dark wood. They did not speak, but leveled their swordpoints at his chest.

"We can give you some money, if that's what you want. Just let us pass," Hamarak said, with no trace of alarm in his voice despite the unnerving noises coming from the merchant and his daughter.

The two robbers exchanged a swift glance. One gave a low snort of laughter with no humor in it.

In the same slow even voice, Hamarak said, "I don't want to fight anybody. I just want to get to Dendorric."

This time the swordsman laughed aloud in a very unpleasant way. He gave a quick nod to his companion and they took a step toward the traveler. The merchant's daughter shrieked. The merchant howled a prayer.

The air rang with a sudden metallic *shingg*, and Hamarak's staff was a staff no longer. He held a black, black sword, so intensely black that no light reflected from it except where the midday sun glinted off the edge of the blade.

The robbers hesitated for an instant, and in that instant Hamarak was upon them like a hurricane sweeping a field of reeds. A single blow shattered the swords of the men before him, and then he turned to face the other attackers. A second blow, with the flat of the blade, laid out the other swordsman; a third splintered the spears of his last assailants.

One man lay supine, a great purple lump rising on his temple. The others stood wringing their hands and gasping in pain from the shock of the traveler's blows. Hamarak stepped to the side of the path, where he could keep all five in view, and raised the black sword. A woman's voice filled the air; it was cold with anger and dreadful to hear.

"You have known the wrath of Panstygia, Mother of Darkness. She has chosen to be merciful. She will not be so merciful again," said the voice of the blade.

The brigands who were conscious whimpered in terror. The fifth stirred and moaned faintly.

"In return for my mercy, answer me truthfully. Who rules in Dendorric?" the blade demanded.

"Mergith, the wizard-king, rules there," one of the thieves blurted, and another nodded vigorously to second his comrade's answer.

"Describe this Mergith."

"I've never seen him. Few people have, Mother of Darkness. I know nothing of his appearance, I swear it!" the man said, falling to his knees. "I'm a banished outlaw—I know nothing of Dendorric or its affairs!"

"I've heard it said that his skin is made of brass, and no weapon can pierce it!" cried one of his companions.

"A woman told me that Mergith has nine fingers on each hand, and iron talons on each finger! His eyes shoot forth flame when he's angry!" the third added.

The fourth robber, trembling, said, "And he has eyes before and behind! And on both sides! A dozen eyes, at least. Maybe more. Maybe hundreds!"

"I never heard such nonsense," said the blade crossly. "A fine lot of brigands you are, babbling like children after a mild thrashing."

"People say such things in Dendorric, Mother of Darkness, I swear they do!" the first brigand howled, groveling.

"Then the people of Dendorric are as silly as you are, and I intend to have as little as possible to do with them," Panstygia said. The other three were groveling by now, and the last brigand had sat up and was holding his head, groaning. "Oh, get away from here, all of you! Get out of my sight!" snapped the blade in exasperation.

As the brigands scurried off, two of them supporting their groggy comrade, Hamarak asked, "Was I all right?"

"You did very nicely, Hamarak. I was quite pleased," the blade replied.

"I'm glad I didn't have to hurt anyone badly."

"I've told you several times that I do what I can to avoid unpleasantness. Don't you trust me?"

"I do trust you, Mother. It's just that—"

"Don't address me as 'Mother,' " the blade broke in angrily. "Step over behind those trees, please. I don't want to carry on a private conversation within the hearing of a merchant and his household.''

When they were well out of earshot of the wagons, Hamarak said, ''Why can't I call you 'Mother'? You just called yourself 'Panstygia, Mother of Darkness.' ''

''I did, Hamarak. And that is precisely what I wish to be called in the future.''

''What's wrong with your own name? Louise is a nice name.''

''It's hardly a name for an enchanted sword. Really, Hamarak, you can be very obtuse.''

Hamarak did not answer for a time. At length he said slowly, ''You think I'm dumb.''

''I didn't say that.''

''You said I was something else, but you *meant* that I'm dumb. I could tell by the way that you said it.''

''Well, you're certainly not a wizard.''

''I never said I was. I'm a farmer. That's all I want to be, Mother. . . . No, Louise. Can't I call you Louise?''

With a sigh, the blade said, ''When there's no one else around, you may call me Louise. But in front of others, please address me as 'Panstygia, Mother of Darkness,' and try to sound respectful.''

''I will. I really want to help you.''

''I know you do, Hamarak, and I'm grateful.''

''But I'm no wizard. I'm no swordsman, either.''

''Now, Hamarak, I don't want to hear any more talk like that. Whoever wields me is the finest swordsman in the world. It's all part of the curse. Look how easily you defeated those brigands, and they were five against one.''

After a pause, to remember and ponder his victory, Hamarak said, ''I don't want to be the finest swordsman in the world. I want to be a farmer. I want to have my own land, and men working for me, and good oxen to plow and pull stumps . . . and a house with two chimneys.''

''You'll have all that, Hamarak. I promise,'' the sword said wearily.

''A new plow, too?''

"Yes, Hamarak. A lovely new one. And now I'm going to go back to being a staff, and you can rejoin your fellow travelers. We'll talk again when Dendorric is in sight."

"What will I tell them?"

"Under the circumstances, Hamarak, I should think you can tell them anything you please."

The air rang like a tapped silver bowl, and the black blade was once more a black staff. Hamarak checked his bearings and made his way back to the trail, only to find it empty. The merchant's wagons had turned aside at the crossroad. Dust still hung in the air from the speed of their flight.

Hamarak sat on a rock and took stock of the situation. If this was the merchant's planned turning point, then Dendorric was two days' walk from here. Without food or money, it would be an uncomfortable walk and a cheerless arrival, but the weather was fair, and there was plenty of fresh water along the way. There might be fruit trees, or wild berries. He idly scanned the ground, trying to raise his spirits, and gave a little grunt of pleased surprise at the sight of a purse lying near one of the fallen weapons. As he rose to take it up he noticed a scrip lying near it. The purse held a few coins, and the scrip contained nearly half a cooked hen and a fist-sized chunk of bread. Beaming, Hamarak returned to his seat on the rock and dined.

He rose when he was done, hefted the purse in his hand and smiled at the comfortable clink of copper and silver. Tucking the purse in his belt, he gripped his staff, turned his face to the east, and set off for Dendorric.

⋯⊰ Two ⊱⋯

simple gifts

THE LITTLE COTTAGE on Silent Thunder Mountain where dwelt the wizard Kedrigern and his wife Princess was a scene of domesticity at its coziest. A fire burned in the grate to ward off the chill of the autumn evening, and Princess and Kedrigern sat before it in comfortable chairs, each absorbed in the work at hand. The fire crackled; Princess hummed softly from time to time as she plied her needle; Kedrigern made occasional low noises of disapproval over a passage in the book on his lap. Save for the clatter of a dish or the rattle of cutlery from the kitchen, attesting to Spot's industry with the dinner dishes, all else was still.

"Well, that's the lot of them," said Princess, holding up a pale blue gown to inspect the two slits she had neatly hemmed in the back, between the shoulders. "And just in time, too."

Kedrigern grunted, but did not raise his eyes from the page.

"It should be wonderful flying weather, as long as the winds aren't too strong. I can't wait to be up again. In a little while I won't be able to do anything but circle the house." With a pleased little sigh, she gathered the garments that lay on either side of the chair and rose with them over her arm. "I think I'll try these on. I want to be sure the wing-slits are roomy enough. I won't be long."

Kedrigern nodded and made an almost inaudible sound of acknowledgement. Frowning, he turned a page of the huge folio volume.

"What are you reading? It can't be anything cheerful," Princess observed.

He looked up gloomily. "It's not. It's a chronicle I took from Arlebar's house."

"Oh, *chronicles*," said Princess with a dismissive flicker of her brows. "They're dreadful reading. All about battles and plagues and famines and horrors. Why don't you read a nice story about kings and queens and princes and princesses?"

"That's just what I'm reading, my dear: the history of Gurff the Strong and Alric the Sly, twin sons of Pollioc and Sming of the Land of the Jagged Mountains. It's very depressing."

"Why do you read depressing things?"

"One must keep up," said the wizard fatalistically. For the first time, he noticed the garments draped over Princess's arm. "Are you cleaning house?" he asked.

"I've just finished altering these. Now I'm going to try them on."

"Good idea. It should be wonderful flying weather as long as the winds aren't too strong."

"I was thinking the same thing."

"You must be impatient to be up and out. In a little while you won't be able to do anything but circle the house."

"My thoughts exactly. *And* my very words. And now, if you'll excuse me . . . ." Princess turned, and with a rapid flutter of her little wings, ascended a handsbreadth from the floor and flew gracefully from the room. Kedrigern returned his attention to the chronicle.

He read on for a time, shaking his head and muttering his disapproval of the goings-on in the Land of the Jagged Mountains, and before he had turned a second page, Princess was back. She stood before him in the pale blue gown she had just been working on. With a smile, she rose into the air and spun around, then landed lightly at his side.

"Lovely, my dear," he said appreciatively, taking her hand. "It's absolutely lovely. Blue is a marvelous color for you. Is that a new gown?"

"I've had it all along. I just wasn't attracted to blue . . . somehow, green always seemed the proper color to wear. Habit, I suppose."

"Well, you look very nice in green, too."

"That's fortunate, considering how long I was a toad."

"Now, now," said the wizard, squeezing her hand gently, "no need to think of that. It's all behind us. You are a spectacularly beautiful woman once again, and will remain so. And you even have those delightful little wings."

"It was a lot of work, altering my entire wardrobe to put in wing-slits, but worth it. Would you just check the fit of these, Keddie?"

He laid the folio aside and stood to inspect Princess's handiwork. The iridescent wings, nacreous and translucent, gossamer-thin yet firm to his cautious touch, jutted from twin slits set close together in the back of Princess's gown. They were shaped like oversized butterfly wings; their tops came to just below her shoulders, their bottoms barely reached to her waist. At the base they thickened slightly, but even there they were no thicker than a leaf. It astonished Kedrigern to see such delicate wings lift a full-grown woman and transport her safely and gracefully through the air at a good rate of speed for considerable distances. True, Princess was slender and slight of frame, and these were magical wings; but he was impressed all the same. And they were quite supple, too. On cool evenings, Princess wore them folded flat against her back; they had the effect of a shawl. This practice was also good for the wings, which had a tendency to become brittle when exposed overlong to cold. They required only a brief fluttering at bedtime and an occasional hop from room to room in order to remain in top condition.

"A perfect fit, my dear," Kedrigern announced. She turned, and he looked on her adoringly. She was in truth a beautiful woman, and the blue robe, which matched the color of her eyes, showed her gleaming black hair to great advantage. A silver circlet set with tiny diamonds ringed her brow. It glinted in the firelight to match the gleam of her wings.

And not only was she a lovely and clever woman, she could work a number of powerful spells and was assidously learning new ones. All in all, Kedrigern reflected, a wizard could not ask for a more perfect wife. He was indeed a most fortunate man.

His contentment must have been manifest in his expression, for Princess kissed him sweetly and said, "We have a lot to be grateful for, you and I."

"We certainly do. Just think—only last spring we were setting off in search of Arlebar."

"And the spring before that, I was still croaking like a toad."

"And the spring before *that*, we hadn't even met." Kedrigern shook his head thoughtfully at the wonder of it all. They settled into their chairs and sat in silent contemplation for a time, gazing into the sinking fire, and at last Princess asked, "Whatever became of that nice man who married us?"

"The hermit, Goode . . . as far as I know, my dear, he still lives in that wood which slopes down to the sea. Pleasant location for a hermit."

"Keddie, do you realize . . . ?"

"Yes, my dear?"

"On our next anniversary, we'll be married three years!"

He looked up sharply and said in a soft astonished voice, "Why, so we shall. Fancy that! Three whole years, and it seems like only the other day I stopped at the Dismal Bog and saw you sitting on a lily pad. . . ."

"I was weeping."

"So you were. Most piteously."

"But somehow, I knew you'd come. You were my only

hope. No one could have despelled me but Kedrigern of
Silent Thunder Mountain, master of counterspells.''

"I've always meant to ask you how you heard of me. I
know that word gets around, but it's hard to imagine
someone spreading my reputation in a bog. Not much
point to it.''

"I don't know how I knew. It might have been part of
the spell. I still can't remember things from . . . from
before.''

"I'm sorry, my dear. But your memory will come back,
I'm certain. Just a matter of time.''

"It's been well over two years since you despelled me!
And I have no idea how long I was in the Dismal Bog
before you found me.''

He nodded sympathetically. "I understand your feelings. Really, I do. I only wish I could give you back your
memories of your family as an anniversary present. I'd do
it in a minute, if only I had some kind of clue to go on.''

"There's no need to talk of presents. What could I
possibly want? I have practically everything a woman
could desire.''

"Sweet of you to say so,'' said the wizard. They exchanged affectionate smiles, and after a brief silence, he
went on, "As a matter of fact, though, it might not be
such a bad thing to know nothing of one's family history.''
She turned a curious glance on him, and he explained.
"Well, as you know, I was a foundling. It's obvious that
I'm of royal blood on one side and wizardry on the other,
but I haven't any names, or coats of arms, or family trees,
or anything of that sort, and frankly, I'm just as pleased to
have things as they are.''

"You may be, but I'm not. I can't understand you,
Keddie. If your mother was a queen, or your father was a
king, wouldn't you like to know about them?''

With a serious frown, Kedrigern shook his head. "My
dear, royal families can be . . . understand, I'm speaking
in the broadest generalities, and I'm sure *your* family
are models of regal deportment . . . but royal families can

be very unpleasant. Take this lot I've been reading about. Pollioc and Sming were a perfectly good king and queen until their twin sons grew up. Right pair of little stinkers those boys were, but parents never notice such things. He favored Gurff the Strong and she idolized Alric the Sly, and before you could say "Gorboduc" there were daggers flashing, and poison in everything, and a nice little kingdom was reduced to absolute chaos. Now, I don't for a moment think that your family—"

"I should certainly hope not," said Princess with hauteur. "Besides, I don't think there were any boys in the family. I seem to recall a sister, but no brothers."

"That's a good sign. You didn't remember anything like that before."

"Well, I can't recall names, or faces. I might even be remembering a fairy tale. Princesses always have sisters in fairy tales."

"True. But sisters can be difficult, too. I was reading about an old king of Albion . . . had three daughters, gave them everything, and they turned on him. Divided up his kingdom and kicked the old man out in a howling storm with only a fool and a lunatic for company. *There's* family sentiment for you."

"I remember that story. Wasn't there one daughter . . . Camellia, I think . . . no, Cornelia . . . who came back to see him and was nice to him?"

"Yes, the youngest one—Cordelia, that was her name— she came back, but she brought her husband's army with her. I suppose that's how members of that family always traveled. And the upshot of it was that everyone died. One sister poisoned the other and then stabbed herself, and one of their boyfriends had Cordelia killed, and it was all too much for the poor old father. Awful doings. And yet they're tame when you compare them to the goings-on at the court of Denmark. I wouldn't touch *that* lot with a ten-foot wand."

At his final word, Princess's expression brightened and she turned to her husband with a sudden eager expression;

but he was gazing dolefully into the fireplace. She settled back, smiling, and put her feet up on the fender, content to wait. After a time she said, "Keddie, I've been thinking. There *is* something you could give me for our anniversary."

"Delighted to hear it, my dear! What would you like—a nice warm set of knitted wing-covers?"

"No. I want a wand."

"A wand?"

"A magic wand, with a little star on the end. It would go so nicely with my wings, and it would help with spells."

Kedrigern was slow to respond. "Well, now, I wouldn't count on a wand to help with spelling. As a matter of fact, any spell that calls for a wand is probably complicating things unnecessarily. I feel very safe in saying that any spell anyone can work with a wand, I can work without one, and probably do a better job."

"Yes, but there's nothing *wrong* with magic wands, is there?"

Again, Kedrigern paused before responding, and the reluctance in his voice was unmistakable. "Nothing actually wrong, no. Not *wrong*. They're just useless. Not like knitted wing-covers."

"I don't want knitted wing-covers."

"They're useful if you have to fly in the winter."

"I want a *wand*. That's clear enough, isn't it?"

"Certainly, my dear. Very clear indeed. I just can't understand why any sensible person would want a wand. Silly things, wands. They leave you with only one hand for making magical gestures, or turning pages, or tracing figures in the air. And you've always got to be thinking about them; can't lay one aside for a few minutes, for fear that it might be stolen. Certainly don't want a magic wand falling into the wrong hand. More trouble than they're worth, wands are, if you want my opinion," said Kedrigern, sounding stuffier than Princess had ever heard him sound in their years together.

"You're certainly not very encouraging," she said.

"Just being frank, my dear. I can't see why you'd want to encumber yourself with a foolish thing like a wand. What do you need a wand for? You have wings."

The room was silent for a brief space, and then Princess turned to Kedrigern, and with a charming smile, said, "If I didn't know better, Keddie, I'd say you were jealous."

"Jealous? Me? Of what?" he replied, astonishment and injury mingled in his expression.

"Of my wings."

"Jealousy is the farthest thing from my mind. What do I want with wings?"

"They help you to fly," she explained.

"If I wish to fly, my dear, I'm perfectly capable of turning myself into a bird. I don't need wings. I'd look like a complete fool with a little pair of gauzy wings."

The smile vanished from Princess's face and her voice took on a distinct edge. "Oh, I see. I look like a fool."

"I didn't say you *do,* I said I *would.* Actually, the wings become you. You look like one of the larger fairies."

Her voice was glacial as she said, "Oh, thank you. I don't just look like a fool, I look like a *fat* fool. Thank you very much indeed."

"No, no, no, my dear! I said nothing of fat. You're not the least bit fat. You have a perfect figure. You're as slender as a . . . as a . . ."

"A wand?" she suggested.

"A willow. Slender as a willow," he said, his voice rising. "I was referring to the fact that while the shape and texture of your wings resemble those of the fairies, you are human-sized. Most fairies are not . . . unless they're attending a christening or a wedding, or are up to something nasty. In short, my dear, you are a beautiful woman with a splendid figure, but you are not smaller than an agate-stone on the forefinger of an alderman, nor could you ride in a chariot made of an empty hazelnut, wielding a whip of cricket's bone. You are not wee, nor are you tiny: you could not dance a jig on the nail of my little finger, nor could you take shelter from the rain under a mushroom."

"Well, no," said Princess grudgingly. "But what has all that to do with my wanting a wand?"

After a moment's thought, Kedrigern said, "If you carry a wand, you'll look like someone impersonating a fairy godmother. Is that what you want?"

"Don't be ridiculous."

"I'm only trying to find out what you really want for our anniversary."

"All I wanted was a wand, and I'm obviously not going to get it from you, so let's just drop the whole thing."

"Don't be angry, my dear."

"I'm not the least bit angry," said Princess in a cool, controlled voice. "I think we've said all these is to say on the subject. Let's discuss it no further, shall we?"

Kedrigern remained silent, pondering the matter. After a time, Princess said softly, as if thinking aloud, "I suppose I *would* look like someone trying to impersonate a fairy godmother. That wouldn't do at all." Again there was silence, and then she observed, "It really would be a nuisance. More trouble than it's worth, a wand is. I'm better off sticking to my spells and not encumbering myself."

Kedrigern's voice, when he spoke, was thoughtful. "They're very difficult to come by, wands are," he said.

"Oh, I'm sure they are. Practically impossible, I should think. No end of bother. And for what?" said Princess, with a little laugh of dismissal.

"There never were that many around in a proper size for you," Kedrigern went on. "I might be able to get one from the fairies, if I catch them in a generous mood on Midsummer's Night, but it would be about the size of a whisker. Not much good to you, I'm afraid."

"None at all. I don't know what I could have been thinking of. What would I do with a wand that I can't do by learning my spells?"

"Actually, a wand can be helpful in transformations and transmutations. Especially if you're close enough to touch the object of the spell."

"Really? Oh, but surely . . . no, it would be too much

trouble. You can't spare the time. I know how busy you are.''

A long silence followed. The room was dark now, as the fire had sunk and no candles were yet lit. Out of the darkness came Kedrigern's voice. ''Mind you, they're not impossible to find. Difficult, but not impossible.''

''Keddie, you don't mean . . . ?''

''My dear, if your heart is set on a magic wand, you shall have one. I can't promise to have it by our anniversary— it may take time.''

''Of course. I understand.''

''I'll have to do some hard bargaining. People who are fortunate enough to possess a magic wand don't just hand it over to anyone who asks for it, you know.''

''Oh, I'm sure they don't.''

''And I'll have to . . .'' In the dark room, the noise of his swallowing was clearly audible, as was the faint gasp of pain as between clenched teeth he uttered the hated word ''. . . travel.''

Kedrigern felt about travel as a cloistered monk feels about debauchery: he knew that people indulged in it, and that they even professed to enjoy it, but in his heart of hearts he simply could not believe that this was so. Travel, to him, meant the expenditure of large sums of money and the loss of irrecoverable time merely to remove oneself from a comfortable home and go to a place one really did not care to be—and then to be faced with a return as bad as the journey out. Travel meant discomfort, inconvenience, squalor, hardship, and danger, not to mention extortion, indigestion, and disappointment. One departed with forebodings and returned with shattered illusions, itching from head to foot, smelling like a kennel, aching in every joint and with a stomach in open revolt. Travel was paying to suffer. Seasoned travelers who boasted of their adventures impressed Kedrigern as the sort of people who would turn themselves over to the local torturer at regular intervals and then regale their friends with accounts of the salubrious effects of wrenched limbs and abused flesh.

Kedrigern's hatred of travel did not blind him to the fact that it might, on occasion, be necessary. Headlong flight from some cataclysmic upheaval of nature was only common sense, and there were times when a client's needs required on-site presence. But even if a wall of flame were racing toward his cottage, or a dozen kings were shoveling gold coins into sacks to lure him away, he would pack his things and mount up with a leaden spirit. Travel was simply not for him.

Princess did not share his views on the subject. "I'll go with you, Keddie. I know how you feel about traveling, and maybe if we're together we can make it a little vacation. We'll relax and enjoy ourselves," she said brightly.

Kedrigern made a low grumbling noise. Talk of enjoying travel was, to him, like talk of enjoying a painful illness. If the filthy business could be got over with quickly— get out, get it over with, get back, one, two, three, no dawdling along dusty roads and being victimized at inns and hostels, no suspicious food, no knee-deep mud, no saddle sores—it might be possible to speak of travel as tolerable. It would never be enjoyable, but it might be made tolerable. Just barely. The trouble was that instantaneous transportation fairly burned up one's resources; there was little point in whisking oneself halfway around the world in the blink of an eye if one had scarcely enough magic left to levitate a spoon when one arrived.

And transforming oneself into a bird, though less costly in magic, was no real solution. The experience of flying was pleasant in itself—not that he was jealous of Princess, not at all, not one bit—but small birds were always being eaten by bigger birds, and big birds were the prey of hunters. Long-distance flying was simply too dangerous. And there was always the problem of the luggage. A bird simply cannot carry enough to provide for a comfortable stay.

There was no way out of it, Kedrigern thought as he sat plunged in both figurative and literal gloom. The only way to travel is to travel, and travel is awful.

Princess rose and lit a taper at the fire. As she lit first the candle on the mantle and then those around the room, the physical gloom was dispelled, but Kedrigern still wallowed in his black mood, and his expression made his feelings plain.

"Our last trip didn't turn out so badly, if you recall," Princess said as she turned her attention to the candle on the table.

"They all turn out badly."

"Well, you certainly seem pleased with the books we got from Arlebar. And I'm very happy with my wings. And you managed to do a lot of good."

Kedrigern grunted. His expression did not change. Princess was not deterred. "You cleared up all that nasty magic in the Desolation of the Loser Kings. People will be talking about that for centuries to come."

"That's true," he said, softening.

"And you saw some old friends and visited some nice places. It wasn't all hardships and grubbiness."

"No, not entirely," he conceded. "But that was last time, seeking Arlebar, a genuine wizard. Now we'd be after a magic wand. It means tracking down some second-rate wizards and sorcerers, and doing a lot of haggling once we find them."

"You could ask someone in the guild. They'd know."

"Oh, dear me, no. The wizards' guild is very anti-wand. I recall one of our discussions in the early days . . . very heated, it was. Hithernils got so excited that he jumped up and shouted, 'Wands are for fairy godmothers— real wizards wear medallions!' That settled it. Wands were out."

Princess looked thoughtful. "Do you have any ideas?"

"Well, I did hear of a fellow, called himself Mergith . . . not his real name, I'm certain . . . shifty little weasel, and not much of a wizard. He was drifting about a few years ago, talking about a magic wand that he could lay his hands on whenever he wanted to. He was almost certainly lying, but he's the only place to start."

"Do you know where to find him?"

Kedrigern nodded. "Dendorric," he said.

"What's that? And where?"

"It's a city. South and a bit east of here, I'd say. About twelve or fourteen days' leisurely riding, ten days if we hurry." He paused, reconsidered, and said, "Actually, it's more a fortress than a city. The people of Dendorric have an outpost mentality. They're located on the pleasant, fertile, sunny side of a river, and they're afraid that someone from the other side will try to seize their city and drive them out."

"Aren't they being silly?"

"Not at all. The other side of the river is all dense dark forest full of thieves, robbers, brigands, outlaws, and wild men. Given half a chance, they'd be on Dendorric like a plague of locusts. But the river's too swift to cross, and the only bridge is heavily guarded."

"So Dendorric is safe."

"Yes, but the people don't really believe it is, so they're always looking out for new guarantees of safety. That's the sort of atmosphere that draws a Mergith and his kind like flies to a stable." Kedrigern gave a deep and heartfelt sigh at the human condition and the way of the world. He drew himself up from his chair. "May as well get an early night, my dear. We'll pack tomorrow, and then . . . Dendorric."

...⚎ Three ⚎...

mergith unspells

THE MORNING SUN was low in the sky when Hamarak had his first sight of Dendorric. It was a sizeable aggregation of buildings, fifty at least, perhaps as many as sixty, clustered in a level area on the lower slope of a hill. The buildings were of every conceivable size, shape, and condition. Atop the hill was a battlemented castle in a poor state of repair. A swift-running river curved in a broad and turbulent arc below the buildings, enclosing settlement, hill, and castle. A single narrow bridge led across.

"We're here, Louise," Hamarak announced.

The staff became a sword again. "Hold me up so I can have a clear view," it said.

Hamarak obliged, wrapping the cloak around his hands and holding the sword as high as he could, grasping the tip. After a brief inspection it gave a little sniff and said, "So that's Dendorric."

"It's one of the great cities of the world," said Hamarak reverently.

"Bring me down," the sword commanded, adding, "Dendorric may pass for a great city in this benighted land, but to one who has heard the bells of many-towered Nimachar or seen the sun rise over the gilded rooftops of Ponnomondira, it is a squalid deposit of hovels. The castle is a disgrace. However, this is where Mergith is to be found, so I suppose there's no avoiding it.''

"Mergith rules in Dendorric. The merchant said so, and the robbers.''

"Yes. Mergith the Wizard-King. Insolent puppy!''

"Why does a wizard want to be a king, Louise?''

"Every man wants to be a king, Hamarak. It's only normal.''

Hamarak thought for a moment, then shook his head, saying, "I want to be a farmer.''

"Well, every *other* man wants to be a king. They crave power, I suppose.''

"But wizards already have greater power than kings. They have magic.''

"Kings have servants, Hamarak. Lots of servants. That means that they can have other people do things for them, and conserve their magic for important things.''

"Like what?''

"Oh . . . spells . . . enchantments, that sort of thing. Turning people into swords, or shields . . .'' The sword gave a sudden little cry of pain and rage, and in a quavering voice said, "Oh, poor William! Imagine being a shield— what a dreadful fate!''

For comfort Hamarak said, "I bet it's nicer being a sword.''

"Marginally. At least our baby sister wasn't turned into a weapon. That has been some consolation.'' Sighing, the blade said, "Enough of this. We must cross the bridge before sunset.''

"Should I go right to Mergith?''

"I think not. Stay at the inn tonight and see what you can find out. I'll be listening. The ideal thing would be to have Mergith learn of your arrival and summon you himself, but I haven't yet thought of a way to manage that. I'll give it some thought along the way,'' said Louise, returning to the form of a staff.

The guards at the bridge let the lone traveler pass without a question. They were sleepy and hungry, and did not care much about one man. He found his way to the inn, where the ale was barely potable but the bread, from a nearby bakery, was delicious. Hamarak drank lightly and ate heartily, but learned nothing to serve his purposes. It appeared that Mergith was not an easily accessible man, and was much feared by his subjects.

The next day was no more fruitful to Hamarak's inquiries. He trudged through Dendorric from end to end, up and down the narrow lanes and alleys, ostensibly looking for a few days' work before he resumed his journey, and found himself answering more questions than he asked. Everyone seemed dubious about his claim that he had traveled from the west, through the forest, alone, and had reached Dendorric alive and whole. The forest was known to be teeming with bands of cruel and murderous men. Each time Hamarak said that he had encountered only five brigands, and had driven them off, he was faced with unbelieving silence.

That evening he feasted on delicious bread and a thick stew, then fell into his customary deep untroubled sleep. He awoke early, roused by cries and shouts. Rubbing his eyes, he sat up and listened closely. Terrified fragments came through the thin walls: a horde of brigands; the bridge unguarded; Dendorric lost.

"Come, Hamarak. This is our opportunity. Mustn't dawdle," said a familiar voice. He looked to where he had rested his staff and saw sunlight from a crack gleaming on the edge of a swordblade.

"What's happening?" he asked, fumbling for his boots.

"Brigands from the forest are attacking the town. The guards have all run away, and the townspeople are in a panic. So we're going to drive off the attackers and save Dendorric. To the bridge, Hamarak! And please remember to call me Panstygia when anyone is listening."

Hamarak strode past barred doors and shuttered windows, through the silent empty streets, and took up his stand, yawning, at the center of the bridge. Figures had already emerged from the morning mists that lay on the road he had traveled not two days previously. He was not skilled at counting, but he could see that there were quite a few men on their way to the bridge, and all were armed in some way.

"Will I have to hurt anybody?" he asked.

"It's possible. I'll do my best to concentrate on their weapons," the sword replied.

"I don't want to hurt anyone, Louise."

"These are not nice men, Hamarak. They're coming here to kill, rape, loot, and burn. They're cruel and filled with hatred. They'll show mercy to no living thing."

After a thoughtful pause, Hamarak said, "Maybe it would be all right if I hurt one or two of them. Just a little. To scare the others."

"Trust me. If we do this properly, Mergith will be begging to meet us."

The brigands advanced on the bridge in something resembling a formation. Hamarak stood his ground, sword in hand. When the first rank came close enough to note his features, one of the men cried out, "It's him! It's the swordsman from the west!" and they all came to a disorderly halt.

"Go away," Hamarak called to them. "No killing, raping, looting, or burning."

"By whose command? That tinpot wizard on the hill?" someone shouted.

"It is I, Panstygia, Mother of Darkness, who command it!" cried the sword, her voice like the clang of a tocsin. "Defy me now, and I will show no mercy."

The brigands huddled together, chattering, gesticulating in a wild manner. Hamarak waited patiently, yawning from time to time. At last one of them came forward. Hamarak recognized him as a member of the luckless forest quintet.

"Let us pass unopposed and we'll spare your life. We'll even give you a share in the plunder," he said.

"No," Hamarak replied.

The man returned to his companions. After more huddling, much shouting, and frequent brandishing of weapons, a different brigand approached him. "Become our leader and help us take Dendorric. We'll give you a tenfold share and obey you in everything," he said.

Hamarak shook his head. "No. You have to go away."

"We won't. We'll kill you and take Dendorric ourselves."

Hamarak saw no point in responding. He waited while the man rejoined his fellows. There was a lot of shouting this time, and some very bad language, and then, without warning, the brigands charged *en masse*, straight for him.

Not one passed. The black blade swept across their path, back and forth, like a scythe, and with each stroke a hail of shattered weaponry went pattering into the water below. The force of Hamarak's strokes sent men reeling, some to collide with their comrades and fall in a tangle, others to topple over the parapet into the swift-running river.

In a very short time, Hamarak stood alone on the bridge, ankle-deep in fragments of metal and wood. A scattered rout of brigands was heading for the forest, some limping from the bridge, others dragging themselves up the far bank of the river.

"My arms are tired. That's hard work," Hamarak said.

"I hope you don't think it was easy for *me*," the sword said petulantly.

"No. But it's harder than cutting down trees, or using a shovel."

Loud noises rose behind him. Turning, Hamarak saw a crowd assembled at the town end of the bridge. They were cheering and waving to him. Women strewed flowers, and men threw their hats in the air.

"Just as I planned. You're their hero," said the sword.

"I am?"

"Of course you are. You've just performed a heroic feat and saved their miserable clutter of hovels. In a little while Mergith will hear of it and send for us. This is really going more smoothly than I had hoped."

"Will they give me breakfast? I'm hungry."

"They'll give you anything you want, Hamarak. Just don't get emotionally involved with any of the young ladies. When Mergith summons us, we must be ready. And please don't forget to call me Panstygia, Mother of Darkness, whenever you refer to me."

Hamarak shouldered the blade and trudged toward the crowd, waving genially. They cheered even louder. Children ran forward to greet him and danced along at his side. Pretty ladies threw their arms around his neck and kissed him with great enthusiasm. Men clapped him on the back and clasped his hand warmly.

With Hamarak at their center, the crowd swept through the narrow streets toward the inn, to celebrate in earnest. On the way, they passed the bakery. The owner, apprised of Dendorric's deliverance, had resumed the morning's work. The aroma of fresh-baked bread filled the air, and at Hamarak's request, the crowd stopped here.

"I'd like some fresh bread," said Hamarak.

"Have some pastry!" a man cried.

"Cookies!" a woman urged.

"A raisin cake!" said a child.

"I only want bread. I like nice fresh bread. Buttered."

"Then nice fresh bread is what you shall have, savior of Dendorric," said the fat little baker grandly. He stepped inside and emerged with three rounded loaves of bread still warm from the oven. "My thanks and my compliments," he announced, amid cheers.

The crowd moved on to the inn, where Hamarak called for butter. While everyone else imbibed, he feasted on the warm bread. Between mouthfuls, he gave an account of the battle on the bridge. Since he was not completely clear in his own mind regarding what had happened, or how, his account was extremely terse. The townspeople were impressed as much by his apparent humility as by his demonstrated prowess. They gazed on him in wonderment.

"That's a fine sword. I've never seen one like it," a man said admiringly.

"It cut right through the brigands' blades," said another. "And look—not a nick in it!"

"It must be magic!" a woman whispered.

"An enchanted blade!" was buzzed about among the assembled townspeople. They gathered more closely around Hamarak to gaze upon the sword in awe.

"This is Panstygia, Mother of Darkness, the great black blade of the west," he said. "I'm Hamarak. I couldn't have saved Dendorric without her."

In the admiring silence that followed this remark, a single figure pushed his way through the crowd to stand before Hamarak. He wore a rust-speckled breastplate and helmet. His cloak was unclean and spattered with mud, and mud was caked on his boots. He carried a pike which he had to hold at an awkward angle because of the low ceiling, and even lower beams, of the inn.

"Are you the one who held the bridge?" the pikeman asked.

A voice from the crowd called out, "He's the one who saved Dendorric from the brigands!" and another added, "When Mergith's guards ran and hid in the castle!" Some angry murmuring followed.

The pikeman turned, knocking his pike against a post and drawing amused snickers from the crowd. "Do you think we were afraid of those raggedy beggars?" he asked defiantly.

"No—we think you were terrified!" someone at the rear of the room called out. There was loud laughter.

"It so happens that we knew someone was going to hold the bridge. Mergith is a wizard, you know. He foresaw the whole thing. We were just keeping out of this swordsman's way so he could fulfill his destiny," the pikeman said.

This announcement silenced the townspeople. It was a possibility that no one had thought of. They looked at one another uncomfortably. Hamarak, having finished his second loaf, broke the third and began to butter it thickly, a look of quiet contentment on his heavy features. He was quite satisfied to enjoy good bread while he could, and let the others go on talking at each other.

"If Mergith knew that the brigands were coming, why didn't he tell us?" a woman demanded.

"He didn't want to worry you," replied the pikeman.

"He could have told us the swordsman would save us."

"He didn't want you getting complacent, either."

"Those wizards are all alike," someone muttered.

"I don't know what you're complaining about," said the pikeman. "You're safe, aren't you?"

The crowd of townspeople began to melt away, grumbling. Clearly the celebration was over. Reluctantly, with wistful backward glances at Hamarak and his enchanted sword, they began to shuffle to their day's tasks.

The pikeman turned once again to Hamarak. "The Master wants to speak to you," he said.

"Do you mean Mergith?"

"Who else? Mergith is the only master around here."

"Is it all right if I finish my bread first?"

The pikeman glanced about and saw a half-filled pitcher of ale on a nearby table. "You go ahead and finish. I'll sit over here and wait for you," he said, commandeering the pitcher.

The castle on the hilltop was smaller inside than it appeared to be from the outside, and very untidy. All the way to Mergith's throneroom, Panstygia was making low sounds of disgust and disapproval, just loud enough for Hamarak to hear.

He said nothing; he was too impressed to speak. This was the first time Hamarak had ever set foot in a castle, and despite Panstygia's complaints, he thought Mergith's stronghold a marvelous place. Rubbish was lying about everywhere, true, but it was rubbish of the very highest quality. Even the rats were sleek and well fed. For the first time in his life, it occurred to Hamarak that owning a farm might not be the finest thing in the world. Being a wizard-king seemed much nicer.

Mergith's throneroom, the state chamber of Dendorric, was a spacious room at the top of the castle. It had an uneven flagstone floor and rough stone walls hung with darkened tapestries that quivered in the constant drafts. A roaring fire warmed the room just a bit, and a half-dozen torches mounted in brackets gave illumination. Beside the hearth stood a crude table and a pair of low stools. The only other furniture was an elaborately carved wooden throne which appeared to have been freshly painted. On the throne sat a lean, sharp-faced man dressed all in black. He was as tense as a tightened spring.

Four guards stood by the throne, and when Hamarak and the pikeman entered, the guards stepped forward, hands on their weapons, to form a box around Hamarak. They said not a word and made no threatening gesture, but their expressions were not friendly.

The pikeman went to the foot of Mergith's throne. "This is the man who drove off the brigands, Master," he said.

"Indeed. All alone?" said Mergith softly.

"Entirely alone, Master. His sword is enchanted, the people say."

"How very fortunate for him. And for them. What is his name?"

"He didn't say, Master. He doesn't say much."

Waving the pikeman aside, Mergith smiled, revealing crooked yellow teeth. "Swordsman, come closer that I might convey my gratitude for your service to my subjects," he called.

Hamarak came to the foot of the throne, the sword still resting on his shoulder. The guards kept close watch, ready to pounce at the first suspicious move.

"What is your name, my fine champion?" Mergith asked.

"Hamarak."

"So. A good name. A fine strong name. A hero's name. And what brings you to Dendorric, Hamarak?"

"I'm going east. Dendorric is on the way."

"So it is, so it is. Particularly if one is coming from the west," said Mergith, a yellowed smile nearly splitting his narrow face. "And you bear an enchanted sword, I'm told."

"Yes. This is Panstygia, Mother of Darkness, the great black blade of the west. She wants to meet you."

Mergith shrank back: a momentary flicker of fear ran through him at the thought that Hamarak's words might be the subtle mocking prelude to a quick and fatal slash; but the sight of Hamarak's homely open features reassured the wizard. There was no subtlety, nor malice, in that face.

"Does she?" he responded, raising his black brows in wonder. "How nice of her. How very sociable. May I hold her?"

"If you want to," Hamarak said, presenting the hilt of the black sword to Mergith. The wizard stood and grasped it in both his bony, long-fingered hands. He raised the blade high and made a few nimble passes in the air.

"It's beautifully balanced," he observed.

"It's a good sword," Hamarak said agreeably.

Mergith returned to the throne, sat down, and laid the black sword across his knees. He pushed back the lank black hair that had fallen over his forehead. Favoring Hamarak with another sallow smile, he gestured to the guards. "You may leave us," he said. "I would speak with the swordsman in private."

No sooner had the door shut behind the last guard than Panstygia said in a clear commanding voice, "Mergith, you must help me."

Mergith gave a start and jerked his hands away from the blade. "Did you speak to me?" he asked warily.

"I did, Mergith. I've come a long way to seek your assistance. Do not disappoint me, please."

Mergith looked suspiciously at Hamarak, who stood gazing at a half-eaten loaf that lay on the table by the fireplace. The swordsman's lips had not moved. He could not be a ventriloquist. And yet Mergith had heard of no enchanted talking swords in the area. It could be a trick.

But who would dare? More to the point, who was capable? The people of Dendorric disliked him; but they were a mob of clods. They could never have come up with such an elaborate ruse. Yet someone had. But was it a ruse, or was this truly an enchanted blade speaking to him, asking his aid?

There was one easy way to make sure of Hamarak. Mergith summoned the swordsman closer and said, "I have been remiss in my thanks. I must reward you for your service to Dendorric." He dug deep into the sleeve of his gown and drew forth a large golden coin, which he held up in two fingers, turning it to catch the torchlight. "Look at this coin, Hamarak. It's a bright, pretty coin, isn't it? Look how it catches the light."

"It's pretty," said Hamarak.

"Look closely. Listen. You've worked hard today, Hamarak. You must be tired. Aren't you tired?"

"A little. It's still only morning."

"But think of all you've done. You need a rest. Wouldn't you like a nice rest?" Mergith asked in a soft, lulling voice.

"I wouldn't mind. My arms are tired."

"Then you must rest," Mergith said, turning the coin, on which Hamarak's eyes were fixed. "You're already beginning to feel very sleepy. Your eyes are getting heavy. It would be nice to sit by the warm fire, and rest your weary bones, and go to sleep. Wouldn't that be nice, Hamarak?"

"Very nice."

"Then you must do it. Go over by the fire and sit on a stool. Have a good long sleep, and don't wake up until you hear the command. Go, Hamarak."

Hamarak walked at his customary slow pace to the fireside, where he settled on a stool and leaned his elbows on the table, resting his chin on his hands and gazing drowsily into the fire. Mergith looked upon his broad, motionless back, smiled, and patted the hilt of the sword possessively.

"And now, my dear sword, we can converse in privacy. What would you ask of me?" said Mergith.

"I am the victim of an enchantment. My brother and sister are victims, too. Only a wizard can help us. Needless to say, you will be rewarded generously."

"I can see your problem. What happened to the others?"

"William was turned into a great iron shield. And Alice . . . dear, sweet little Alice . . . was turned into a golden crown."

Mergith's brows rose. He nodded slowly and appreciatively. "That's a very impressive triple enchantment. Whatever did you do to bring it upon yourselves? And at whose hands?"

"It was the work of Vorvas the Vindictive," said the blade coldly

"I've heard of Vorvas. He was legendary for his transformation spells. He's dead now, you know. Died about twenty years ago, in his cave."

"Was it painful?"

"I should think so. Slow, too, in all likelihood."

"Good," said Panstygia grimly.

"It was also quite humiliating."

"Better and better. Tell me all about it."

"Not much to tell, really. Vorvas became rather absent minded in his last century or so. One day he turned himself into a vole for some reason, and forgot to notify his familiar of the change. His familiar was a large black cat."

"Serves him right. But if Vorvas died, why am I still a sword?"

"He wasn't called 'Vorvas the Vindictive' for nothing, good blade. He placed an exceptionally strong spell on you to make sure it would outlast his own life. What did you do that got him so angry?"

The blade hesitated for a moment, then plunged ahead with her story. "When our parents died, the neighboring kingdom seized disputed lands on the western border. William and I went off to fight them—his battle name was Shield of the Realm, and I was called Sword of Righteousness—while Alice stayed behind to act for the crown. During a lull in the fighting, when the three of us were home together, Vorvas came to offer his magic in our cause. In return, he wanted to marry me.''

"But you refused him.''

"Vorvas was three hundred and eighty-nine years old at the time, and exceedingly ugly. He smelled like a dead goat. I spurned him. William threatened him. Alice denounced him. He enchanted us on the spot and carried us off with him. He even put enchantments on distant cousins who happened to be visiting us at the time. He was extremely cruel. I ended up sealed in an oak tree. I don't know what's become of William and Alice. Or our cousins,'' the sword concluded.

"It may be difficult to find out. You were sealed in that oak tree for a long time. Just a few months before his fatal oversight, Vorvas celebrated his five hundredth birthday.''

"One loses track of the days when one is sealed up in a tree. But surely you can help me find the others, and free us from our enchantment,'' said the blade confidently.

"I'm afraid I must disappoint you,'' the wizard said, gripping the sword firmly and rising from the throne. "In the first place, I much prefer not to tamper with one of Vorvas's spells. He was far more powerful than I, and very nasty. And in the second place, I have little need at present for a pair of grateful princesses and a grateful prince, but I could do very well with an enchanted sword. Oh, yes, very well indeed.''

"Then you won't help us!'' the blade cried.

"On the contrary, *you* will help *me* . . . Panstygia, is it? Very impressive name. What is your real name?''

"I'll never reveal it to you!''

"You will, sooner or later. We're going to be together for a long time, Panstygia. I know a bit about these enchantments, and I know that you're bound to obey and protect the one who wields you.''

"But I don't want to be a sword! I insist that you change me back!"

"Not for a long time, if ever. I suggest that you learn to enjoy being a sword. It will save you no end of frustration."

"I hate being a sword!" Panstygia cried in anguish. "All that hacking, and smiting, and hewing, and slashing . . . and the noise! And the *crowds*! It's no fit work for a princess. I was better off sealed in the tree! Help me, Mergith—I'll reward you generously."

"With what?" he asked, and laughed in a cruel, superior way. "After all this time, your kingdom is lost irretrievably. It's gone and forgotten."

"You'll have my undying gratitude and respect!"

"I'd rather have an enchanted sword."

"But you're a wizard, Mergith—wizards don't need enchanted swords."

Mergith glanced sharply around the room, checking all the dark corners; then, in a lowered voice, he said, "Since I know that I can speak to you in confidence, my faithful blade, I will admit you to my secret: I am not a very good wizard. Oh, I can work an effective little spell now and then, but nothing like what Vorvas accomplished. And every time I do work a bit of magic, I'm exhausted for weeks afterwards. Consequently, my hold on Dendorric has become rather tenuous. Sleight of hand and conjuring tricks can keep the townspeople looking over their shoulders and behaving themselves, but I won't be able to keep the brigands from the woods at bay much longer. They're too hungry. But with an enchanted sword . . ." He raised the dark blade high and looked lovingly on the glinting edge. "Great days lie ahead for Mergith the Magnificent, the warrior-wizard-king. And great deeds for his sword Panstygia."

"I'll never help you! I'll miss every stroke and wiggle around in your grip!" Panstygia said defiantly.

"I think it would be best if you learned at once who is in charge of this partnership, Panstygia," said the wizard, striding to the hearth. He plunged the blade into the bright embers and stepped back. "Perhaps when you've toasted for a while, you'll feel more agreeable."

"You'll destroy my temper!"

"Quite the contrary. I expect to improve it."

"You'll ruin me! Hamarak, get me out of this fire!"

"I'm afraid Hamarak is in a long, deep sleep, thanks to my hypnotic powers," said the wizard with a thin smile of triumph.

"Hamarak, wake up!" Panstygia cried in desperation.

Hamarak gave a start, turned, blinked, and looked at the wizard and the sword in obvious bewilderment. "What are you doing in the fire, Panstygia? Do you want to get out?" he asked.

"Yes! Immediately!"

Mergith reeled back, astonished. "You're supposed to be in a deep sleep! I hypnotized you! What's going on here?"

Rising and drawing the blade from the fire, Hamarak turned to him. "I'm sorry. I wasn't really asleep," he said slowly. "I never sleep during the day. A man told me it isn't good for you to sleep during the day."

"But you were . . . you looked . . . you did as I said! You sat by the fire and didn't move," Mergith said, his voice tight and squeaky.

"I thought that was what you wanted me to do, so I did it," Hamarak said, raising the smoking blade and inspecting it with apparent concern. "I never met a king before, and I wanted to be polite and do what the king told me to do."

"You were right about one thing, Mergith," said Panstygia. "You aren't a very good wizard. You can't even hypnotize a peasant."

"Wait a minute, Hamarak," said Mergith, backing away and skipping behind the throne. "Don't do anything hasty."

Panstygia's voice was like an arctic wind. "We will not be hasty, Mergith. We will deal with you slowly and deliberately."

"No! Wait! I'll unspell you—how's that for an offer?"

"Too late, Mergith," Panstygia said solemnly. "You've already given me a clear idea of your ability."

"But I'll try! At least let me try!"

"The way you do things, Mergith, I might wind up as a kettle. No, thank you."

"I'll be careful. Please."

After a moment of tense, expectant silence, the blade said, "All right. You can try."

"Good! Fine. Now . . . you just hold her steady, Hamarak. Hold her by the guard. Parallel to your body, point down, hilt just above your head. That's it. Hold it there," Mergith said rapidly. He poked about in the recesses of his sleeve and took out three stubby black candles and a bit of blue chalk. "Stay still," he directed. He then proceeded to draw a shaky triangle enclosing Hamarak, and placed a candle at each point. Extracting a small black book from another recess in his clothing, he leafed through the pages with tremulous hands until he came to the desired place. He glanced at Panstygia and Hamarak, licking his lips nervously.

"I want you to know that this is a very dangerous undertaking. There's no telling what backup spells Vorvas placed on you. A man like Vorvas hates having his work tampered with," Mergith said, his voice strained.

"I'm not afraid," said the blade stoutly.

"I'm not afraid, either," Hamarak added.

"I'm so afraid I can hardly stand," Mergith whimpered. "This is the most dangerous thing I've ever attempted. Are you sure—"

"Start the counterspell," Panstygia commanded.

The words were harsh and ugly, great thorny blocks of gargling gutturals and tussive gouts of consonants unsuited to human articulation. Mergith struggled through the first invocation. Pale and sweating, he paused for a breath, his eyes wild. Suddenly he jerked his head up, dropping the book. His mouth gaped, and he pointed to the fireplace with a pathetic little squeak of terror.

Something whooshed past Hamarak's legs. It moved

quickly, sinuous as a giant serpent, a swirl of dark, oily colors bearing altogether too many glowing eyes, peculiarly arranged. It enveloped Mergith, who gave one awful scream, and then it whooshed back the way it had come. Mergith's cry faded up the chimney. The trail of the apparition was a smoking ribbon of molten stone.

"Well, he knew it was dangerous," said Panstygia.

"It was a lot more dangerous than he thought," Hamarak added softly.

····} *Four* }····

a crown, like alice

THE DOOR of the throne room burst open and a score of guards rushed in, swords drawn and pikes leveled at Hamarak. They saw the smoking stone, caught a whiff of sulphur, and stopped in their tracks.

"Where is Mergith?" the guard captain demanded.

Panstygia's voice rang through the chamber. "Mergith has been vanquished by a greater wizard. He will return no more. On your knees, all of you! All hail Hamarak the Invincible!"

The guards glanced uncertainly at one another and backed away. The pikeman who had conducted Hamarak to the castle drew them together and began to speak to his comrades in low, urgent tones. They looked at Hamarak, at Panstygia, at the pikeman, back at Hamarak; then one by one they stepped forward to kneel before their new ruler.

"Proclaim the coming of Hamarak among the people," Panstygia commanded. "And bring back enough help to get this place cleaned up. It's in a shocking state."

"As our master wishes," said the guard captain. "Are there further commands?"

"Would you bring back a couple of loaves of nice fresh bread and some butter?" Hamarak added.

"At once, my lord Hamarak," said the captain, bowing and backing from the chamber.

When they were alone, Panstygia said, "A very fortunate thing you didn't have to fight the guards. I'm sure Mergith made me lose my temper. I'm useless as a sword until I have my temper restored, and I don't think it will be a pleasant process."

Hamarak, his brow furrowed, was silent for a time, and then he said, "If I'm king, you could be my ceremonial sword. I wouldn't hit anybody with you."

"Thank you, Hamarak, but if I must be a sword, I prefer to be the real thing, not a decorative object. I have my pride."

"Would you like to be my staff? A king needs a staff."

"A staff is all right as a disguise when we're traveling, but I don't enjoy being one. I certainly don't want to spend the rest of my life as a stick." She paused for a moment, then blurted, "Why did that wretched man have to make me a sword? Why couldn't I be a crown, like Alice?"

Hamarak paced the room once, then a second time, and finally took his place on the carven throne, which proved to be a snug fit. At last he said, "I get to wear a crown, don't I, if I'm king?"

"You get to wear anything you like if you're a king. I don't even have a *sheath*, but you can have a crown, robes, sashes . . . the full regalia."

"Would you like to be my crown?"

"Your crown? I don't understand, Hamarak."

"It would mean being heated up again, and hit with a hammer a few times, but they might have to do that anyway, to give you back your temper. You could be a crown. Like Alice."

"But I'm not gold, Hamarak."

"I don't care. You've been a good sword, and a good staff, and you'll be a good crown, gold or not."

"Why, Hamarak, what a sweet thing to say! I'm touched."

Embarrassed, Hamarak ducked his head, stared down

into his lap, and squirmed uncomfortably on the narrow seat. In a subdued voice, he said, "Well, if it hadn't been for you, I'd still be working for other people. Now I'm a king."

"You're a wizard-warrior-king. You can even be a wizard-warrior-farmer-king, if you like."

"I can?" Hamarak looked up, smiling. "It's nice to be a king."

"My father always spoke well of it," Panstygia said. "I'm not absolutely certain I want to become your crown, though. I'll need time to think about that. Meanwhile, you'd better summon your guards and servants, and give them orders."

"What orders?"

"Any orders will do. The thing is to let them know at once that you're decisive and demanding. You are Hamarak the Invincible, and you're not to be kept waiting. That's the secret of successful kingship."

At the very moment that Hamarak commenced to impose his regal presence on the castle staff, Kedrigern and Princess were crossing the narrow bridge to Dendorric. They rode mounts acquired on their recent travels, creatures of tractable mien but singular appearance, especially useful for passing through dangerous country. Princess was on a transparent horse; in the proper light, she appeared to be comfortably seated in midair, her stately passage marked by the clopping of unseen hooves. Kedrigern's horse was jet black, a gigantic red-eyed stallion with massive silver hooves and a redoubtable silver horn spiraling from his broad forehead. This was no mincing unicorn, fit only to recline a milky head on a maiden's lap and roll its mournful eyes in abject surrender; it was a spiked juggernaut that could rampage through an army, leaving a wake of bloody pulp. Thanks to the spectral appearance of one steed and the awesomeness of the other, the travelers had had, thus far, a peaceful trip.

As the horses picked their way through the oddments of

splintered wood and shattered metal that cluttered the bridge at midpoint, Kedrigern and Princess exchanged a puzzled glance. Clearly, a pitched battle had been fought here by a sizeable body of warriors, and not long ago. But by whom? And why? And who had won? There was no smoke rising from Dendorric, no cries of victims or roaring of conquerors; nor had they passed a retreating army on their way through the forest, or encountered wounded stragglers, or seen abandoned campsites. It was decidedly odd.

Even odder was the fact that the bridge was unguarded. Far from showing concern at this dereliction, the citizens of Dendorric were in a holiday mood that even the sight of two bizarre horses could not dampen. They greeted the travelers with waves and smiles and shouts of welcome. Several little girls threw flowers.

Here and there, knots of small boys flailed away at one another in mock swordplay. When all had gone down before the onslaught of one, the victor would cry, "I am Hamarak, and I wield the great black blade of the west, Panstygia! Bring me my bread!" The others would then spring up and begin to shout, "Now I get to be Hamarak!" or "My turn! My turn!" or "I'm Hamarak this time, and you're the robbers!" Kedrigern smiled benevolently on their play and turned to Princess.

"It appears we've arrived on the festival of some local hero."

"Yes. It's odd, though . . . the people don't seem to be the least bit nervous, as you said they'd be."

The wizard looked about. "They don't, do they?" he said thoughtfully. "They're not even curious about our horses."

"Maybe Mergith has done something to make them feel more secure."

Kedrigern raised an eyebrow and shook his head slowly, skeptically, but said nothing. This was certainly not the fearful, suspicious city he remembered. He doubted that Mergith had the power to bring about such a change, but clearly someone or something had, and his curiosity was aroused.

At the inn, a trembling hostler took the horses only after Kedrigern tipped him lavishly and smothered him under assurances of their gentle natures. This evidence that courage had not become endemic to the people of Dendorric only heightened the mystery.

Withindoors, a crowd was gathered around the innkeeper, listening in worshipful silence as he pointed out where Hamarak had sat and held up the plate from which he had eaten buttered bread, a few crumbs of which were still available at a modest price. For a bit more, he offered to point out the very room in which Hamarak had slept only the previous night. There was a respectful murmur from the crowd, but no takers, and the innkeeper's withdrawl behind the bar, and his call for orders, had the effect of clearing the room of all but himself and the two travelers.

"Good day, sir and madam. Are you new to Dendorric?" he asked.

"My wife is," said Kedrigern. "I was here before, when Linran was king."

"Oh, yes, poor Linran. Deposed by his own guards, he was. That's when Joder became king."

"So Joder is now king in Dendorric?"

"Oh, no, sir. Joder didn't last at all, bless him. Died in his sleep one night, and Hildebad took over. Then Hildebad fell from the tower and Zill became king, and when Zill had an attack of food poisoning—"

"Who's king of Dendorric now?" Kedrigern broke in.

"Oh, that's Mergith, sir. 'Mergith the Wizard-King' he calls himself, and a very careful gentleman he is, too, sir. Keeps himself to himself, if you know what I mean. Very seldom leaves the castle."

"One can hardly blame him," said Princess with a disarming smile.

"Tell me, innkeeper, is Mergith a difficult man to see?" Kedrigern asked.

"Well, he is and he isn't, if you know what I mean, sir.

If it's you as wants to see him, that can be very difficult indeed. On the other hand, if it's Mergith as wants to see you, well, then, there's nothing to it. He just sends a few guards and fetches you up to the castle. And sometimes you come back and sometimes you don't, if you take my meaning," said the innkeeper, winking and laying a finger alongside his many-times-broken nose, tapping one hairy nostril meaningfully.

"I think I do," said the wizard. "And it would seem to be the wisest course to rest and refresh ourselves and do a bit of thinking. Do you have a room and a bed we will not be obliged to share with strangers?"

"We do, sir and madam, and a lovely room it is," said the innkeeper, hurrying out from behind the bar. He snatched up their packs and started for the stairs, saying over his shoulder, "You're at the other end of the hall from where Hamarak stayed, so you won't be disturbed by the people coming up to look at where he slept."

"We seem to have missed a significant chapter in Dendorric's history. Who is Hamarak, and what did he do?"

The innkeeper stopped on the first step of the stairs, turned, and said, "Why, sir, he's the savior of Dendorric. This very morning, all by himself, with not a soul to stand at his side, he drove off an army of brigands from across the river. He must have slain threescore men with that great black sword of his, and then he came back here and sat in the very room we've just left and called for a loaf of fresh bread. And butter." The innkeeper shook his head in wonderment. "And now he's up at the castle. Mergith wanted to see *him* in a hurry. Poor lad. I don't think he'll find Mergith as easy to deal with as a hundred ruffians."

From outside came the sound of distant shouting. It grew louder, and more distinct, until they clearly heard a number of enthusiastic voices crying, "Long live Hamarak! All hail Hamarak the Invincible! All hail the king of Dendorric!"

"That's that for Mergith," said the innkeeper with a

fatalistic shrug. "I hope Hamarak lasts a while. Kings do
come and go here in Dendorric."

"Bring our things up to the room. We'll be back as
soon as we can," snapped Kedrigern.

"To the castle?" Princess asked.

The wizard nodded. "To the castle."

Panstygia was giving instructions while Hamarak listened patiently. "For the first few days, it's best you see
no one. Let the people build up a healthy uncertainty about
their new lord and master."

"But everyone's already seen me," Hamarak objected.

"They're only had a glimpse. Just enough to whet their
curiosity."

"Can't I see people? I like to have people around."

"It's lonely at the top, Hamarak. Fortunately, there are
compensations."

A guard entered and fell to one knee at the foot of the
throne. "Visitors, my Lord Hamarak. They would see you
at once," he announced.

"Who are they?"

"A man and a woman. The woman has little wings, like a
fairy godmother. The man is plainly dressed and carries no
weapons. His name is Kedrigern, but the lady is known
only as Princess," said the guard.

"Is she really a princess?"

"She appears to be, my lord. Except for the wings."

His expression solemn, Hamarak said, "Leave us for a
time, while we ponder the matter. We will summon you."
When the guard was gone, he asked, "How did that
sound? Was I kingly?"

"I was impressed, Hamarak," Panstygia replied.

"I'd like to see these people. I never saw a woman with
wings. If she's a fairy godmother, maybe she can help
you."

"I don't wish to go to a ball, Hamarak, I wish to be
restored to human form. That is work for a wizard," said
the sword. "Since the woman is a princess, you may

admit her, but the man really must wait outside. A stranger plainly dressed, without a sword, has no right to take up a king's time."

At that moment, the guard burst in and fell trembling before Hamarak. "Wizards, my lord! They are wizards! What shall we do?" he cried in terror.

Panstygia's voice was like a trumpet as she cried, "Show them in at once, you unmannerly idiot, and fetch comfortable chairs for them, and plenty of pillows! Bring the finest wine from the cellars, and dainties from the kitchen! Bid the cooks prepare the most sumptuous dinner they've ever made, and see that it's served on clean dishes!"

"Well, go ahead. Do it," Hamarak said.

For the better part of an hour, Kedrigern and Princess were the objects of a courtesy that stopped just short of worship. In chairs piled with soft pillows, their feet on cushioned stools, superb wine in delicate crystal vessels on one hand and a tray of sweetmeats on the other, they were feted like conquerors and coddled like harem beauties, indulged almost to the point of embarrassment. Finally, when every pillow had been plumped up for the twentieth time, and every decanter refilled, every delicacy sampled, every word of welcome spoken and every smile of greeting smiled, the servants withdrew with orders not to disturb them, and they were left alone with Hamarak the Invincible.

At once Panstygia spoke, and her voice, cloaked in authority and slightly metallic, brought the visitors bolt upright among their pillows. "I have not always been a sword," she promptly explained. "I am currently under an enchantment from which only a powerful and benevolent wizard can release me."

"I'm sure my husband can do something. He's a master of counterspells," said Princess.

"I'll help if I can. I assume my lord Hamarak has no objection?" said Kedrigern.

Panstygia snapped, "Certainly not," and Hamarak shrugged. At the wizard's request she related her history in full, from her happy girlhood as Princess Louise of the

Kingdom of the Singing Forest to the arrival of her present visitors. Kedrigern listened attentively, without interrupting, and his expression grew ever more grave as the narrative proceeded. When she ended, a long silence followed, broken at last by the wizard.

"I've heard of Vorvas. He was one of the big names when I was just starting out. People used to say, 'When Vorvas enchants them, they stay enchanted.' "

"Was he really vindictive?" Princess asked.

Kedrigern's eyebrows rose. "Was he ever. What he did to Tirralandra, the Musical Princess of Gaspenberg, was absolutely . . . Well, no need to go into that. You see, Vorvas never stopped believing that he was irresistible to women, beautiful young princesses in particular." Turning to the sword, he said, "I take it you were a beautiful young princess at the time of your misfortune."

"I had many admirers," she said with dignity.

"Of course. And Vorvas expected you to fall at his feet, whimpering for a smile and a caress. Actually, women used to gag when Vorvas was still fifty paces off. Men didn't enjoy having him around, either. A totally repulsive person, Vorvas. Rejected by everyone. And the more rejected he felt, the more vindictive he became. He turned more beautiful young princesses into grotesque objects than any wizard I know. And you're one of the lucky ones. I'm sure it's not pleasant being a sword, but you got off a lot better than Tirralandra. He turned her into a hautboy."

"Better a hautboy than a sword," Panstygia said impatiently.

"Ordinarily, one might think so, but Tirralandra was a very musical person. She was born with perfect pitch. Hand her a strange instrument, and before you could cross the room she'd be playing it like a virtuosa."

"Then I should think she'd enjoy being a musical instrument," said Princess, looking perplexed.

"That's where Vorvas's vindictiveness comes in. A hautboy is difficult to play well. Vorvas saw to it that this particular hautboy came into the possession of Bertrand the

Bumptious, a local nobleman who fancied himself—erroneously—to be a musician. It was said of Bertrand that he couldn't carry a tune if he had six strong minstrels to help him. Think of poor Tirralandra's sufferings at his hands!''

"I'd prefer to think of my own sufferings, thank you. As if things weren't bad enough, that wretched Mergith made me lose my temper. There's no telling what inconvenience I'll have to put up with to regain it,'' said Panstygia.

"That's no problem. You're an enchanted sword. You'll never lose your temper, nor your edge.''

"I won't?'' said Panstygia with happy surprise.

"Not a chance of it. Do you mind if I heft you? May I, Hamarak?''

Hamarak, who had remained cautiously silent and watchful during the conversation, obligingly handed Kedrigern the black blade. Hamarak wore the expression of a man who was in deep waters, and knew it.

Panstygia was heavy, and Kedrigern was about half the size of Hamarak and a modest swordsman. Nevertheless, the dark sword was so perfectly balanced that his practice cuts through the air had the smooth grace of a master's, and he felt no more strain in his shoulders than if he had been flicking a willow switch.

Returning the sword to Hamarak, he said candidly, "When Vorvas turns you into a sword, he turns you into the very best. That's real workmanship.'' With a gesture toward the hearth, he added, "You could shear through that poker as if it were a broom straw.''

"That's very reassuring, but I'd prefer not to,'' said Panstygia, and Hamarak blurted, "She's not going to be a sword anymore, she's going to be my crown. We worked it out, didn't we, Louise?''

"I said I'd think about it, Hamarak. Actually, I'd prefer to be a princess once again.''

"I think that's your smartest choice,'' Princess said.

"Crown? What's this about a crown?'' Kedrigern cried in sudden alarm. "You haven't tried any homespun magic, have you?''

"No. I thought we'd just get a good blacksmith and have him make Louise into a crown. Like her sister," said Hamarak defensively.

Kedrigern placed a steadying hand on Hamarak's beefy shoulder. "Good thing we got here when we did, my boy. You tamper with one of Vorvas's spells, and there's no telling what might become of you. When Vorvas turns someone into a sword, he means for that person to remain a sword."

Hamarak's small dark eyes widened. "Really?"

"You saw what happened to Mergith."

They had, and they recalled it vividly. Kedrigern's words brought an uncomfortable silence over the throne room. Hamarak slumped dejectedly on the throne, Panstygia across his knees. Kedrigern perched on the edge of his chair, rubbing his chin. Princess reclined among the pillows, her small feet placed daintily on the cushioned footstool, her pensive gaze fixed upward. Kedrigern wondered at her silence. Having experienced some nasty enchantments herself, Princess might be expected to take a level-headed view of the present situation; but she was a naturally compassionate woman and Panstygia—or Louise—was—or had been—a sister princess, and Princess was offering her cold comfort at a time when heartfelt consolation seemed in order. Perhaps, thought Kedrigern, there were memories too painful to discuss before strangers.

"Must I remain a sword forever, then, wizard? Can you do nothing? Tell me the truth," said Panstygia.

" 'To every spell there is an equal and opposite counterspell, and to every enchantment an equal and opposite disenchantment.' That's the Third Law of Magic," Princess announced in a loud clear voice.

"That's absolutely correct. The problem is, some of the counterspells and disenchantments are so subtle, or so obscure, or difficult, or dangerous, that they're of no practical use," Kedrigern added.

"I don't believe you've answered my question," said the sword coldly.

"I can't, if you interrupt me. Now, just listen. Vorvas has obviously backed up his original enchantment with all sorts of traps and pitfalls for anyone who tries to disenchant you. Only when I learn precisely what he inflicted on you—his exact words, if possible—will I have any hope of undoing it."

"But I can't recall the spell. I've tried, and I can't."

"Naturally not. Vorvas would see to that. If the enchantee recalls the details of the enchantment, disenchantment becomes child's play. And since you, your brother and sister, and two cousins, were the only ones present except for Vorvas, and Vorvas is dead and you're all enchanted, then there's no one who remembers it. Under such circumstances, any attempt at disenchantment might well lead to disaster for all concerned. Your situation appears hopeless. I'm terribly sorry to have to say it, but I don't see how I can assist you."

The poignant silence was broken by Princess's urgent voice. "Keddie, you must do something. If you don't, who can?"

"My dear, I fear that no one can."

"Don't say that. It's bad enough to be enchanted, but to be hopelessly, irrevocably, irremediably enchanted . . . "

"A moment, wizard," said Panstygia sharply. "One of the cousins was my second cousin Hedvig. From childhood, Hedvig had been strangely immune to magic in all forms. No one could make anything of Hedvig. I cannot say for certain that she escaped the spell, but I do recall seeing the others transformed, and not Hedvig. I can picture the scene distinctly."

Kedrigern frowned, deep in thought. "Yes. It's possible I've heard of such people. But after all these years, and the dissolution of the kingdom . . . "

"There was the shield. That was William. Alice became a plain, simple golden crown," Panstygia went on dolefully, headless of the wizard's objections. "And Wanda. Oh, poor Wanda! I can see her now, lying there so slender and helpless. She's the most tragic figure of us all. William and Alice and I insulted and threatened that dreadful man, but Wanda did nothing to offend him. Wanda never offended anyone. His cruelty was completely gratuitous. When he heard her name, Vorvas actually laughed and said that he couldn't resist the opportunity. . . ."

Shaking his head slowly, Kedrigern said, "We'd be looking for Hedvig's great-great-grandchildren, and hoping that one of them could tell us something that Hedvig overheard a century ago. No, it's hopeless. The odds must be millions to one." He fell silent, gazing gloomily down at the flagstones.

"What did Vorvas do to Wanda?" Princess asked.

"He turned her into a wand!" Panstygia cried.

Kedrigern's head snapped up. He turned to Princess. They shared a glance, then a smile, then an eager nod, and the wizard sprang to his feet and boldly declared, "But we defy the odds! We'll take that chance, however remote it may be!" With a shake of his fist, he added, "We'll go to the west and seek out Hedvig's descendants. And we'd better leave at once—Princess and I want to be home before the first snow."

"Then you'll help me!" Panstygia cried.

"Of course," said Kedrigern, with a gallant sweeping bow.

"I want to come, too!" Hamarak said excitedly.

Kedrigern turned to him, his expression solemn, and shook his head. "My good Hamarak, you are a king. You can't just dash off on a quest, like ordinary people."

"Why can't I?"

"First of all, it's very bad politics. I take it you enjoy being a king."

"It's been a little confusing so far, but I think I'm going to like it," Hamarak said.

"Well, one of the hard truths about kingship is that it's much easier for a king to go away than it is for him to return. And besides, you can't abandon Dendorric. *Noblesse oblige*, and all that."

"All what? What's that you just said?"

Before Kedrigern could speak, Panstygia's stern voice said, "He means that when you're a king, certain things are expected of you, and you jolly well *do* them. There's no getting around it, Hamarak. Duty is duty. You're a king now, like it or not, and you can't let the side down."

"Remember, Hamarak," said the wizard, "You're the only one who stands between Dendorric and that wild gang from the forest. If you leave, they'll be back here the next day, and there'll be no champion to stop them."

Hamarak weighed that for a moment, then said, "If Louise goes, I won't be able to stop anybody anyway."

"But Hamarak," said the black blade in a tender maternal tone, "you never liked wielding me. You were always afraid of hurting someone."

"I wouldn't have to wield you anymore, Louise," Hamarak said earnestly. "All I'd have to do is let people see you, and that would scare off the robbers and give courage to the people of Dendorric."

"I think you've hit on the solution. A brilliant idea," said the wizard. "You're thinking like a king."

"What idea?"

With a wink, Kedrigern stepped to the hearth and took up the poker. It was of iron, very black, and about the length of Panstygia. Murmuring softly, he traced a design along its length with his fingers, then raised it high, brandished it, and plunged it down dramatically into the table top. There it stood embedded, a great dark blade the exact twin of Panstygia.

Hamarak clapped his hands and cried out in astonishment and pleasure. Kedrigern acknowledge this tribute, and Panstygia's brusque "Well done, wizard," with a dignified nod.

"The enchanted sword of Hamarak the Invincible, King of Dendorric," he said with a gesture toward the slowly swaying blade.

"This one won't make me the finest swordsman in the world, will it?" asked Hamarak wistfully.

"No. But you could always practice on your own," Kedrigern pointed out.

Hamarak accepted the suggestion with a resigned shrug. He took up the genuine Panstygia and handed her to the wizard, then rose to inspect the duplicate. When he was out of earshot, the sword gave a little hist to attract Kedrigern's attention.

"I'm not happy about leaving Hamarak," she whispered. "He's a decent young man, but he needs a firm hand to guide him."

"He'll learn," Kedrigern assured her.

"I'm not so sure. He's a peasant, and they're all a bit—"

A sharp knock at the door of the throne room interrupted her observation. "The servants were told not to disturb us," Panstygia said with vexation.

"You mentioned dinner. Perhaps it's ready. But we can't let the servants see two blades. If you'll permit me—"

"No need, wizard," said the blade coolly. She twitched in his grip, the air reverberated with a clear chiming tone, and Kedrigern held a black staff. With a low whistle, he said, "Vorvas may have been a consummate swine, but he certainly knew his stuff. That's first-rate magic."

A guard opened the door and peered in cautiously. "My lord Hamarak, the bread you requested has arrived," he announced.

"Send it in," Hamarak ordered.

"And the people to clean the palace are here, as well, my lord."

"Tell them to wait."

The door closed behind the guard and reopened to admit a girl bearing a tray on which three fragrant loaves lay under a clean white napkin. The aroma of fresh-baked bread filled the throne room. Hamarak looked on hungrily as the girl uncovered the loaves. Then he looked at the girl, and a light came into his eyes that had been summoned up previously only by the sight and scent of raisin pumpernickel bread hot from the oven.

The girl was young and very comely, buxom of figure,

sweet of expression, light of foot. Her brown hair hung in thick curls nearly to her slender waist. She was simply and neatly dressed, with only a smudge of flour on cheek and forearm to attest to her haste. She held out her tray and looked up at Hamarak with wide violet eyes and a shy smile. King and subject gazed at each other for a long time, unmoving, in profound silence.

"Your bread, my lord Hamarak," she said in a breathy, childlike voice.

"Are you the baker?" he asked.

"I am Berrian, the baker's daughter," she replied with a bow. "You met my father earlier today, after your victory."

"A little fat man gave me bread. I didn't see you, Berrian."

She lowered her eyes, and with a catch in her voice, said, "I was within, recovering from my fright. Had it not been for you, Dendorric was lost, my bold lord Hamarak."

"You don't have to be afraid anymore. Panstygia and I will protect you," said Hamarak, plucking the sword from the tabletop, setting his jaw grimly, and gazing with narrowed eyes into the distance.

Setting down the tray, Berrian stepped closer. "You're so brave . . . and so alone," she said huskily.

Hamarak shook his head and reached out to take her hand. "A wise woman once told me, 'It's lonely at the top, Hamarak. Fortunately, there are compensations. You must stay and dine with me, Berrian."

Princess caught Kedrigern's eye and winked. Clearing his throat, the wizard approached the throne and said, "If my lord Hamarak will excuse us, we will make ready to depart on our quest."

Hamarak looked at him for a moment in utter bewilderment, but recovered himself and said, "Go, friends of Dendorric. I wish I could go with you, but . . ." He sighed, smiled wearily, and concluded, "As we kings say, 'Noblesse oblige.'"

"It certainly does," said the wizard sympathetically.

···⚜ *Five* ⚜···

*once upon a time and
happily ever after*

KEDRIGERN AND PRINCESS left Dendorric early the next
morning, to the great relief of the hostler and stable boys.
They crossed the river at sunrise and rode into the misty,
silent forest, their destination a forgotten, perhaps vanished, kingdom in the west, their way unknown, their
plans unformed.

Despite the early hour and the chill air, Princess was in
the best of spirits. She considered their undertaking a
glorious adventure, a high quest in the noblest tradition.
Kedrigern was less enthusiastic. He had begun to have
doubts before they were halfway back to the inn the previous day, and his doubts had grown overnight. Now, in the
morning's clear light, he felt as if he were involved in
some monumental act of lunacy, angry at his impulsive-
ness and unable to do a thing about the situation.

Any decent wizard would be happy to assist a princess
in distress; any proper husband would go to great lengths
to secure for his wife the gift her heart was set on. But
surely there were limits. And just as surely, dashing off on
less than a day's notice, without a map, without a guide,
without even a clear direction to pursue; with each day
shorter than the one before, the mornings chillier, the
leaves falling, the winds rising, and every sign foretelling

an early and bitter winter; surely such behavior exceeded all reasonable limits. And he could see no way out of it that did not involve guilt, recriminations, and long silences in the winter evenings. He felt trapped.

Princess swooped past him, circled, and came back to hover at his side with a soft hum of wings. "Isn't it a glorious morning?" she asked ebulliently.

"It's cold and wet."

"It's bracing, Keddie. It's invigorating!"

"You're awfully chipper for someone who was up half the night talking."

"Oh, what a delight to have a mature, intelligent woman to talk with! When this is over, we must invite Louise to visit. She can have the room overlooking the garden. It's lovely in the summer."

"When this is over? We could spend the rest of our lives on this quest," said the wizard glumly.

"Don't be so negative. There's nothing to it. We just have to find the Kingdom of the Singing Forest, look up Hedvig's descendants, find out the wording of Vorvas's spell, and undo it. Why are you so grumpy? You've done much harder things."

After a brief peevish silence, Kedrigern said, "You must realize that if I disenchant Panstygia—"

"Louise," Princess corrected him. "She's Panstygia in public, but among friends she prefers Louise."

"Louise, then. If I disenchant her, I'll have to offer to do the same for her cousin Wanda. Wanda may even disenchant automatically when Louise does."

"Well, of course. I know that."

"But I thought the whole point of this was to get you a wand!"

"Really, Keddie, do you think I'd use the relative of a sister princess as my wand? Naturally I want Wanda despelled. According to Louise, she's a charming girl."

"What about your wand?"

"Having been one herself for so long, Wanda can give us the best idea of where we're likely to find the genuine item. She may have met dozens of other wands who are looking for a princess. She may even be able to tell you how to construct your own. Doesn't it make sense to try to find her?''

Kedrigern gritted his teeth and forced out an exasperated ''Yes.''

Princess laughed merrily, blew him a kiss, and flew off, leaving him to grumble to himself. After a time she drew up beside him on her translucent mount, which looked milky in the morning light, covered with fine moisture. In a cool matter-of-fact voice, Princess said, ''And on the other hand, if Wanda turns out to be permanently enchanted, I've got my wand.''

''No enchantment is permanent. That would go against the Third Law of Magic.''

''Well, Arlebar was supposed to be a great, great wizard, and he told us that I could never again be turned into a toad. That's permanence, as far as I'm concerned.''

''Arlebar was talking about disenchantment. That can be permanent. I know quite a few people who are permanently disenchanted.''

Princess had no immediate response, but after a brief silence she turned to him with a triumphant look and said, ''But *you* told Louise that some disenchantments and counterspells are so difficult, or so dangerous, that they might as well not exist. So an enchantment could turn out to be permanent for all practical purposes, even though a disenchantment exists for it.''

''That's true,'' the wizard admitted. ''And I fear we may run into something like this in Louise's case. Vorvas was as skillful as he was villainous.''

''But you'll try, won't you?''

''Certainly, my dear.''

She patted his hand, smiled, and said no more on the subject.

As the day warmed up, so did Kedrigern's mood. The forest was bright with the brilliance of autumn, the sky a clear blue free of cloud, the air crisp and tangy. They saw no one, and came upon no sign of human passage. Apparently the brigands' raid on Dendorric had been a last-ditch attempt, and defeat at the hands of Hamarak had persuaded the robbers to seek their fortunes elsewhere without delay.

Toward evening, they found a pleasant glade near a stream, and here they camped for the night. After a simple but filling meal, Kedrigern kindled a fire and heaped up leaves into a comfortable bed. Laying a warning spell about the campsite, he rolled up in his blanket and stretched out.

Princess sat by the fire, her knees drawn up, her cloak thrown loosely over her shoulders and wings. Louise, once again in her sword mode, in which she could both speak and hear, rested against Princess's knee. They conversed in low voices, with occasional laughter, and the sound of their *tête-à-tête* and the soft crackling of the fire in the background was pleasantly lulling.

Kedrigern listened as one listens to distant music: not eavesdropping, only half hearing, drifting in and out of a comfortable dozy state. The leaves rustled beneath him when he moved: the night breezes passed overhead soft as a breath. He went at last into deep sleep feeling that all might yet be well.

For two more days they saw no sign of life except for birds and squirrels, and then, on the third day at midmorning, a small black-and-white dog burst from the woods, took up a stand in their path, and filled the air with high indignant yipping. Kedrigern's great black steed snorted and pawed menacingly at the ground with a hoof the size of a punchbowl, but the dog was not intimidated. It barked all the louder, skipping from side to side, darting forward and then as quickly retreating, its bright black eyes on the travelers. It seemed intent on arresting their passage.

"This is obviously not a wild beast of the forest. There must be someone dwelling nearby," said Kedrigern.

Princess reined in beside him. "Someone sociable, but cautious," she said judiciously.

"How can you tell?"

"The owner must be cautious, since he—or she—has a watchdog. But this dog is too small to attack people, or frighten them off, so the owner must be sociable at heart, and would welcome visitors," she explained.

"Very astute, my dear. And since he—or she—lives deep in the forest, the owner must be someone who values privacy."

"True. And a kindly man—the dog is well fed and clean."

"So it is. But are you sure the owner is a man?"

"Quite," said Princess calmly.

"Then shall we seek the fellow out?"

"No need for that. He's over there, behind the beech tree," said Princess, waving in the direction indicated.

From behind the tree stepped a very tall, slender man, youthful in his appearance but aged in his manner. He returned Princess's wave tentatively. When Kedrigern smiled, and also waved cheerily to him, the man came forward.

"Rumpie didn't frighten you, did he?" he asked anxiously.

"Surprised us a bit, that's all," said the wizard.

"He's really very friendly. Wouldn't hurt a soul," the man said, picking up the dog and scratching it behind the ears, to the dog's evident delight. "It's all right, Rumpie. They're friends," he assured it. Then he saw the horses clearly for the first time and looked up with wide fearful eyes. "You *are* friends, aren't you?"

"We are indeed. This is Princess, my wife. I am Kedrigern, of Silent Thunder Mountain. We're on a sort of quest."

"A quest? How exciting!"

"Yes, we're seeking a lost kingdom for an enchanted friend," Princess explained. "My husband is a wizard. And I fly." She let the cloak fall from her shoulders in a dramatic gesture—which she had carefully practiced—and with a soft humming of her wings, rose from the saddle, circled the men, and landed gently before the stranger, smiling.

"Are you a fairy godmother?" he asked.

"No. I'm too big to be a fairy godmother," she replied, with a sharp glance at Kedrigern, who looked quickly aside. "I'm a princess. I just have these wings."

"Oh, this is wonderful! This is more than I dared hope for! Will you stop for dinner tonight? And stay over? My cottage is very near, and I have a nice clean room for you. You could help me so much if you'd just stay for a while and listen to a few of my things."

"What sort of things?" Princess asked.

"My fairy tales. My name is Zorilon. I'm a maker of fairy tales. I'm having a few problems."

"What can we do to help?" asked the wizard, perplexed.

"You're experts!" Zorilon cried. "A wizard and a princess—a princess with wings—on a quest for a lost kingdom—why, you must know witches, and dragons, and elves—and—and—"

The air rang and a woman's keen voice cried, "And an enchanted sword!"

"Oh, marvelous! Wonderful!" Zorilon dropped the dog and clapped his hands in glee, skipping about like a child given free run in a toyshop. The dog leaped and yipped and scooted back and forth, as happy as his master. "Oh, please say you'll stay! Just one night, please!" Zorilon pleaded.

Man and dog were so eager and happy that there was no possibility of refusing the request. Zorilon led them down a narrow path, through a clearing full of waist-high weeds to a pleasant, if somewhat untidy, cottage, apologizing at every step for the narrowness, the weeds, and the untidyness. Dusting off chairs for them, he said, "If only I were a wizard, I could just work a little spell and everything would be clean and bright in the wink of an eye."

"Don't believe it, my boy," said Kedrigern. "Any wizard who uses up his magic on housework won't last beyond his first century. We have servants."

Zorilon's face lit up. "That's just the sort of background information you can help me with, Master Kedrigern! The housekeeping methods of wizards . . . how a witch talks to her broom . . . what sort of furnishings one might find in an ogre's cave . . , Details like these lend authenticity to a fairy tale, but they're very difficult to check out." Gesturing to Panstygia, who rested against a chair by the table, he said, "For instance, I never knew that enchanted swords had no scabbards. I just assumed that every sword, enchanted or not, had its scabbard."

"As far as I know, young man, they do," said the dark blade. "I've never come across one that fit properly. They've all been tight up toward the hilt."

"I see," Zorilon said, reaching for a pen on a nearby worktable and scratching down a quick note.

They enjoyed a leisurely dinner of stewed wild fowl and vegetables, and afterward spent time over the empty dishes sharing news of recent events. Zorilon, aware of considerable movement in the forest in recent days, was beside himself to learn of Hamarak's deed and his assumption of power in Dendorric. He filled three sheets with notes and enthused aloud repeatedly over what a grand fairy tale this would make.

After clearing the table, Zorilon went to a cupboard and removed a folder full of sheets and scraps of parchment and vellum, all of them covered with close, tiny writing. Joining his guests at the hearthside, where they sat with Panstygia between them, he pulled up his chair facing them and cleared his throat shyly.

"I was wondering if you'd mind . . . I'd like to read you . . . I've got these fairy tales I've been working on," he muttered, eyes fixed on the papers lying in the opened folder.

"We'd love to hear them, Zorilon," said Princess.

"Oh, thank you!" Zorilon gushed. "Now, I really want your frank opinion. Don't hold back, please. I know there are rough spots, and intelligent people like yourselves, knowledgeable in the field, can point them out and even suggest improvements. These are all my own original work, you see.''

"Whatever got you into this field? I should think there are quite enough fairy tales about already," said Panstygia.

Furrowing his brow earnestly, Zorilon said, "I thought the same thing myself when I started out. All I planned to do was travel about the countryside, gathering up the fairy tales told by the local peasants, polish them up a bit, and bring out a nice collection for children. But when I started doing my research, I found that I kept hearing the same stories over and over. If I stopped at a miller's house and asked for a fairy tale, I'd hear the one about the miller's beautiful daughter who married the handsome prince. If I stopped at a farmhouse, they'd tell of the farmer's beautiful daughter who married the handsome prince. Blacksmiths would tell of the blacksmith's beautiful daughter who married the handsome prince, and innkeepers . . . well, you see the problem. Once in a great while it would be a farmer's, or miller's, or blacksmith's handsome son who married a beautiful princess, but nothing else ever changed. I must have heard that story three hundred times. The other one I kept coming across was the one about the miller, or blacksmith, or farmer, who encounters a strange little man in the woods and manages to trick the little fellow out of a pot of gold.''

"That's commoners for you," Panstygia sniffed. "Nothing on their minds but sex and money.''

"You surprise me, Zorilon," said the wizard mildly. "I always believed the common folk were veritable repositories of fairy tales.''

"That's what everyone thinks, Master Kedrigern, but it simply isn't true. And I saw this as a great opportunity. Everyone assumed—as you did—that hundreds of fairy tales were circulating out there among the people. But everyone was wrong. So I decided to go ahead and make them up myself.''

"Very enterprising of you," Kedrigern said, and Princess smiled approvingly.

"Thank you. And instead of dealing in wish-fulfillment and fantasy, I planned to write the truth, and deal with the realities of life—spells, and witches, and dragons, and magic rings—"

"And enchanted swords. Don't forget enchanted swords," Panstygia broke in.

"Certainly not, I assure you, sword. So I came out here, where I could work in peace, and now I've got scores of drafts. May I read you one?" Zorilon asked. They nodded and murmured obligingly, and he rummaged among the sheets of parchment, finally drawing one out, and began to read:

THE DEMANDING PRINCESS

Quite some time ago, there was a king who had a daughter so beautiful that no words could possibly describe her. A handsome young prince in a neighboring kingdom had a single glimpse of her as he rode by her family castle, and immediately fell into a swoon from which he did not wake for seven days and nights. When he finally awoke, his first words were, "I can love no one but the beautiful princess, and I must have her for my wife." But the beautiful princess was a very mean princess, and she told her father to send forth word that she would accept no suitor unless he swore to meet any three demands she made, on pain of losing his head. When the handsome prince's father and mother heard of this, they tried to discourage him, but he said that if he could not marry this princess he would as lief be dead, so they let him go. But before he left, the prince his brother gave him a green ribbon and said, "Wear this on your arm, under your tunic," and he did. And the king his father gave him a silver chain and said, "Wear this around your neck, under your scarf," and he did. And the queen his mother gave him a glass ring and said, "Wear this on your finger, under your glove," and he did, and then he set out alone for the kingdom of the mean princess.

When he arrived, she met him at the palace gate and said, "Are you prepared to have your head cut off if you cannot meet my demands?" He was so overcome by the sight of her beauty that he could only nod, so she said, "Very well, then. First, you must give me a green ribbon." And he gave her the green ribbon from his arm. "Now I want a silver chain," she said, and he gave her the silver chain from around his neck. "My third demand is a glass ring," said the mean princess, and so the handsome prince gave her the glass ring from his finger. So they were married, and lived a reasonably pleasant life, all things considered.

Zorilon looked up proudly at his guests. "Do you like it?" he asked, smiling.

Guardedly, Princess said, "It's very . . . interesting."

"Yes. Interesting," said Kedrigern, while Panstygia remained silent. The little dog burst into action as soon as Zorilon was finished speaking. He bounded about the room, frisking and leaping, jumping up, wagging his tail, and generally behaving in an agitated manner.

"Rumpie enjoys hearing my little stories," Zorilon said, smiling fondly on the dog. "He always acts this way when I tell them."

"Rumpie is an unusual name for a dog, isn't it?" the wizard observed, covering a yawn.

"It's short for Rumpelstiltskin."

"That's an even more unusual name," said Princess.

Zorilon looked at them in surprise. "It is? It's not an unusual name in my family. Not at all. I have an older brother with that name. And an Uncle Rumpelstiltskin on my mother's side."

"Interesting," Kedrigern murmured sleepily.

"Maybe if I read another fairy tale or two you can get a better idea of my style. I've got one right here," said Zorilon, leafing through the folder. He jerked up his head

at a sudden metallic ringing in the air, and saw that
Panstygia had become a staff. Princess and Kedrigern
gazed on her enviously as Zorilon held up a sheet of
parchment, then smoothed it out on the folder and began to
read it aloud:

ROSEBUD AND THE JEALOUS QUEEN

Some years back, a king and queen had a daughter
named Rosebud, whom everyone in the kingdom loved
because she was so beautiful and sweet-tempered. When
the queen died, the king married a very lovely woman
who possessed a magic mirror. Every day the new
queen would look in the mirror and ask:
>   "Mirror, mirror, in my hand,
>   Who is fairest in the land?"
and every day the mirror would reply:
>   "You, my dear—you're looking grand."
But one day, when Rosebud had just turned sixteen,
the queen asked her question and the mirror answered:
>   "Please, dear queen, don't be distressed,
>   But you'll slipped to second best:
>   Rosebud's fairer than the rest,"
and the queen became very, very angry and wanted to
do something that would get Rosebud out of the way
and win back her standing as fairest in the land.

While she was thinking it over, a handsome young
king from a distant kingdom came to the castle on a
state visit. When he and Rosebud saw each other, it was
love at first sight. The queen noticed, and urged her
husband to arrange a match between them, and he did,
and Rosebud married the handsome young king and
moved halfway across the world to live in his faraway
kingdom, and they were very happy. And the queen was
once again the fairest in the land, so she was happy,
too. Rosebud's father missed her now and then, but on
the whole, he was happy enough.

"Is that the end?" Princess asked. Zorilon nodded, and she said, "Ah. I see." Kedrigern remained silent, his eyes glassy.

"Maybe if I read one more, then we could discuss them . . . really do a good critique . . . no holds barred," said Zorilon eagerly. They responded to his suggestion with faint apathetic murmurs that served only to make his eagerness the keener. "Here's a good one. It's my own version of the stock theme of the miller's beautiful daughter marrying well, but I think it has a rather ingenious twist to it. I'll just read you this one, and then we can discuss all three," Zorilon said, much animated.

Princess smiled a wan smile. Kedrigern fidgeted and tried his best to conceal a yawn, but the set of his jaw and his flared nostrils gave him away. Zorilon paid no heed. He cleared his throat, took up his parchment, and began to read.

THE MILLER'S BEAUTIFUL DAUGHTER AND THE LITTLE MAN

Years and years ago, a poor miller had a very beautiful daughter. The king heard of her beauty and decided to marry her, but he insisted on a generous dowry, for he was a proud and greedy king. The miller could provide no dowry, so in desperation he told the king that his daughter could spin straw into gold. The king had her brought to the castle at once and put in a room full of straw. "Spin this straw into gold and you shall be my queen. But if you fail, it's off with your head, and your father's as well," he said, and locked her in the room.

Now the girl could no more spin straw into gold than you and I can, so she began to weep bitterly and wish that her father had kept his mouth shut. In the midst of her weeping, a little man appeared before her and asked why she was carrying on so. When she explained, he said, "If it's straw spun into gold that you want, I'm your man. But I must have my price." "And what's your price?" she asked. "I must have your firstborn child," said the little man. The miller's beautiful daughter wept even more bitterly and wailed, "Is there no way out?" and the little man said, "If you can guess my true name, you may keep the baby. That's fair, isn't it?" She agreed, and the little man went to work.

When the king unlocked the door in the morning and found the room full of gold, he married the girl at once. Within a year, they had a beautiful baby girl, and the very day after the child was born, the little man came to claim it. "If I can guess your true name, I get to keep her," the miller's daughter reminded him. "All right, guess," he said. She thought for a moment, then said, "Your name's Larry." "Someone told you!" he cried angrily, but she swore that it was just a lucky guess. So the little man went away, and the miller's beautiful daughter kept the baby, and that was that. They lived long lives, but nothing much happened to them after that.

Zorilon leaned back in his chair, spread his arms in an expansive gesture, and smiled proudly and expectantly.

"Nice," said Kedrigern.

"Interesting," Princess said. "Really quite . . . interesting."

"Yes. And nice," the wizard agreed.

Zorilon leaned forward and looked at them with a pleased, but earnest expression. "I'm glad you liked them. But is there anything you think might be improved? Perhaps a word here or there that I might change for the better?"

His guests exchanged a glance. Princess frowned, bit her lip, and said, "Well, I thought . . ."

"Yes? Please go on, my lady. I really want to hear your frank opinion. Do be blunt with me."

"There's no conflict," she blurted.

"Conflict?"

"That's right, conflict. Struggle. Opposition. Insurmountable obstacles to be overcome. Insoluble problems to be solved. Don't you agree, Keddie?''

''What? Oh, yes, my dear, conflict. That's the thing.''

Zorilon's face fell. ''But there's so much conflict in the world already. . . . I want my characters to be happy, not to be struggling and overcoming obstacles. Happy tales are what people want these days. Success stories, not a lot of gloom and suffering. Are you sure you understood what I was trying to do? Maybe if you heard them again—''

''No! We understood!'' the two of them cried with one desperate voice, and Princess added, ''We liked them very much, too. But we think that if you introduce the element of conflict they'll be ever so much better. More true to life.''

''Couldn't I just add some details of magic? You could advise me.''

Princess shook her head. ''Conflict,'' she said firmly.

Zorilon, crestfallen, nodded absently and gazed into the fire. At last he said, ''Could you be more specific? Could you point out places where I might put in conflict? Maybe suggest the kind of conflict to put in?''

''Well, you ought to make things tougher for little Rosebud, for a start,'' Princess said. ''Have the queen try to poison her, or hire a huntsman to take her into the woods and cut her throat. Something along those lines.''

Zorilon looked horrified. ''Do queens ever do things like *that*?''

''More often than you think,'' Kedrigern assured him somberly.

''I suppose . . . as long as nothing really happened to her, and everything worked out for the best . . .''

Kedrigern, warming to the subject, said, ''The lovesick prince in your first story has it much too easy, too. The mean princess ought to demand outrageous things of him. He should be in terror of his life, yet driven by his burning love.''

''What sort of demands could she make? I thought a

princess would *like* a nice ring, and a silver chain, and a lovely green ribbon.''

"Most princesses have such things," Princess pointed out.

"And this one is a mean princess. You said so yourself. So she'd ask for . . . oh, for an eagle's feather from a nest on the very top of the highest mountain in the world," the wizard suggested.

"And a black pearl from an oyster at the bottom of the deepest ocean!" Princess added, clapping her hands gleefully.

"And a ring from the nose of a man-eating ogre," Kedrigern said, "Or a scale from the chin of a fire-breathing dragon. Do you get the idea?"

Zorilon shook his head confusedly. "You seem to want me to make life difficult for my characters. But aren't people in fairy tales supposed to live happily ever after?"

"Only the good ones. And they only get to do it after a lot of misery. It makes them appreciate getting through the nasty spots," Princess said. "It's a lot like real life, only in real life there aren't as many happy endings."

"Yes . . . I think I see. . . ."

"And they shouldn't be *too* happy, either. I mean, 'happily ever after' is saying quite a lot. No married couple is happy all the time."

Kedrigern turned to her with a look of pained surprise. "My dear, I always thought that we . . . it seemed . . . aren't you . . . ?"

Princess reached out to give his hand a reassuring squeeze. "Of course we're happy, but we're an unusual couple. I was speaking of all those other people. They have problems even after they've married their handsome prince or beautiful princess or whatever. Just think of some of your clients. Even the great kings and queens don't just sit around being happy all the time."

"Too true, my dear. In fact, they probably spend less time at it than anyone would believe."

Enlightenment came over Zorilon's features, and he

cried, "They could live happily for a while, and then *wham*! I'd fix them! The beautiful princess would get these terrible headaches, and the handsome prince's leg would start acting up from an old wound that never healed properly, and their oldest son would turn out bad, and a dragon would carry off their daughter, and . . . and a plague would threaten the kingdom! Oh, a plague would really shake them up!"

Princess nodded. "You've got the idea. Just don't overdo it."

Leaning forward and raising a preceptorial forefinger, Kedrigern said, "My wife is absolutely right about kings and queens, my boy. They're an unhappy lot, on the whole. Take your story about the miller's daughter: you should make the king a lot greedier. He could force the miller's daughter to spin gold a second and third time—"

"And lots more of it! A barnful!" Princess added.

"And instead of having her promise her firstborn child right away, you could lead up to it."

"Build the suspense! Create unbearable tension!"

Caught up in the excitement, Zorilon said, "She could give him a bracelet the first time . . . and then . . . then a ring, and then, when she's desperate, only *then* would she tearfully and reluctantly promise her firstborn! Of course!"

"And she mustn't get his name on the very first guess," said Princess. "That will never do."

"And that name has to go. I mean, after all, 'Larry.' Quite a few little men are named Larry, you know."

"They are?"

"Oh, dozens of them," Kedrigern assured him.

"I don't know any little men. They're not easy to meet. I was just guessing at a suitable name. What can I call him?" Zorilon asked, picking up his dog and scratching him under the chin.

"How about 'Rumpelstiltskin'? It may be a common name in your family, but it's very infrequent among little men."

Rising and thrusting the dog into the wizard's hands,

Zorilon took up pen and parchment and cleared a space at the table, saying to his guests, "You've been very helpful. I'd like to copy down your suggestions while they're still fresh in my mind."

"Good idea. We'll toddle off to bed and leave you to your work," said Kedrigern, putting down the dog and taking Princess's hand.

In the morning, Zorilon greeted them red-eyed and yawning but in good spirits. He had sat up much of the night rereading his fairy tales and making notes, and was bursting to talk of his planned revisions. Only the repeated admonitions of Princess and Kedrigern not to talk away all his good ideas but to start working on them at once kept him from submitting his entire *oeuvre* to their scrutiny then and there.

Zorilon followed them to the stable, all the while protesting that his hospitality was but feeble recompense for their literary insight and counsel, and lamenting that he could not hope to repay them properly. He kept up his apologies as Kedrigern saddled the horses and packed their gear, and then, abruptly, the wizard rounded on him with a smile.

"Zorilon, I've thought of a way you can repay us," he said, laying his hands on the young man's shoulders. "You've traveled far and wide in the course of your research. Have you ever heard reference to the Kingdom of the Singing Forest?"

Zorilon pondered the question, frowned, and said, "No." As Kedrigern turned away with a fatalistic sigh, Princess asked, "Perhaps you heard a tale of a wicked sorcerer? A nasty man who turned a royal family into a sword, a shield, and a crown?"

"Oh, that one. Yes. 'The Vengeance of Vorvas the Vindictive,' they called it," said Zorilon matter-of-factly. "I only heard it once. It wasn't nearly as popular as the ones about someone's beautiful daughter marrying a handsome prince, or someone tricking a little man out of a pot of gold."

"Did the story-teller say where it took place?" the wizard asked.

"Long ago, in a kingdom in the west."

"Was there any mention of landmarks?" Kedrigern asked in growing frustration.

"Let me think. . . . There was something about a river. Yes, you must cross the Moaning River, that's what it was. And there was a warning. 'Beware the Green Something-or-Other,' the man said."

"Anything else?"

"No. Sorry."

"Don't apologize, Zorilon. You've been helpful," said Princess. "We'll head west and listen for a moaning river. What could be simpler?"

"Getting a ring from the nose of a man-eating ogre. Or a scale from the chin of a fire-breathing dragon," Kedrigern said under his breath.

Princess looked at him sharply. He shrugged his shoulders and gave her his most innocent smile. She fluttered gracefully up to the saddle, Kedrigern mounted his black beast, and they started on their way. They had proceeded only a few paces when Princess snapped her fingers sharply, reined in her diaphanous steed, and turned to Zorilon.

"One more observation, Zorilon: Your openings need more life," she said.

"More life, my lady?"

"They're flat. They don't create that immediate feeling of involvement and curiosity and wonder that every story-teller strives for. I mean, 'Quite some time ago . . .' or 'Some years back . . .' just won't grab an audience."

"She's right, Zorilon. They certainly didn't grab me," Kedrigern said. "How about, 'Once, a long time ago . . .'?"

"Yes, something like that. 'Once, years and years ago . . .' "

"Or maybe, 'Once upon a time . . .' " Kedrigern suggested.

Zorilon's face lit up. "That's it! That's a perfect opening! I love it! Oh, thank you both so very much!"

"I'd work on the ending, too. People don't like their stories to trail off. They want a punch line . . . something to tie it all together," Kedrigern said.

"Keddie's right. Your endings need work." Princess pressed a hand to her brow and closed her eyes in thought, then said, "You used a phrase last night when we were discussing the need for conflict. You wanted your characters to live happily . . . oh, what was that phrase?" All were silent, expectantly, and then Princess cried, " 'And they lived happily ever after!' That's it, Zorilon. I think it would make a lovely closing line for a fairy tale."

"But, my lady, last night you spoke so persuasively on the other side!"

"I did?"

"You did, my dear," Kedrigern said.

"You persuaded me that except for yourself and Master Kedrigern, people don't live happily ever after. They can't. Maybe they shouldn't even try. In any case, they don't."

Princess looked thoughtfully into the distance for a time, then said, "Oh, let's give them a break, Zorilon. What are fairy tales for?"

"But, my lady, what about all those disasters? The suffering? The plagues and dragons and misfortunes and ogres and all that?"

Princess leaned down to pat him softly on the cheek. "Give it a try, Zorilon. Let them live happily ever after. Do it for me."

He took her hand and kissed it reverently. "For you, my lady."

"Thank you, Zorilon. And remember: if you really want to fix them good, you can always write a sequel."

···⟨ *Six* ⟩···

o cursed spite

THE STOP at Zorilon's cottage had been a pleasant interlude. The young man's information, though sketchy, had been helpful. But as Kedrigern proceeded westward, his old doubts returned. Autumn was in full glory all around him; and if autumn came, could winter be far behind? Surely not. All too soon there would be ice and snow and bitter cold and impassable roads and wolves and frostbite; desperate searching for shelter; meager food; wretchedness and misery; and worst of all, an ever-lengthening absence from the warmth and comfort of their home on Silent Thunder Mountain.

Winter mornings could be quite pleasant when one awoke to them in a warm bed, under a cozy comforter or two, or three, with Princess nestled at one's side. Very pleasant, indeed. A snowstorm was an exhilarating sight when viewed through a window, with the warmth of a fire at one's back. The distant howl of wolves was a kind of stark music, all the more musical for being muted by intervening doors and walls. But a winter in the open, in the rugged trackless west country, in search of a half-remembered kingdom and an unknown distant relation, was certain to be unpleasant at the very best, and at the worst, horrendous.

The scant directions they had were nothing to inspire

confidence. For a start, cross the Moaning River (not the Happy River, or the Laughing River, or the River of Hope. No, the Moaning River). The Singing Forest, if they ever reached it, would probably sing only dirges. And who—or what—was the Green Something-or-Other, and what did he—or she or it or they—have to do with this affair?

Even if they somehow found their way to Louise's former home, there was no guarantee that they would be near their goal. What if Wanda and the rest of the family had, like Louise, been placed in a tree? Were they to go through the forest asking every tree if a relative of Louise's was inside? The more Kedrigern thought on the situation, the worse he felt.

He kept his misgivings to himself. Princess, knowing his moods, did not inquire into his long silences. He contained himself for several days, until at the end of an afternoon of cold, drenching rain he erupted in a wild tirade. Princess let him go on, and when he was out of breath she patted his hand and said sweetly, "You'll think of something."

The next morning was dry and sunny, almost summery in its warmth. The leaf-paved trail was misty, the forest curtained in gray, and Princess laid her cloak over her saddle and flew above the treetops to scout out the way. It was pleasant to escape the closeness of the lower world, and stimulating to exercise her wings. She swooped, and turned, and dipped, and circled, and then quite unexpectedly she came speeding back to Kedrigern's side.

"Three armed men ahead!" she cried breathlessly.

"Robbers?"

"Don't think so. They're dressed . . . as guardsmen."

"That's a good sign. All the same . . ." Kedrigern brandished the black staff. The air rang, and in his hand was Panstygia, Mother of Darkness.

"Is there any trouble?" she asked.

"It's possible," Kedrigern replied.

"I saw three armed men on the road ahead. They may be friendly, though," Princess explained.

"I thought they'd be a lot friendlier if I were carrying a big black sword," Kedrigern further explained.

Panstygia sighed. "If you absolutely must use me, you'll be the greatest swordsman in the world, but I do hope you can avoid violence. I don't enjoy hewing and smiting."

"I'm not fond of it myself," the wizard assured her.

Princess flew back to her horse, mounted, and drew up close behind Kedrigern. They rode on slowly, alert for any sign of the guardsmen. As they passed into the shadow of a pair of giant oaks that rose like sturdy columns on either hand and formed a shaded vault overhead, a figure loomed before them and a voice called out, "Halt, if you please, travelers."

Kedrigern, in the lead, drew in the reins and his black steed was still. Princess rode to his side before stopping, and said confidently, "He's too polite to be a robber."

"Let's hope so," Kedrigern replied; then, raising his voice, he addressed the figure in the road. "What business have you with us? Speak, stranger."

"None, if you are ordinary travelers. My lord and master, King Ezrammis, is sore afflicted," said the man, starting toward him. "A curse has come upon him, and he seeks the aid of a . . . of a . . . a wuwuwu . . ." His voice shrank and was still. He stopped in his tracks, his eyes displaying much white. His mouth hung open.

"A wizard?" Kedrigern asked gently.

The man nodded. He looked at the slitted red eyes and beaded silver horn of the black steed that towered over him, and the black blade resting on the rider's shoulder. The rider himself seemed quite ordinary. He was dressed in simple garments of homespun stuff, neat but not gaudy, and his features were alert but not particularly striking. The woman beside him was dressed rather better than he, and wore a circlet of silver. She was breathtaking in her beauty. She was on a horse that seemed to be only half there. These people were no commonplace travelers.

The guardsman stood gaping. Two others joined him and were transfixed in their turn.

"Perhaps we can help your king. I am Kedrigern of Silent Thunder Mountain. This is Princess, my wife. We have some knowledge of the subtle arts," said the wizard.

"Quite a lot, as a matter of fact," Princess added.

With a sigh of relief, the first guardsman said, "My master and mistress will be pleased to see you. You will be richly rewarded. If you care to follow us, it's just—"

"No tricks!" said a clear ringing voice, and the three guards jumped back and huddled together. "I am Panstygia, Mother of Darkness, the great black blade of the west. No army can stand before my wrath!"

"You heard her," said Princess.

"No tricks, I swear! Honest, no tricks!" the guard cried.

"Very well, then. Lead on," Panstygia commanded.

It was a bit pushy of her, Kedrigern thought, but he kept his opinion to himself. Princesses, he had found—with the single happy exception of his wife—were spoiled and willful creatures. In their way, they were as bad as the princes he had known, and the princes were impossible. And kings and queens could be much worse. He could only hope that King Ezrammis, of whom he had heard very little, was not like most of his class.

A short ride brought them to a tidy castle on a hill, with a pleasant garden and a lovely view to the south. They were brought directly to the throneroom and presented to a small gray-haired woman with a sweet, sad, motherly face. She was almost spherical in shape. She cast an envious glance at Princess and burst into tears, but recovered herself quickly.

"The wizards are here, Your Highness," said the guardsman, bowing low.

"Oh, good dear kindly wizards, can you help us?" asked the queen in a voice to wring the heart of an ogre.

"I trust we can, Your Highness. In cases of cursing, the main thing is to determine the facts. Can you give us a complete account? It's particularly important that we know the exact wording of the curse."

"Oh, I can tell you that," said the queen. "Let's just introduce ourselves, and then we'll sit down to a little snack, and then get to business."

Her name was Queen Pensimer, and her idea of a little snack was enough food for a healthy family of twelve. While Kedrigern and Princess ate moderately, the queen wolfed down dish after dish, stuffing herself indiscriminately with fruit and bread and meat and butter and cake and pudding and fish and gravy and nuts as they came within her reach. When the meal was completely consumed she sank back into her oversized chair, gasping, and covered a queenly burp with her pudgy hand.

"I never used to eat like this. It's all part of the curse," she said despondently.

"Perhaps you could tell us more about this curse," Kedrigern said, leaning forward, placing the tips of his fingers together and peering intently across the table at her.

"Well, I don't know exactly how it all started. I walked in while Ezrammis—that's the king, my husband—was in the middle of a bitter quarrel with the wizard Ashan. They've been friends for a long time, but they're both getting cranky, and they argue a lot these days. Apparently Ashan had threatened to put a curse on our children for some reason, but when I entered he changed his mind and cursed Ezrammis and me instead. It was terrifying. He raised a skinny hand and pointed at my poor husband and began to recite:

> 'May your teeth drop down like hail,
> One each month, and never fail;
> While you live on whey and batter,
> May your wife grow ever fatter,
> Eating double lunch and dinner
> Every day, as you get thinner,
> Till at last you vanish utterly,
> And she's round and fat and butterly.'

That was three months ago. Since then, Ezrammis has lost two molars and a bicuspid, and I've doubled my weight," said the unhappy queen.

"I think we can do something about this, Your Highness," Kedrigern said with professional solemnity. "It's a straightforward curse, and though I've never met Ashan personally, he's known in the profession for being an impulsive sort—not a man likely to plot out a complicated curse in advance and brood over it for years. May we see your husband?"

They were shown at once to the royal bedchamber, where King Ezrammis, a sunken-cheeked, gray-bearded man late in his middle years, lean as a lath, was sulking. Kedrigern reviewed the situation with the king, who remained silent, communicating in nods and gestures of varying degrees of emphasis. When all was clear, Kedrigern had the royal couple sit side by side on the royal bed while he worked the appropriate counterspell.

When the last word was spoken, King Ezrammis looked up. Cautiously, he ran his tongue around his mouth. He tried a front upper tooth against the ball of his thumb, and grinned at the result. Very carefully, he gritted his teeth. With a whoop of glee, he shouted, "Solid as the dungeon walls! Well done, wizard! Now let's get some decent food in here. Three months on milk and mush could kill you!"

"Ugh! Please don't mention food, dear. The very thought of food revolts me. Isn't that wonderful?" Queen Pensimer exulted.

Kedrigern and Princess bowed graciously and withdrew to leave them to their rejoicing. Later that evening they were summoned to the royal presence. King Ezrammis was cheerfully picking his teeth after a snack of cold fowl, celery, nuts, and apples, while Queen Pensimer, already looking a bit thinner, sipped a small glass of water. A faithful old retainer sat by the king's side, dozing.

"You do nice work, wizard. Very nice," the king said in greeting, underscoring his praise by holding out a hefty purse of gold. "And you, too, my dear lady," he added, taking Princess's hand and slipping onto her finger a ring containing a diamond the size of an acorn. "I don't know how things got out of hand, but I appreciate your help. It's

not like Ashan to hold a grudge. I expected the curse to
last a few days, maybe a week . . . but three months! I'm
glad you came along."

"You never explained that to me," Pensimer said. "You
never said anything to me at all."

"Who could talk? If I tried, it sounded like I had a
mouthful of dominoes. Besides, you were always too busy
eating to listen to me."

Kedrigern, puzzled, said, "Then it was all a misunder-
standing?"

"You could say that. I never realized how sensitive
Ashan was about his cursing. He was telling me how he
laid this curse on some no-good knight and his whole
family, gave all the sons indigestion and the daughters bad
breath, and I laughed. 'This is a curse?' I said. 'This is
family history! When my sons gather in the courtyard
after dinner, it sounds like an earthquake in a thunder-
storm. My boys eat a crust of bread and sip a mouthful of
water, and for two hours they rumble like volcanoes. And
my daughters can etch glass just by breathing on it.' "

"I wish you wouldn't talk about the children that way,
dear," Pensimer said, frowning.

"Am I lying? Anyway, Ashan got very touchy and said
that my kids' troubles could be cured by an apprentice
alchemist, but the knight's family would need a first-class
wizard to straighten them out. One remark led to another,
and first thing I knew, Ashan was climbing out the window, my teeth were waving around in my mouth like shirts
on a clothesline, and Pensimer was eating everything that
couldn't run away." Ezrammis paused, sighed, and shook
his head sadly. "I hope Ashan is all right. It's not like him
to stay away so long."

"Where did he go?" Kedrigern asked.

"The guard said he headed west. Nasty country out
there."

"Is there anything particularly nasty we should know
about? We're heading that way ourselves."

"Must you? Nice people like you don't belong out there," said Queen Pensimer primly.

"We're seeking a lost kingdom for a friend."

"Well, be careful," Ezrammis said. "You've got that big green idiot to watch out for—some crazy giant who leaps out at travelers and forces them to answer riddles."

"What if they don't answer?" Princess asked.

"He eats them. And there's an enchanted patch of forest, too. You want to watch out for that. And the Moaning River. Depressing place, they say."

"Does either of your majesties know of a Kingdom of the Singing Forest out there anywhere?" Kedrigern asked.

"Never heard of it myself, but I'll ask around the castle. Maybe old Jossall knows something. He's been here since my grandfather was a boy," said the king, reaching over to nudge the old retainer at his side. The man's eyes flew open and he exclaimed in a high thin voice, "Yes, indeed, Your Majesty, that's absolutely true. Oh, true beyond a doubt, no question at all, Your Majesty. Well said and wisely put, not a word wasted, just as—"

"It's all right, Jossall. I only want to ask you something," Ezrammis broke in. "Have you ever heard of a Kingdom of the Singing Forest somewhere off to the west?"

The old man looked at the king, then at the wizard, and then at each of the ladies, with an expression of growing bewilderment. His eyelids slowly closed, he nodded, and just when he seemed to be falling asleep he jerked his head up and said, "Yes! I heard the story long ago . . . a sad tale, Your Majesty . . . a treble curse . . . a bold young warrior prince and two valiant princesses . . . the malice of a sorcerer known for his vindictiveness . . . oh, a tragic story it is, Your Majesty, and a lesson for us all," concluded Jossall with lugubrious voice and rueful shaking of his white-haired, white-bearded head.

"Do you know the way to this kingdom?" Kedrigern asked.

"No one goes there now."

"If someone wanted to go there, could you give him directions?"

Jossall looked at him steadily with pale, searching eyes, and at last said, in a soft and distant voice, "The way lies across the Moaning River, beyond the enchanted wood, through the domain of the Green Riddler. But you are not—"

"What's the Green Fiddler?"

"Riddler. He is a giant who forces travelers to solve his riddles. If they cannot—"

"He eats them. We've been warned," said Kedrigern. The name sounded vaguely familiar, but he could not fix it in his memory. Was it a name he had read, something out of a traveler's tale, or a legend? Might it be someone he had once dealt with? He could not recall. In all likelihood it was a lot of nonsense, but the half-remembered name was bothersome.

"As I started to say," Jossall went on, "you are not the one who is to find it."

"I'm not?"

"The land is empty now," Jossall went on, oblivious to Kedrigern's question, speaking like a man reciting the remembered prayers of his childhood, "and the royal hall stands deserted, but one day a great hero will restore the glory of ancient times. So says the prophecy. Even now, he wanders the earth, an empty scabbard at his side, in his unceasing quest for the great black sword that will enable him to undo the curse of Vorvas."

"Vorvas? Vorvas the Vindictive?" King Ezrammis asked sharply.

"The very man, Your Majesty."

"What did Vorvas do, go around cursing everyone he met? He put a curse on one of my great-grandfather's sisters. You must know about that, Jossall."

The old man was silent for a long time before replying, "I was very young at the time, Your Majesty, but I remember a period of extreme consternation. Princess Gazura was cursed with blunt speaking. All her suitors vanished.

It eventually became necessary for her to go off and live in seclusion.''

"Vorvas was a fiend," said Princess vehemently.

Ezrammis nodded in agreement, but added, "He had imagination, I'll say that for him. What sort of curse did he lay on this friend of yours?''

With the king's permission, Kedrigern withdrew to fetch Panstygia, so she could tell her story in her own words. Ezrammis and Pensimer listened with growing sympathy, while Jossall was absolutely fascinated.

"This is the sword of the prophecy!" he proclaimed when she was done. "It is the sword foretold! When the hero comes, the curse will be lifted!''

Rather waspishly, Panstygia said, "I don't plan to wait for some hero to come along, thank you very much. If you'll just direct us to my kingdom, we'll see about this curse.''

"You've got a good wizard there. He got the curse off us like *that*," Ezrammis assured her with a snap of his fingers.

Modestly, Kedrigern said, "Counterspells and disenchantments have long been my specialty.''

"Have you heard of the Desolation of the Loser Kings?" Princess asked the company. "It was a terrible conglomeration of nasty magics, all stewing and seething and breeding even nastier new magics of their own. Kedrigern cleared it up single-handed.''

Kedrigern smiled benignly and said nothing. The king and queen appeared suitably impressed, but Jossall said solemnly, "You may be a skilled wizard, but you would be wise to withhold your power in this matter and let the prophecy run its course. Vorvas was the greatest of them all when it came to cursing.''

"No, he wasn't," Kedrigern said flatly. "He's right up there near the top, I grant you that, but Vorvas isn't the greatest. That title belongs to Flaine of the Four Fates.''

Sounds, gestures, and facial expressions indicative of wonder and eager curiosity made it clear to Kedrigern that his auditors were ignorant of Flaine's accomplishments. He waved them closer, and as the darkness deepened outside the castle and the candles in the royal bedchamber burned low, he began his amazing tale.

FLAINE OF THE FOUR FATES

PART I: THE CURSE

Not so very long ago, four miscreant knights spread fear throughout the land. They were very wicked and very bold. So bold were they, in fact, that they were known as Giles the Bold, Otto the Bold, Bruce the Bold, and Dennis the Bold, or the Four Bold Blackguards. Their greed, ferocity, and wickedness grew with each evil deed, and no one dared to resist them.

One winter day, as they rode back to the castle of Giles the Bold after doing something particularly terrible to a group of harmless pilgrims, the Four Bold Blackguards came upon a little cottage in the woods. The day was cold and gloomy, and they were in a peevish mood. They decided to take whatever food and drink was within the cottage and then burn it and its occupants, so they might warm themselves at the flames and take pleasure in the screaming.

Unknown to the miscreant knights, the cottage was the home of Flaine, a wizard who had grown weary of the wickedness of men and retired to the depths of the forest to study and meditate. When Dennis the Bold pounded on her door, she told him to go away. When he and Bruce the Bold began to smash the door down, she cast a spell to render the cottage inviolable. Finding their plans thwarted, the Four Bold Blackguards withdrew to form a new one.

The preceding autumn had been a season of violent storms. Fallen wood was scattered everywhere. The four gathered a great supply and piled it around the cottage, then warned the occupant to let them in or they would burn it to the ground. Flaine responded by summoning up a rainstorm; but Flaine was getting on in centuries, and her power was diluted by the necessity of keeping up the spell of inviolability, so she managed only a brief shower. The Four Bold Blackguards were able to light the fire, and soon the cottage was surrounded by a high wall of flame.

All through the night, Flaine held the fire out. But the four fed it generously and she found herself weakening. At dawn, knowing that the end was near, she opened the door and stepped into the flames, which shrank from her. The four knights drew their swords and rushed forward, but with her last strength she sent the flames at them, driving them back. Raising her hand, she pointed to them and intoned these words:

> "For this wicked deed you do,
> Wizard-slayers, hear your fate:
>   Ice and iron, wood and water,
>   Shall requite this cruel slaughter;
>   Wood and water, ice and iron
>   Shall entice you, like the Siren,
> To the secret rendezvous
> Where my vengeance shall await
> You, and you, and you, and you."

At the last word, her power gave out. The flames closed in and rose up around her with a great roar. In an instant, all was consumed.

"A very impressive curse. It rhymes, even," said King Ezrammis.

"And you must remember, it was impromptu, and done with her dying breath," Kedrigern pointed out.

Jossall waved a skinny hand for attention. "Yes, yes, but what of the curse? Did it work?"

Kedrigern smiled. Clearing his throat, he settled back and went on with his story:

PART II: FULFILLMENT

The Four Bold Blackguards were annoyed by this turn of events, but unshaken. They had been cursed by dying victims so many times that they had become connoisseurs, and while they found Flaine's style and delivery impressive, they dismissed the content as the same old blustering.

In the course of the siege they had finished their food and water, so they set out again at a goodly pace for the castle of Giles the Bold. About midday, as they crossed a meadow, a knight dressed entirely in red appeared from the woods at the far side and blew a challenge on his horn.

Pleased with this opportunity for sport, the four reached for their weapons, that they might gang up on the lone knight. But the red knight charged at such speed that he took them by surprise, unhorsed Dennis the Bold, and disappeared down the path they had come.

Dennis the Bold lay groaning and uttering foul oaths, run through the chest with an iron-tipped wooden lance that had broken off in the wound. He begged for water. Having none, they gave him water from a puddle and placed him on his horse, binding him upright in his saddle and pressing on to the castle of Giles the Bold, where help might be found. The clouds gathered, and it grew bitter cold. Dennis the Bold began to rave and cry out wildly, and they realized that the water had been tainted. Before they reached the castle, he was dead— but whether he had frozen to death, or died of the tainted water or the iron-tipped wooden lancehead in his chest, no one could say.

At his castle, Giles the Bold was first to reach the drawbridge. For some reason, he dismounted and started across on foot. He tripped over an iron spike, slipped on a patch of ice, hit his head on a wooden beam-end, and plunged into the deep murky waters of the moat. It was morning before his servants recovered the body.

Otto the Bold and Bruce the Bold slept fitfully that night, and after replenishing their supplies they left for their own strongholds, traveling together to gain whatever sense of safety they could from companionship, though in truth there was little feeling of companionship in either of them, and no feeling at all of safety. They knew that their doom was closing in.

As they made their way along a stony ridge above a shallow stream, Bruce the Bold heard a sharp cracking noise overhead. He looked and saw an ice-coated branch break free and strike Otto the Bold from his horse and send him rolling down the slope into the stream, where he lay face down in the water, immobilized by the weight of his armor. By the time Bruce the Bold reached him, Otto the Bold was dead.

In panic, Bruce the Bold rode until his horse dropped like a stone from exhaustion and died without a sound. Stripping off his armor, telling no one his true name, Bruce the Bold made his way ever southward, until he came to a desert. Here he stopped. He hid in a cave, eating uncooked food out of clay vessels. He never washed, and drank no water, subsisting on goats' milk When he regained his self-possession to some extent, he set down a full account of the fates of his companions and himself. He had once been a student, and knew how to write.

The last entry, in a shaking hand, told how he awoke one morning in an agony of thirst, feeling as if his body had been wrung dry of all fluids. He began to shiver uncontrollably as a chill came over his ravaged frame. With no wood about, he could not make a fire, so he dragged himself from the cave to seek the warmth of the sun.

He managed to struggle to the top of a small rise. A goatherd saw him and shouted, but Bruce the Bold was dead before anyone could help him.

"Now, that's cursing," said King Ezrammis. "I'm glad I never had an argument with Flaine. She knew her business."

"Flaine was the best there ever was," said Kedrigern. "She was a true professional."

Jossall would have none of this. "She wasn't better than Vorvas! Her curse fell apart at the end, with Bruce the Bold, didn't it? All the other deaths involved ice and wood and water and iron, but there wasn't any iron in the death of Bruce the Bold."

Unruffled, Kedrigern said, "I didn't finish the story."

PART II: FULFILLMENT (CONCLUDED)

The goatherd, though he had lived long and seen many strange sights, had never seen anything like this. The Fearful One, as the local people had come to call Bruce the Bold, crawled from his cave and dragged himself up the side of the rise. He struggled to his feet and stood with his arms spread wide and his face turned to the sun. As he stood there, something plummeted from the skies and hit him squarely in the chest, knocking him flat. It was a chunk of solid iron the size of a man's head, very badly pitted and warm to the touch. The desert people call such an object a "meteorite."

A profound silence followed the end of Kedrigern's tale. At last Jossall said in a low disgruntled voice, "Maybe Vorvas is the second greatest of them all when it comes to cursing. But he's a *close* second."

···⁕ *Seven* ⁕···

in the grip of the green riddler

KING EZRAMMIS was firm. "I don't like to see you going off to the west on your own. You may be good wizards, both of you, and have an enchanted sword to help you, but it's dangerous out there. I'm sending one of my guards along."

"Your Majesty is very kind, but there's really no need," said Kedrigern. The horses were saddled and packed, and he was eager to be on his way. But the king was not to be dissuaded.

"His name's Dyrax. He showed up here one day last fall and asked to be taken into my service. Done very well here, too. He's a gloomy sort, but he gets along with everyone."

"I'm sure he's a sterling man, Your Majesty, but we—"

"He's been out there. Knows his way around. He can guide you to the Moaning River without wasting a lot of time. Get you there and back before the weather turns bad."

"Oh. I see."

Ezrammis nudged him and laughed slyly. "I thought that would change your mind. Besides, if you should come across Ashan, or news of him, I want to know, and you may not come back this way, so I'll need a messenger.

Dyrax is good and dependable. Quiet lad, brave as a lion, nice and polite. Never talks about himself, but he comes from good stock. I can tell.''

"We thank Your Majesty once more. If we hear word of Ashan, we'll send Dyrax back at once."

"No hurry, wizard. Let him take you to your destination first, and give you good clear directions for the rest of the way." Ezrammis paused, then added in a softer tone, "Try to find Ashan for me, though. He probably thinks I'm furious about the spell, but I'm not. He was a good arguer. I miss him. Tell him so. He'll believe another wizard."

"I'll tell him if I see him, Your Majesty."

Princess, having taken her leave of Pensimer, said a last affectionate goodbye to Ezrammis. When she turned to her horse, grooms sprang forward to help her mount. Kedrigern looked about, but saw no guardsman.

"Go ahead and mount. Dyrax is waiting at the gate. He doesn't like crowds," said Ezrammis. And as they approached the gate they saw him, a sturdy, well-built young man with noble features and an air of deep gloom. He rode a handsome chestnut stallion and led two heavily laden packhorses.

"I am Dyrax, your guide and protector," he said in a somber, cultured voice. "My sword and my life are at your service."

"That's very nice of you, Dyrax, but I think all we're going to need is someone to point out the way," said Princess.

"I have traveled in the western lands, my lady. Strange and perilous are the things to be found there."

"Well, my husband and I both know magic, and we do have an enchanted sword. We really don't expect trouble. Just the usual inconveniences of wayfaring."

With a stately, sweeping gesture in the direction of the packhorses, Dyrax said, "King Ezrammis, with his accustomed generosity, has made provision against the worst inconveniences."

"He's a kind man," said Kedrigern, "and I'm sure you'll be a great help to us, Dyrax. Shall we be off?"

Dyrax took the lead, with the two packhorses directly behind him. Princess followed, and Kedrigern rode at the rear of the little column. From time to time he and Princess rode side by side, chatting or simply enjoying one another's company in silence, but Dyrax never looked around and spoke only when directly addressed. In the evenings, he set up camp in some pleasant spot, prepared a simple but tasty meal, and erected a shelter for the wizards. He spread his own blanket in some dark and gloomy spot. On the first night he had announced his willingness to keep watch while the others slept, but they would not hear of it. A simple spell provided a more dependable warning system than a small army of heavy-eyed humans, and they wanted their guide to be alert along the way; and aside from such practical considerations, they did not like to see a healthy young man deprived of his rest. Dyrax seemed doleful enough already. There was no need to add fatigue to his problems.

On the fourth evening after their parting from Ezrammis and Pensimer, as Princess and Kedrigern lay side by side in their shelter, snug under blankets light as gossamer but warm and cozy as plump comforters, Princess yawned and said, "Can't we do something for Dyrax? He's so sad."

"He is, isn't he? Always sighing." Kedrigern paused for a yawn, then said, "I don't know any good jokes. I was never much of a hand at telling jokes."

"It's not jokes he needs. He's thwarted in love, that's Dyrax's problem."

"How do you know?"

"The sighing. Deep, heartbroken sighs are a giveaway."

After a thoughtful silence, Kedrigern asked, "What can we do?"

"First we ought to find out the whole story. We won't know if we can help until we know what's the matter. Listen—he's sighing again!"

Cautiously they raised their heads and peered outside. Dyrax sat by the fire, his chin cupped in his hands, gazing morosely into the flames. From time to time he heaved a deep, desolate sigh. Occasionally he groaned. At last he rose from the fireside, and with bowed head and slow, sad steps he walked to where his blanket lay and threw himself down.

"I'll talk to him tomorrow," Kedrigern said.

But when morning came, Dyrax was much too melancholy to be approached. He prepared breakfast for the wizards, then went aside to nibble a crust of bread and sigh. Kedrigern answered Princess's urgent glances with calming patient gestures, and they started the day's travels in silence. Three times during the morning Princess fell back to ride at Kedrigern's side and exhort him in angry whispers to make good his word and speak to the sad young man, and three times he put her off. At last, near midday, the wizard braced himself, reassured his wife, and leaving the black staff that was Panstygia in her care, rode forward to Dyrax's side.

"Lovely day, isn't it?" he said with a cheery smile.

Dyrax raised his head and looked upward and around. "The sky is blue. It is neither too warm nor too cool for comfort. The leaves are highly colored. Yes, Master Kedrigern, one might speak so of this day."

"It doesn't sound as though *you* would."

Dyrax sighed profoundly and said, "*Lovely* is a word I have purged from my vocabulary, along with *beautiful* and *fair* and *happiness* and *joy*."

"That's too bad. Is there any way I can help? I'll be glad to do whatever I can, honestly."

"No one can help me. Nothing can undo what has been done, unsay what has been said. I live in an abyss of pain, seeking forgetfulness, cursed with remembrance."

They rode on in silence for a time, into a darker, denser part of the forest where the road narrowed and overhanging branches shadowed the way. In these surroundings Kedrigern found himself falling into the dismal mood of his companion, and thinking that it was not such a lovely day after all. But he shook off such thoughts and said confidently, "If it's forgetfulness you want, I may be able to help you."

"No, kindly wizard. If I were to forget the cause of my unceasing anguish, I would forget my reason for being."

"I have some very selective spells. I could work it so that you only forget the bad parts."

Dyrax shook his head slowly. "I must remember. It is my fate to remember, and to suffer."

Kedrigern could see that he was getting nowhere, and changed the subject, observing, "The forest seems to be thicker here."

"Yes. We are in the domain of the Green Riddler. We must be wary. He is as cruel as he is strong, and his strength is the strength of ten. He is twice the size of ordinary men. Our lives are in great peril at every moment," said Dyrax in the same weary monotone.

"Do you think it might be wise to take another way?"

"There is no way to avoid the Green Riddler. If we should encounter him and his minions, be assured that I will defend you to the death, and fall with my sword in my hand."

"It may not come to that."

"No one can withstand the Green Riddler."

Provoked by this unending flow of negativism, Kedrigern said, "I may not have the strength of ten, Dyrax—on some mornings I have barely the strength of one—and I am not twice the size of anyone but dwarfs and children, but I am a wizard. I have magic at my command."

"So, it is said, has the Green Riddler."

"He has? No one mentioned it before."

"Perhaps people assumed that you know."

"I wish people wouldn't make that assumption. I'm not fond of surprises," Kedrigern said with some annoyance. They rode on a few paces, neither man speaking, then the wizard brightened and exclaimed, "Wait a minute, now. I *do* know the Green Riddler. Never met the fellow person-

ally, but I've read of him. Yes, of course. He's a friend of
Sir Gawain's; something of a prankster, but a decent sort.
He has some rudimentary knowledge of magic, but he isn't
the sort to misuse it.'' He paused to chuckle in a warm and
friendly way, and concluded, ''We have nothing to worry
about, Dyrax. All those tales about the Green Riddler's
eating people are nonsense. He's a pleasant chap. We'll
get along.''

''I fear you are mistaken, Master Kedrigern. The Green
Riddler is said to have an amiable brother with connections
at Camelot, but he himself is a monster of wickedness,''
said Dyrax.

''Oh. And he has magic powers, you say?''

''So I have heard, and believe.''

Kedrigern looked somber. ''Well, then, we will just
have to see whose magic is stronger.''

The opportunity to put this question to the test came
sooner than the wizard had expected. Scarcely had they
gone a hundred paces farther on this dark portion of the
trail when they reached a clearing, and as they entered the
clearing from one side, the Green Riddler strode from the
forest opposite them. One by one, his followers stepped
from behind the trees around the clearing. The Riddler's
men were common forest ruffians, scruffy-looking, dressed
in rags and animal skins, carrying clubs and daggers and
rude spears, and all of them bore an expression of stupid
malice. Their leader was unmistakable. He was bright
green from head to foot—hair, beard, skin, and clothing
were all green as spring grass—and the distance between
these points was at least twice the height of an ordinary
man.

The travelers halted, ringed by sullen men and facing
their giant leader. The Riddler stood with folded arms,
looking the trio over, and then he laughed, a deep slow
rumbling laugh that suggested a very unpleasant sense of
humor.

''Arm yourself, wizard,'' said Dyrax in a steely undertone. ''Side by side, we will fight to the death.''

"Don't be hasty. There may be another way out of this," Kedrigern said.

"There is none. The Green Riddler is merciless."

"I don't intend to appeal to his mercy."

The Green Riddler raised one hand in greeting. Kedrigern returned the salute. Dismounting, he approached the giant, stopping just out of reach and working, as he walked, a quick protective spell to cover his companions and himself.

"Good afternoon, big fellow," he said politely.

"Good afternoon to you, traveler, and welcome to my domain. You have arrived just in time for a wonderful dinner," the Riddler boomed.

"Kind of you to invite us, but we're just passing through on our way west. It's too early for dinner, anyway," Kedrigern replied.

"Not a bit early. You're right on time. You're the dinner!" the Riddler cried, roaring with unnerving laughter as he pointed at the wizard. "You yourself will be the appetizer. This husky swordsman will be our main course. And the lady will be a most delicious dessert."

When the amused grunting of the Riddler's men had subsided, Kedrigern said, "I'm afraid we must disappoint you. We are not staying."

"They all say that. But they all stay."

"All? Does that mean that you spare no one?"

Self-righteously, the giant proclaimed, "I am the Green Riddler, traveler. I have a reputation for fair play. If any who come this way can solve three riddles, they may pass in safety and enjoy my protection all the way to the banks of the Moaning River."

"Excellent, excellent. Let's hear the first riddle. No sense standing here all day," said Kedrigern, folding his arms to match the giant's stance and looking up with an expression of anticipation.

The giant looked around, gloating, and smiled to display very large greenish teeth. Stooping a bit, he recited:

> "I am no woman, yet I bear
> Children made of living air,

Invisible to every eye.
Unless I choose to slay them,
My daughters never die;
My sons live on forever.
Now say—what man am I?''

Kedrigern had never heard this one before, but he felt that he knew the proper answer. It was right there, fresh in his memory, close to the surface. He scratched his nose, and rubbed the back of his neck, and stroked his chin, and screwed up his face in an expression of profound concentration, while the Riddler leered at Princess and bared his teeth at Dyrax. Then the wizard flung up one hand and cried, ''A maker of tales!''

The Green Riddler scowled. His men muttered in a sour, ominous tone. Kedrigern smiled and bowed graciously. ''I can tell from your expression that I gave the right answer. Next riddle, please,'' he said, snapping his fingers.

''You won't get this one. You think you're clever, but you won't get two of my riddles in a row,'' sulked the giant.

''Oh, get on with it.''

The giant snarled and ground his teeth while his men nodded confidently to one another and hefted their weapons. Kedrigern ignored it all, and at last the Riddler said:

''Motherless and fatherless,
Born without a skin,
I speak when I come in the world
And never speak again,''

and placing his arms akimbo, he glowered down on Kedrigern.

The wizard chewed on his lip. The riddle was familiar. He had heard it somewhere, years and years ago, but his mind was a complete blank and the harder he thought the blanker it got. He had a vague memory of long-ago days, of himself as a boy, the servant of old Tarrendine. The work was hard, but Tarrendine was a kindly master and left him plenty of time to himself. There was an inn nearby. He would go there sometimes, on the hot summer days, and drink beer. Sometimes the innkeeper had a tale, or a song, or a riddle. Often they were rather coarse . . .

The Green Riddler began to chuckle in a nasty way. He swept the trio of travelers with a hungry glance. Kedrigern scowled. The answer to the riddle popped into his head, and he reddened, and shaking his fist, he cried furiously, "You boor! You churl! You base barbaric lout! You lumpish lubberly uncouth booby! How dare you pose such a riddle in a lady's presence!"

Abashed, the giant retreated a step. "It's only a riddle," he said.

"It's an extremely vulgar riddle that no one but a giant would repeat within a lady's hearing, and I demand that you apologize to my wife this instant. Go on, apologize."

Lowering his head, the Riddler muttered, "I'm sorry, my lady."

Princess averted her eyes and acknowledged the apology with a dignified nod. Kedrigern, slightly mollified, said, "Go on to the next riddle. And mind it's in good taste."

The Green Riddler paused, pondered, and turned narrowed suspicious eyes on the wizard. "Wait. You didn't get this one yet."

"Of course I did, but I'm not going to shout it out." Kedrigern motioned for the Riddler to bend down, and when he had, whispered in his ear, "The riddle is about a fart."

The Riddler howled in frustration. Thrusting several of his men aside roughly, he stalked to a tree at the edge of the woods, wrapped his arms around the trunk, and with a great straining grunt tore it from the ground and flung it from him. Shaking the dirt from his feet, he shook his fists at the sky, thumped his chest loudly, and roared.

Kedrigern, unperturbed, said, "When you're quite ready, I'd like to get on with the riddles."

With another roar, the giant ran to the uprooted tree. Raising it high above his head, he slowly bent the trunk, his skin darkening to the color of holly leaves with the effort, until the tree broke in two with a terrible splintering noise. Hurling the pieces aside, he returned to take up his place before Kedrigern. When his breathing was back to normal, he glared at the wizard and spoke his third riddle.

> "One, holding one, under one;
> Two tops bare to the sun;
> Three white sticks in a line;
> One taps; one makes a whine;
> No sound at all from three.
> Say what this scene may be."

With a disdainful sniff, Kedrigern said, "A pale, bald, one-legged beggar with a white crutch standing under a birch tree in winter." The Riddler gaped at him and his green eyes grew wide. The wizard turned, walked to his horse, mounted, and in a kindly voice added, "If that's really the best you can do, I think you ought to consider going into another line of business. Lumbering, perhaps. And now, if you'll tell your men to step aside, we really must run."

"How did you guess my riddles?" the Green Riddler demanded in a voice squeezed small by anger and frustration.

"Sheer brilliance," Kedrigern replied off-handedly.

"No! You cheated!"

"We must fight, Master Kedrigern. We'll cut our way through this rabble or die in the attempt," said Dyrax.

"Patience, my boy. We'll save the cutting for a last resort. Let's try using our wits first," Kedrigern said in a lowered voice. Addressing the giant, he said aloud, "You're not playing fair, Riddler. I solved your riddles and you must let us pass. You need not accompany us all the way to the Moaning River, but we would appreciate knowing of any shortcuts."

The Green Riddler did not move from their path. His men shifted irritably from one foot to the other, sensing trouble, impatient to stop all this talk and get to work. Folding his brawny arms across his huge chest, the giant said, "It's obvious to anyone that you cheated. Nobody could solve my riddles without cheating. So we're going to eat you. That should teach you a lesson."

"Before you do anything you'll regret, let me pose a riddle of my own. I'll be happy to tell you the answer if you're stuck," said the wizard.

"Don't try any tricks on me."

"No tricks at all. I *want* you to solve this riddle. Ready?"

At the giant's nod, Kedrigern said, "Who is it that rides in the forest at peace with the world, no man's enemy, wishing good to all, yet has the power to turn anyone who attacks him into a fieldmouse?"

"That's not much of a riddle. It doesn't even rhyme," said the Green Riddler scornfully.

"Indulge me. Give it a try. Come on."

The giant muttered to himself. He scratched his head loudly and dug his fingers into his tangled green beard. He rolled his eyes skyward, shook his head, and at last said, "I don't know. Who?"

"Kedrigern, the wizard of Silent Thunder Mountain. And I am he," the wizard announced. "I hope I make myself clear."

The Green Riddler was not easily convinced. "You're no wizard. You don't even look like a wizard."

"Observe my horse," Kedrigern said patiently. "Would anyone but a wizard ride a horse like this? Would they dare? And look at my wife's horse, if you can."

The giant studied the great silver-horned steed and squinted helplessly in an attempt to see Princess's horse, which was all but invisible in the bright sunlight. For a moment he seemed to waver, but then he cried in frustration, "I don't care what kind of horse you ride, I don't believe you're a wizard! You look like . . . like a merchant!"

"Do you suppose I'm going to dress up as a wizard to please the likes of you? It so happens, Riddler, that I am secure in my professional identity. I require no pointy hat, and no long robe covered in cabalistic symbols, to prove my status. I feel no need to dress any other way than the way I choose, and if you think I dress like a merchant, that's your problem and not mine. Why do *you* have to go around all green and overgrown, I'd like to know. What are you trying to prove? You're probably not even a giant,'' said Kedrigern disdainfully.

"I am so a giant! And I'm not afraid of wizards, either. Just this summer, I caught the wizard Ashan trying to sneak through the forest. He couldn't solve my riddles, so I ate him!''

Kedrigern gave a little jump in the saddle, and his motion made the black steed snort and toss his head and the silver horn to flash menacingly in the sun. The Green Riddler's men started back. The circle came apart. Things began to happen all at once. Kedrigern heard a soft *whitt* at his side and turned to see Dyrax brandishing his sword. The air tingled and smarted with the presence of magic, and the Green Riddler flung out his hand in the first movement of a spell, but it shattered against Kedrigern's own protective spell, and before the giant could recover his wits, Kedrigern channeled all his power into a great transformation that lanced out before and behind them, and to the sides, touching the Riddler and all his followers. They vanished from sight, leaving nothing behind but a small commotion in the grass.

Dyrax, his sword poised for a blow, looked wildly about and cried, "Where have they fled? What has become of them?''

Kedrigern blinked, caught his breath, and replied in a strained voice, "They're still around here somewhere. I turned them into fieldmice.''

"Keddie, are you all right?'' Princess asked, hurrying to the wizard's side.

"I'm fine, my dear,'' he assured her, squeezing her hand weakly. "Just dizzy for a moment, that's all. I had to put a lot into that spell, and do it quickly.''

"Let's get away from this place,'' she urged.

"Yes, at once. Lead on, Dyrax.''

They rode at a faster pace than before, wanting to get
away from the clearing and its ugly memory. Ashan's fate
had come as a shock, and Kedrigern could not drive it
from his mind. For all his bulk and bluster, the Green
Riddler was a quick hand with a spell, and the spell he had
tried to cast was a strong one; had Kedrigern not been
prudent, and protected himself and his companions at the
very outset, the situation might have been grave. Poor
Ashan must have been taken completely unprepared. It
was a sobering thought, and it led Kedrigern to some
serious brooding on the vicissitudes of wizardry and the
general hostility of the world and its inhabitants. It was
hard enough to be safe in one's own cottage; to go traveling in strange lands was sheer recklessness. And all for a
wand. Surely, he thought, there must be an easier way to
find a wand.

But then there was Panstygia—or Louise. One had to do
what one could for a princess in distress. Not that much
could be done after all this time. A fool's errand, that's
what this was. If he was not careful, alert every second,
they might all end up like Ashan, or worse.

Kedrigern rode for the rest of the day in sullen silence.
Princess, aware of the strain that working spells can place
on one, kept a close protective eye on him but did not
fuss. She knew how much pleasure he could derive from
solitary brooding, and let him indulge himself.

The brush with danger seemed to have had a salutary
effect on Dyrax. He rode a bit taller in the saddle. His eye
was brighter, and there was a spring to his step. When
they made camp that evening, he even chose a comfortable
and picturesque spot overlooking a small waterfall to spread
his blanket.

Princess insisted on casting that night's warning spell,
and Kedrigern made not even a token protest. He was still
weary, feeling weak, and glad to avoid anything that
would further drain his powers. He turned in as soon as
they had eaten, and slept like a man entranced—until
Princess shook him awake in the dark.

"Someone's coming, Keddie. Can you feel it?" she whispered.

"Yes," he said groggily, rubbing his eyes. "A lot of people. And they're coming fast. Let's go."

Dyrax sprang up at a word, and they were quickly on their way. Just before dawn, as they came to the top of a rise, Kedrigern called for a halt and reined in his great black steed. Turning to face back down the trail, he raised the medallion of his guild to his eye and peered through the Aperture of True Vision at the medallion's center.

"Can you see them?" Princess asked anxiously.

"There's a man all in black . . . a very big man . . . with twenty-two . . . no, twenty-seven . . . thirty . . . thirty-six followers. All big, all dressed in black. Thirty-six of them, and their leader, and they're hot on our trail."

"What shall we do?"

"We will meet them sword in hand and fight to the death!" Dyrax cried joyously.

"Are you mad, Dyrax? We will flee!"

"This is dangerous ground, Master Kedrigern. The enchanted wood lies near, and in the faint light, we might easily lose our way."

"Princess and I can usually tell when there's magic around. We'll be safe enough, Dyrax."

"I could cast a small spell to mislead the people following us," Princess offered.

"An excellent idea—but make it very small, my dear. I'll need a few days to get my strength back, and we mustn't deplete yours."

"Can't we just stand our ground and challenge them? I'd appreciate the opportunity to perform a heroic deed."

"Heroic, yes; suicidal, no," said the wizard flatly. "We flee, Dyrax. Cast your spell when ready, my dear."

Princess faced down the road and rolled back her sleeves. Turning to Kedrigern, she said, "I'll confuse them for a day. There's no point in doing more. We're not even sure they're after us. They *could* be friendly."

"Great big scowling men dressed in black from head to

foot may be friendly souls, but somehow I doubt it. Confuse away, my dear.''

Princess extended her slender arms. She shut her eyes tightly and murmured in a soft, barely audible voice. "There. It's done," she announced, adjusting her sleeves and brushing back a stray lock of hair. Kedrigern, who had observed their pursuers through the Aperture of True Vision, seized her hand, kissed it, and raised it high in a victorious gesture, crying, "And very well done, too! I'm proud of you, my dear. They're already milling around and blaming each other for losing the track. We should have ample time to elude them.''

They rode all morning, stopped for a short rest at midday, then pressed on, steadily westward. About midafternoon Kedrigern felt a faint tingle in the air, and rode to Princess's side.

"I have a feeling of magic near. Do you feel anything?" he asked.

She looked about, rubbed her hands, and at last said cautiously, "No, nothing. But I'm still not good at sensing magic.''

"It takes practice," he admitted. "The magic seems to be over that way," he said, waving vaguely to his left.

"Then let's go *that* way," said Princess, raising the black staff and pointing to their right.

"Look at those woods, my dear. Impenetrable. We'll just have to wait until we come to a side road. By the way, I'll be glad to carry Louise for a while. You've had her since yesterday.''

"I don't mind, Keddie. I'll carry her until you're fully rested.''

"Well, as long as you don't mind . . . Look, I'd better warn Dyrax about the magic. We don't want him blundering into anything," Kedrigern said, urging his mount forward.

Princess watched him as he rode past the packhorses and drew up at Dyrax's side. Kedrigern spoke, and Dyrax replied, and their conversation became quite animated as it went on. Princess could not hear the words because of distance and the noise of the horses' hooves, but she could see the gestures, and she smiled. Men seemed to have such difficulty talking to one another in a calm, reasonable way. Always such flurry and bluster and emphasis.

Then, suddenly, the air shimmered, as if a ripple had passed over still water, and both men were gone. The lead packhorse whinnied, stopped short, and pawed the ground, but then calmed down and proceeded on the way. There was no other sound, no motion, not so much as a breeze; only a faint tingle in the air that faded even as it touched her.

·····⁊ Eight ⁊·····

princess without kedrigern

"OH DEAR ME," said Princess softly. She rode to the spot where Kedrigern and Dyrax had last been visible and looked in all directions, even up and down. They were gone without a trace. The track of their horses ended abruptly, without a suggestion of struggle or hesitation, as if they had gone in a single step from this plane of being into another; which, as she thought of it, was probably just what they had done.

"Keddie? Keddie, can you hear me?" she called. There was no reply. "If you can't speak, give me a sign." There was no sign. "Keddie, do something! Anything!" There was nothing.

She drew her cloak close around her, for protection; then she flung it off, to free her wings, in case flight became necessary. The packhorses were plodding on, and she knew she ought to go after them; but she was reluctant to leave the place where Kedrigern had vanished. He might be in danger. He might need her help. He might be safe, but as worried about her as she was about him. He might be, or think, or feel, almost anything.

She tried to put herself in Kedrigern's place and think as he would. That was no help at all. Would he try to return here, or would he press on to the Moaning River, or

perhaps all the way to the Singing Forest, in the assurance
that she would go on herself and trust in him to meet her?
She found convincing reasons to support every possibility,
but none so overwhelming that she was forced to accept it.
She longed for someone to talk to, someone who could
help her weigh the alternatives, suggest different approaches,
plan calmly; but she was alone in the middle of this
gloomy wood, miles from friends and companions and
kindly counsel.

It suddenly dawned on her that she was not really alone.
She raised the dark staff and gave it a little shake. "Louise, I'd like to talk," she said.

The staff twitched in her hand. The air rang, and she
found herself clutching the black blade. It was massive, a
weapon for a mighty swordsman thickly thewed and steel-
sinewed, and yet it rode gracefully in her grip. Although
she had always—as far back as she could remember, in
any case—felt an aversion towards weapons and a dislike
for those who used them, she now found herself thinking
that with this blade in her hands, she might be a pretty fair
swordswoman. As she shifted her grip and hefted the
blade, she became certain that she would be a very good
swordswoman; in fact, she would be the best ever, anywhere. Barbarians, recreant knights, and obnoxious giants
like the Green Riddler would go down like stalks before
the scythe when faced with the might of Princess. It was a
heady moment.

"You called?" said Louise in a cool businesslike voice.

Princess blinked and gave a start. "Yes, I did. It's
Kedrigern. He's vanished, and Dyrax with him. We're
alone."

"Did the packhorses vanish, too?"

"No. They're going on ahead."

"I suggest you get them before they wander too far.
You'll need the supplies."

"What if they should return here? Shouldn't we wait
and see?"

"Kedrigern won't return here," the sword said confi-

dently. "He'll find his way to my kingdom, and expect
you to do the same. He certainly won't expect you to
mope about in the woods, waiting for him to show up."

"No, I suppose not. Surely not. He can take care of
himself, and the sooner we're out of these woods, the
better I'll feel," said Princess, spurring her translucent
mount.

"You needn't worry about your safety. If you find it
necessary to wield me, you'll be the finest swordswoman
in the world."

"I felt that as soon as you became a sword, Louise. You
have a knack for inspiring confidence."

"It's kind of you to say so. One likes to feel helpful.
All things considered, though, I'd prefer to be a princess
again," said the blade. After a moment she added, "If it
should become necessary to wield me, I hope you'll remember to refer to me as 'Panstygia.' "

They caught up to the packhorses in a very short time,
but once they had, Princess was not certain what to do.
She had been raised as a princess, not as a drover, or
herdsman, or whatever one called people who deal with
large animals. She noticed a rope trailing behind the lead
horse and managed to catch hold of it, then rode alongside
the horse for a time simply holding the rope and feeling
rather foolish. This was certainly not the way things were
done. At last she rode ahead and looped the rope around
her saddle horn. The packhorses trailed behind her obedi-
ently, and after a few glances over her shoulder to monitor
their progress, she rode on feeling a bit more in command
of things. She had her supplies; the trail was plain and
easily followed; and Louise would help her to beat off any
attackers her magic could not handle; in emergencies, she
could fly. If only she could be sure of Kedrigern's safety,
she thought, this might almost be a pleasant little adventure.

Kedrigern could, of course, take care of himself, as she
had assured Louise. His magic was not at peak strength,
and that put him at a disadvantage; but he was a resourceful wizard, as more than one adversary had learned. She

was pretty resourceful herself, Princess reflected, recalling
the sight of Grodz, her would-be ravisher, turned into a
toad and trapped in his own boot. The memory of her first
big spell encouraged her, as did the knowledge that she
had learned a thing or two since then. It will all work out,
she told herself.

Her complacency received a jolt when the rope suddenly
went slack, and turning, she saw that the packhorses had
vanished. There had not been a sound, and there was none
now. No bandits swarmed from the woods or dropped
from overhanging branches. No tyrant's bullying guardsmen
appeared to seize the reins of her horse. This was the work
of no human agency. It could only have been magic. She
drew in the severed rope and found the end fused as
smooth as glass. Yes, it was magic, beyond a doubt.

This was a bad turn of events. The packhorses had
carried all their gear—tent, tools, cooking utensils—and
all the food except for some dry bread and cheese she
carried in a scrip. Without the horses, she was helpless.
Upon further reflection, she realized that she would have
been every bit as helpless if they had remained, and en-
cumbered as well. She had not the remotest idea of how to
unload a horse, or do anything else with it but ride. She
could not light a fire or put up a tent, and though she
occasionally baked a bit of fancy pastry at home, the
cooking was all left to Spot. She had never had to concern
herself with such matters, either as princess, toad, or wife
of a wizard. Louise, with a life experience limited to
princess and sword, could offer no helpful advice.

"Fine mess this is turning out to be," Princess muttered.

"Things could be worse," Louise said by way of consolation. "You're better off without those horses, if you ask
me. Just something else to worry about."

"It's easier for you, Louise. You just turn yourself into
a stick, and that's that. I have to find water, and a place to
sleep, and I have to make a fire, and do something about
my horse . . . if *he* disappears, I don't know what I'll
do!"

"He's practically disappeared already," Louise pointed out, with a hint of suppressed amusement.

"You can see him quite clearly when the light is right," said Princess irritably. "Really, Louise, this isn't funny."

"Don't get upset. You can always fly, you know."

"Well, yes. I suppose . . . yes, I could." Princess sighed. "You're right, Louise, I mustn't get upset. I just have to concentrate on finding a good place to spend the night. We'll worry about the other things as they arise."

"That's the attitude I like to see. Remember, you're a princess," said Louise stoutly.

Before the sun was down, Princess had found a huge oak with a nice clean dry depression high up in the trunk where she could pass the night in safety, if not very much comfort. A brook ran nearby. She drank, washed the dust of the road from her hands and face, filled her water bottle, and watered her horse. The transparent steed seemed quite comfortable and untroubled, so she tethered it to a sapling within reach of the brook and flew up to her place in the oak. She spread out her cloak, seated herself, and settled down to a supper of hard bread, dry cheese, and water.

"It's not easy, being a princess," she observed glumly.

"Easier than being a sword," Louise retorted.

"Yes, certainly. Or being a toad, for that matter. But there's so much they don't teach us. I can't remember the details, but I'm sure I had a typical princess's education—embroidery, court etiquette, the lute, singing—that sort of thing."

"Dancing, too, I'm sure. I used to have dancing lessons every Monday and Thursday, just after Recitation. Hated it."

"I must have had dancing. I still remember some of the steps. But what I'm getting at, Louise, is what good has it all been?"

"It improves the carriage. My mother always said that."

"I mean *practical* good. Here we are, out in the woods, and if it weren't for my wings and my magic, I'd be helpless. If I were a peasant, I'd know how to kindle a fire, and make a shelter, and catch food, and cook it. I'd know what to do about horses, and how to keep the smoke from blowing in my face, and how to make a comfortable bed out of leaves and boughs, and find my way by the position of the sun and moss on the sides of trees. Peasants learn all those things. Why don't we?''

Louise answered without hesitation, "They have to—they're peasants. We don't—we're princesses.''

"That's not much of an answer, Louise.''

"It's the only one I ever got,'' the sword admitted. "I thought it might help.''

"Then you must have asked the same question!'' said Princess, delighted.

"Not exactly the same. I always wondered why Alice and I weren't taught to fight, as William was. The kingdom was in constant danger and every additional warrior would have been a help. But my mother always said, 'Soldiers do the fighting, Louise. They have to—they're soldiers. You don't—you're a princess.' It used to upset me terribly. I'd kick the dancing master black and blue out of sheer pique.''

"But you learned to fight, didn't you?''

"I watched my father's men training, and practiced in secret. My brother William got me a sword and taught me everything he knew. I learned quickly. Alice never got the knack of swordswomanship. Her heart wasn't in it. She liked politics. So when the invasion came, William and I led the troops and Alice ran things at home. It worked quite well, until that disgusting old Vorvas . . . oh, the wretched man!''

"He must have been awful,'' Princess sympathized.

"They're all awful. The only decent men I ever knew were my father and William. I learned very early in life that men are out for only one thing—they want to turn you into something nasty at the earliest opportunity.''

Indignantly Princess said, "I don't see how you can say they're *all* awful, Louise. Kedrigern has gone out of his way to do you a good turn. And he would never have met *you* if he hadn't gone to Dendorric to look for a present for *me*. That's two good turns right there.''

"Well . . . he's an exception," Louise grudgingly conceded.

"He certainly is. And Hamarak was decent enough, wasn't he?"

"All right. Two exceptions. But most men are absolute devils. Can't wait to find a beautiful princess so they can turn her into a sword, or a toad, or a rosebush. It's all they think of.''

"It's not only men, Louise. I was turned into a toad by a female bog-fairy. And I know a charming little princess— Lalloree is her name—who was imprisoned behind a wall of fire by a jealous sorceress.''

"At least Lalloree stayed a princess. She wasn't turned into a toad.''

"Not then. That came later.''

"Aha!" Louise cried in triumph. "And it was some man who did it!''

"No, it wasn't. It wasn't a woman, either. It was a magic mist. It did all sorts of things, good as well as bad. Our horses were perfectly ordinary until the mist turned them into . . . well, into what they are now. And it turned me from a toad back into a woman and gave me wings, besides.''

"I thought your husband had turned you back into a woman," said Louise suspiciously.

"He did, the first time. The second time, it was the magic mist that did it.''

"You seem to have had a run of very bad luck with spells.''

"I certainly did. For a long time, it was just one thing after another." Princess fell silent, looking into the gathering darkness, thinking about those days; then she set her chin firmly, raised her head, and said, "But I came through it, and we'll come through this, Louise. You'll see.''

The sword did not reply at once. Finally, in a listless

voice, she said, "It hardly seems to matter. You can never feel secure. I mean, I might get out of this spell, and wander into a magic mist, and find myself turned into a spear, or a warming pan, or heaven knows what." They were both silent for a long time, and at last Louise sighed and said, "You were right. It's not easy being a princess, Princess."

"It's no better for princes," said Princess gloomily. "I've known them to be turned into toads, and bears, and swans, and monsters. Your own brother is a shield."

"It all seems terribly unfair. You don't hear of these things happening to kings and queens, or the lesser nobility, and almost never to the common people. It's always the beautiful princess or the handsome prince. What does everyone have against us?"

"Just jealous, I guess." Princess wiped her fingers daintily on a leaf, took a final sip of water, and stretched out, pulling the cloak around her. "I'm going to turn in, Louise. I'm exhausted."

"It's been a hard day for you. I think I'll stay on the alert for a while. One never knows what's likely to happen in a place like this. Oaks tend to attract an odd crowd."

Princess mumbled an indistinct and sleepy reply. Louise, propped up securely in the fork of a branch, surveyed the dark forest. Scarcely anything was visible now, nor could any sound be heard save the soughing of the wind in the treetops. It was a restful, lulling sound, and in a short time Louise was ready to turn herself into a staff and rest, but then she had a glimpse of light far off. It disappeared for a moment, then she saw it again, and saw, out of the corner of her eye, another light in the opposite direction. They seemed to be converging on this spot. She watched them closely, to make certain, and when she saw a third light approaching on a course to meet the other two, she decided to wake Princess.

When she had explained the situation, she said, "It's probably a band of brigands meeting to divide their spoils.

Nothing to worry about. Just take a good grip on me and do what comes naturally. I'll take care of the rest.''

Covering a yawn, Princess asked, "What if it's fiends, or demons? Or witches? We're near enchanted ground, and this is the high season for witches."

"Use your magic."

"I don't know if I could handle three of them. Especially if they're major witches. The Witch of the Isles, or the Witch of the Cold Seas, could turn me inside out," said Princess uneasily.

Louise did not reply for a moment. They both watched the lights closing on the tree, and finally the blade said softly, "Let's just keep quiet and hope they don't notice us."

"Good idea," said Princess. She stretched out on her stomach so that she could peek over a limb, through the leaves, to the open ground below, and arranged Louise in a good viewing position at her side. There they waited.

A cloaked figure arrived at the oak, joined almost at once by a second cloaked figure. Each bore a globe of swirling light in one hand. They dropped their lights to the ground, where the two flowed together to form a pool of brighter light, growing still brighter when the third traveler, and the third light, arrived. The figures threw back their hoods, revealing stringy white hair, warty faces, and pointy chins, and at once began to cackle with laughter and exchange greetings.

"Welcome, my sister, Witch of Sticky Little Things! Where have you traveled, and what have you seen since last we met beneath this venerable oak?" asked the first arrival. Her question was preceded and followed by a great deal of cackling from all three.

The second witch to arrive answered, "I have traveled to the sea and raised a squall to cause mild seasickness in threescore and seven sailors. And what has my sister, the Witch of Over There Someplace, seen and done, and where has she gone?"

After more cackling, the last arrival said, "I have been

to the castle of the King of the Murky Lake, where I caused the roof to leak and the chimneys to smoke, to everyone's annoyance. And where has our sister the Witch of Mud been, and what things has she seen and done?''

The witch who had been first on the scene said, "I have made the rounds of the fairs, where I caused jugglers to drop plates and balls and apples, and soured the cider and made flat the ale and burned the cakes.''

They cackled once again, with noticeably less enthusiasm. The cackling dwindled and died out, and there was a long silence. Someone sighed. One of the witches said in a dull dispirited voice, "Another year shot."

"Makes you wonder, doesn't it?'' said one of her sisters. "Might as well sit home by the fire, gumming a crust of bread.''

"If I *had* a crust of bread, I'd sit home and gum it, believe me.''

"It's the walking that does it. It I wasn't so worn out from walking, I could do a nice bit of evil now and then, but I've been at this since I was a slip of a girl and I still haven't scraped together the price of a broom.''

"A broom? I can't even afford to keep a *cat*!''

"I had to sell my cauldron last year to pay the rent on my hovel.''

"Look at my cloak. It's a rag. Shameful, I call it.''

The complaints came flooding out.in whiny querulous voices. Princess and Louise listened from the darkness above. When the three witches began to argue over who had the largest holes in her shoes, and whose garments were most ragged, Princess whispered to the blade, "These are not major witches.''

"Obviously,'' Louise replied.

The complaining went on until the witches had gotten it all out of their systems, long after each of them had ceased to pay any attention to the grousing of her sisters. They trailed off into a diminishing three-part harmony of grievance. Indignation slowly modulated to annoyance, thence to a sullen despondency that silenced all three. For some time no one spoke. Finally, one of the witches rose and scratched herself vigorously.

"Maybe things will get better," she said without conviction.

"Can't get much worse," one of the others muttered.

"Has anyone heard any news? There must be something going on that will give us a chance for some decent mischief," another said.

"Well, someone's gone and cleared up the Desolation of the Loser Kings, that's what I heard. A pair of wizards went in and blew all the magic to bits."

"No! What did they want to do that for?"

"Just showing off, I suppose. You know wizards."

In the tree, Princess nudged Louise and smiled proudly. "That's Keddie and me they're talking about," she whispered.

One of the voices below said, "Lovely place, the Desolation. Hideous spells and curses and enchantments all bubbling and stewing together. Lots of fiends lurking about . . ."

"And demons. Mustn't forget the demons."

"Oh, ever so many demons, yes. It was grand, the Desolation was."

A pause, then a nostalgic sigh, and one of the sisters said, "It's a shame to see the old places change. You'd think wizards would have a little consideration for the rest of us."

"They're an independent lot, those wizards."

"Out for themselves, wizards are. That's what I always say. Wizards are out for themselves."

Princess's nostrils flared a bit, and she gritted her teeth audibly, but did not speak. Louise whispered to her very softly, "Pay no attention to them."

"I hear tell the Knight of the Empty Scabbard is at it again, dashing about with his band of loyal followers," a witch said.

"A great simpleton, that one."

"Oh, yes. Just like his father. And his grandfather."

"He'll never find it. The Mother of Darkness has been lost since I was a girl. Longer than that."

Louise gave a little jump at the words. Princess laid a steadying hand on her hilt and patted her pommel to calm her and keep her from crying out. "I'm all right now," Louise said after a moment. "It gave me a turn, hearing my name."

"I understand, Louise. Let's listen to what they say," Princess whispered.

The witches' mood had improved. They were cackling again, now and then emitting a bloodcurdling shriek of laughter.

"Ah, that Vorvas. There was a wizard for you," said one fondly.

"Never did a kind thing in his life. You wouldn't find Vorvas mucking about with the Desolation of the Loser Kings, except to make it even nastier."

"A great one for putting uppity princesses in their place, Vorvas was," said one witch, eliciting a fresh outburst of happy cackling.

"That little snip Blamarde has been snoring away for nearly a century because of her proud tongue."

"And those redheaded twins from off beyond the mountains. Fixed them good and proper, Vorvas did."

"His best one was right nearby, in the Kingdom of the Singing Forest, when he changed that great cow Louise and her brother and sister and—"

"Wretches! Villainous, venomous crones!" cried Louise in a voice that set Princess's ears ringing. The blade was fairly vibrating with passion. "You've gloated your last gloat, hags! I, Panstygia, Mother of Darkness, the great black blade of the west, will be avenged!"

With shrieks and howls, the witches snatched at the pool of light and caught up their glowing spheres. They raised them high, hopping about in jerky motion, staring upward, pointing at every quiver of the leaves above them. The lights blazed up. Cries of "There! No, over there! It's a demon! Where?" overlapped.

"Well, you've done it now," Princess said.

"I couldn't help myself," Louise replied, still quivering with barely controlled anger.

"I suppose not. Do me a favor, and let me handle things from now on. I'm going down there and talk to them."

"Talk to them? Carve them to bits! That's what they deserve! Just swing your arms, Princess, and leave the slashing and smiting to me."

"There will be no slashing, Louise. And no smiting, either."

"Just a few good whacks with the flat of my blade. Please."

"These witches know things that may be helpful."

"Well . . . if they try anything, I'll be ready for them."

"So will I, Louise." Gripping the sword firmly by the hilt, Princess lifted off with a soft hum of her wings, circled the tree, and landed lightly and silently behind the shouting witches. "Looking for someone?" she asked.

They turned, emitting startled cries. In the lurid light of the globes, Princess was a formidable sight. She stood erect, gripping the great dark sword with both hands, the flat of the blade resting lightly on her shoulder. Her expression was severe. Her circlet twinkled and glittered in the glow of the swirling lights.

"It's a fairy godmother!" cried the Witch of Mud.

"They don't come that big," said the Witch of Over There Someplace.

"I don't care how big she is, sisters, look at her wings. Those are the wings of a fairy godmother, mark my words."

"That's no wand she's carrying."

The third witch wailed, "It's Panstygia! It's the Mother of Darkness!"

"The great black blade of the west!" cried the first.

All three began to shriek and mill about desperately, throwing up their hands in wild gestures of abandonment and despair and crying out incoherently about swords, curses, and revenge. Princess looked on, silent and unmoving. Eventually the three weird sisters ran out of breath. They turned, panting, to inspect Princess more closely.

"What are you doing here, a pretty little thing like yourself?" asked the Witch of Over There Someplace sweetly.

"Gave us a turn, you did," said the Witch of Mud.

"Oh, yes. You don't expect to have anyone drop in like that in the middle of the forest," said the Witch of Sticky Little Things, baring a single grayish tooth in a grin.

"Especially someone carrying a big black sword," said the Witch of Mud.

"Much too big for you, my dear. But it's ever so becoming. Matches your hair, you know," said her sisters, nodding eagerly.

"It must be terribly heavy, though. Your poor little arms must ache from carrying that thing around," said the Witch of Over There Someplace with great solicitude.

"Why don't you just put it down and come over here and sit with us? We can have a nice chat," said the Witch of Mud.

"Oh, that would be lovely, wouldn't it? So seldom we get to meet the young people and have a little talk with them," said the Witch of Sticky Little Things. "Let's do that. Come, dearie, put the nasty old sword down and join us."

The blade vibrated angrily. Princess whispered reassurance until Louise was calm, then said to the witches, "This is not a nasty old sword. This is Panstygia, Mother of Darkness, as you well know."

"Well, now, dearie, we might have shouted out all sorts of things in our surprise. Hearing voices up in a tree, and then seeing a sweet little thing like yourself right in our midst with a big black sword on her shoulder . . . oh, my, there's no telling what we might have yelled out," said the Witch of Sticky Little Things.

"Now that I can see it clearer," said the Witch of Mud, shielding her eyes with one hand, "I'm beginning to have my doubts. That blade's not broad enough to be Panstygia.''

The metallic voice of the sword rang through the darkness. "Wretched hags! Know that I am Panstygia, and I am returning to my kingdom!''

"No! You can't do that!'' the weird sisters shouted in unison.

"I can and I will,'' the sword declared, and Princess stoutly added, "And I'll see to it that she does.''

The witches were staggered by these words. They gaped at Princess and her dark blade, then turned to one another.

"The spell will be broken,'' said the Witch of Over There Someplace, her voice quaking.

"The curse will end!'' cried the Witch of Mud.

"Our power will vanish!'' wailed the Witch of Sticky Little Things. "We must seize her, and take the blade!''

They turned on Princess, their skinny hands outstretched. She lowered the sword and cocked her slender arms for a swing. Louise—now Panstygia—was comfortable in her grip, perfectly balanced. "Don't try it, girls. You know what this sword can do,'' Princess said evenly.

They faltered and fell back. Princess advanced a step, raising the sword aloft. That was too much for the witches. With cries of "Flee, flee!'' and "Every witch for herself!'' and "Fly to the farthest corners of the earth!'' they seized their globes of light and vanished into the dark forest. The little residual pool of afterglow faded and slowly dwindled, like water seeping into the ground.

"I wonder what all that was about,'' Princess said.

"Apparently, once the enchantment on me is lifted, something is going to happen to those three. Serves them right,'' said Louise.

"I wish we could have found out more before they ran off.''

"What more do we have to know? We're close to my kingdom, and the fact that those crones were so worried must mean that I have a good chance of becoming myself again.''

"But *why* were they worried? They seemed to be involved in your spell. They knew Vorvas. This whole affair may be more complicated than we suspect."

"I refuse to be troubled by the babbling of a few tenth-rate witches," said Louise grandly.

"And who's the Knight of the Empty Scabbard? Whoever he is, he's looking for you, and he probably expects you to be a sword."

"I certainly hope he'll be disappointed."

"Louise, you're not taking a very helpful attitude. We're talking about magic, an enchantment of great potency that has lasted for several generations, and the more involved it gets, the more lightly you treat it. You really must take these things more seriously."

Louise did not reply at once; then, with a tremble in her voice, she said, "Oh, Princess, I so detest being a sword, and I want so badly to be a real woman again! I simply can't face the possibility that I'll have to go on this way. I can't bear to talk about it, and I don't even want to think about it!"

"There, now," said Princess, laying a gentle hand on Louise's pommel, "I understand. I often felt the same way back in the bog. I hated being a toad."

"Then you know how I feel."

"Oh, I do. And I sympathize. But it was worse being a toad. I mean, I was just one more ugly toad. The bog was full of them. At least you're something special."

"Don't tell me how much worse it could be, and how fortunate I am, Princess. I don't think I could bear it," Louise said pettishly.

"All right, Louise. I guess we're both tired. Let's fly up and get some sleep. We'll make an early start."

·····⚹ Nine ⚹·····

kedrigern without princess

A Warning To The Reader

Several very nasty scenes occur in this chapter, and those who are reading for delight and diversion may be upset by them. However, anyone who skips to the next chapter will miss important information and key details regarding the life of Dyrax, the useful but seldom-seen herb *Haemony*, and the shocking malice of Vorvas the Vindictive. It would be best to read this chapter in its entirety, but cautiously. And not too soon after eating.

"OH DEAR ME," said Kedrigern softly.

"What's wrong?" Dyrax asked.

"Princess is gone. She must have strayed into the enchanted wood. The pack animals are gone, too."

"Maybe it's we who have strayed, Master Kedrigern. This place is odd."

"What do you mean, odd?"

"It feels strange. Tingly. Like cool breezes blowing on

you from all sides, very gently, only they're not really cool and the air is still.''

Kedrigern looked around, sniffed the unstirred air, and then looked around once more, studying the sky, the trees, and the path. "I think you're right, Dyrax. We've crossed over somehow, but I don't understand how I did it without knowing,'' said the wizard, looking uncomfortable.

"You said your magic was low," Dyrax pointed out.

"It's not *that* low. I should be able to sense enchantment when I'm riding straight into it. Unless . . . maybe this is a very complicated and subtle bit of enchantment.''

"It's an old one. Or so I've heard.''

Kedrigern grunted irritably. "I've heard that, too. And an old enchantment, as a rule, loses a bit of its strength as the centuries go by unless it's very conscientiously maintained. But this one is still powerful. It must have been a masterpiece when it was new.''

"Maybe if we just rode very carefully back the way we came . . .''

"It wouldn't do a bit of good. You can wander into an enchanted wood, but you can't wander out again. You have to break the enchantment to escape.''

"We could shout to your good lady. She could use her magic.''

Kedrigern shook his head. "She wouldn't hear us. These things are soundproof. I'm sure she's calling to us right now, but you don't hear her voice, do you?''

"Not a sound.''

"Well, then.'' Kedrigern rubbed his chin thoughtfully, and at last said, "Princess will be safe, I think. She can fly. She's got her magic, and she's got the packhorses with all the supplies. And if worse comes to worst, she's got Louise. What we have to do, Dyrax, is concentrate on getting out of here and making our way to the Singing Forest. She'll go there and expect us to meet her.''

"Then you plan to . . . to go on? In there?'' Dyrax asked in a shrunken voice, pointing to the dark path ahead.

"We might as well. We're sure to end up there anyway.

Enchanted woods are tricky that way. The paths have minds of their own. I want to get out of here as soon as possible, don't you?''

"Oh, yes. Yes, certainly," said Dyrax, but he kept his horse reined in.

"What's the matter? A little while ago you were itching to fight an army. Don't you want to perform a heroic deed?''

"I do, but I'd rather perform it against an army. Enchantment makes me nervous.''

"A little enchantment won't hurt you, Dyrax. Trust me. Once my powers are back to full strength I'll be able to handle anything we encounter.''

"What if we encounter something *before* your powers are restored?''

Kedrigern gestured confidently. "I'll improvise. Or you can perform a heroic deed." He urged the great black horse forward at a walk. A few paces on, he turned and motioned to Dyrax. "Come on," he said cheerfully. The young man followed, glancing from side to side and keeping his hand near his sword.

Though he put up a convincing show of confidence, Kedrigern was well aware of the potential danger. Enchanted woods were, as a rule, places to be avoided whenever possible. The fact that no one knew for certain just how, and why, and by whom, and for how long this particular wood had been enchanted did nothing to reassure him. Even at the peak of his power he would have stayed clear of such a place. Now, still weakened in magic by his clash with the Green Riddler, he would have to be doubly wary and trust to luck.

He had his medallion; that was some comfort. And he felt a bit stronger now than he had the previous evening. In fact, he thought, with the proper herbs he might even now be able to throw together a magic that would keep Dyrax and himself safe from most threats, lead them to the source of the enchantment, and help him to undo it. He slowed his mount and began to study the ground. Dyrax looked on

curiously, but asked no questions for a time. Finally, when
they had ridden the greater part of a league with Kedrigern
hanging half out of his saddle, peering closely at the
herbage and sniffing the air like a hound on the scent,
Dyrax could contain himself no longer.

"Is something wrong? Have we wandered off the way?"
he asked.

"No, we're doing very well so far. I'm just looking for
herbs."

"Herbs?"

"Yes. You can work some useful magic with herbs if
you can find the right ones. And if you know what you're
doing."

"I thought herbs were just for fixing upset stomachs and
toothaches and such."

"Not at all, my boy. You can do great things with
herbs. Nice clean kind of magic, too. And if it doesn't
work, you've at least got the beginnings of a decent salad.
You can't go wrong with herbs."

Dyrax could think of no appropriate response, and attempted none. They rode a bit farther, until Kedrigern
gave a happy shout, reined in his steed, and jumped to the
ground, dropping to his knees in a patch of bright golden
flowers.

"Haemony!" he cried. "The real thing, Dyrax, genuine
haemony! I almost didn't recognize it with the flowers in
full bloom!"

"Is haemony good, Master Kedrigern?" asked Dyrax,
dismounting.

"It's wonderful! Haemony is of sovereign use against
all enchantments and ghastly apparitions. It's also good for
mildew and damp."

"Is it really? Do you mind if I gather some? In case I
return home someday, it might help around the castle. My
father was always—" Dyrax checked himself with a sharp
intake of breath and began to pluck up the small yellow
flowers, keeping his eyes lowered.

Kedrigern studied him for a moment and at last said,

"Make sure you get the roots. That's where their strength is."

"The roots. Yes. Thank you," said Dyrax, keeping his eyes averted. "Tell me, Master Kedrigern, how did you learn of this wondrous plant? I've never seen it myself."

"You may have seen the plant, but never in bloom. It needs a special soil for that. Most of the time it has darkish leaves with prickles all over them. Rather unattractive. I heard about it from a shepherd lad. He wasn't much to look at himself, poor chap, but he knew every virtuous plant and healing herb under the sun, and he loved to talk about them. He showed me a little dried-up root and said that it was called 'haemony.' Better than moly for protection, he claimed, and that's saying a lot. He told me how to recognize it, but from that day to this I never saw so much as a stalk of it," said the wizard, rolling up his sleeves. "I intend to lay in a good supply. So your father's a king, is he?"

"Yes, my father is Lutermine, King of the—" Dyrax said, taken off his guard by the unexpected question. He groaned and looked sheepishly at the wizard.

"I thought so. Hard to disguise good breeding. It's nothing to be ashamed of, my boy."

"It isn't my birth I'm ashamed of, Master Kedrigern. On the contrary, I'm proud of my parents and I miss them greatly."

"Why did you leave them in the first place?"

Solemnly, the youth said, "I have loved and lost, Master Kedrigern."

"Not an uncommon condition among healthy young males. But that's just the time when a man needs his family to cheer him up."

"Ah, but you see, they would expect me to pine and mope for a time, grow pale and sigh and wander about the castle in a disheveled state, and at last get over my sorrow and find a new love."

Knocking a bit of dirt from a haemony root, Kedrigern said, "It's been known to happen."

"To other men, perhaps. But I know in my heart that I can never love again. Being a prince, I have obligations, and being a devoted son, I would accede to my parents' wishes. For reasons of state, they would have me enter a loveless marriage with some beautiful young princess."

"Give it a try, Dyrax. You might be pleasantly surprised."

The youth sighed, shook his head sadly, and tugged at a haemony stalk. "No, good wizard. For me there can be no one but the fair Kressimonda."

"That's a pretty name."

"A name befitting her matchless beauty," said Dyrax reverently. "Kressimonda, Kressimonda! Hair the color of blown embers, eyes like the midday skies at harvest time, skin like cream, a breath as sweet and fragrant as a meadow of flowers . . ."

"Sounds lovely," Kedrigern murmured.

"Graceful as a cat, gentle as a doe, blithe as a butterfly, laughter sweet as birdsong, a voice like crystal chimes in a spring breeze, a silken hand, a tiny foot . . . ah, Kressimonda, Kressimonda!" the youth rhapsodized.

"Clearly, you are fond of the lady. Is there any possibility of a reconciliation?"

"She has married another," said Dyrax in a doomed voice. "Forced by her calculating parents, she has wed an aging lecher, a wealthy lord who lives in a gleaming palace, where he dines off plates of gold with diamond-encrusted tableware. We, who had been sweethearts since childhood, who had sworn to love forever while we could barely lisp one another's names, were torn asunder. She was driven by others' greed into the arms of a doddering miser."

"How old is this miser? Maybe it's only a matter of waiting a year or two. . . ."

"He is quite twenty-eight, at least. Perhaps as much as thirty," said Dyrax with scorn.

"I see. That could mean a long wait."

"I am not a man for waiting, Master Kedrigern. Immediately I learned of Kressimonda's wedding, I armed myself and rode to the villain's castle. I fought my way through a hundred guards to reach her side, and shouted in a great voice, "I have come for you, my Kressimonda! The ordeal is over! I shall carry you off to my mountain stronghold, and there we shall live and love through all our days!"

"And . . . ?" Kedrigern asked in a hushed, expectant voice.

Dyrax heaved a deep despairing sigh that seemed to empty his body of breath and hope. He tore up a cluster of haemony with a violent gesture and shook the dirt free with a vehemence that scattered petals around him in a golden shower and got little bits of dirt all over Kedrigern, who went on with his own gathering and said nothing more. After a long pause, Dyrax said in a choked voice. "She told me that her husband was kind and generous and very affectionate. She praised his wonderful sense of humor. She said that they were happy together, and expressed her fond wish that I become as a brother to them both. I spurned the words she had been tricked into uttering, Master Kedrigern. I left the castle, broken-hearted, but first I proclaimed to all present that I would love no one but Kressimonda, and never marry another. I have spoken strong words, Master Kedrigern, and cannot retract them."

"There are extenuating circumstances. You spoke in a moment of extreme stress."

"No, Master Kedrigern, I will keep my word and win back my Kressimonda. If I perform some great feat, she will hear of it. Her eyes will be opened."

"But if she really is happily married . . ."

"I have said what I have said, Master Kedrigern. Honor's at the stake. I must be firm."

"Whatever you say, Dyrax. It's your life. How are you doing with the haemony?"

"I have a great sufficiency. More than I can carry."

"I'll take whatever you don't want. I know a few

people who'll be glad to get a sprig or two of this. Are you ready to move on?''

"Quite ready, Master Kedrigern. You say that this plant will protect us against enchantment?''

"It will indeed. Just carry it next to your skin, or hang it around your neck,'' said the wizard as he stuffed plants into his saddlebag, retaining one which he rubbed clean with his fingers and knotted around the chain of his medallion. "Like this. Or tuck it securely into your waistband. Just be sure it touches your skin.''

He mounted the black steed, who had been contentedly browsing in the haemony patch beside them, and led the way, feeling much more confident and secure. Dyrax, too, rode with a bit more assurance, and his glances to the side were belligerent rather than apprehensive. Thus they rode until late afternoon, when they came to a promising campsite: the ground was flat and dry, firewood was abundant, and a clear stream ran nearby.

"This seems a goodly place to pass the night,'' Dyrax observed.

"Looks fine to me. Do you feel any tingling in the air?''

"None whatsoever.''

"Neither do I. It must be safe.''

And so it was. They built a fire, dined simply from their own meager store, and slept without alarm or disturbance until first light. They washed in the stream, but to be on the safe side, did not drink from it, relying instead on their own water-bottles. After a hasty breakfast, they were back on the road.

In a short time they emerged from the forest into an open meadow covered with an odd grayish-white stubble. It looked much like an new-mown field, except that the stubble, instead of being brittle and dry, was quite lively. The tiny stumps writhed in rippling waves of motion.

Their path led directly across the field, bisecting the carpet of wriggling stubble. Kedrigern's steed went on unperturbed, but Dyrax's horse whinnied in fear, reared up with rolling eyes, and set its feet firmly.

"He won't go on, Master Kedrigern. He's frightened," Dyrax called to the wizard.

"What's there to fear? It's only an empty . . ." Kedrigern's voice faltered as he looked more closely at the grayish-white stumps beside the path. Motioning to Dyrax to hold his ground, he dismounted and hunkered down for a serious inspection.

The stumps were not vegetation. They were fingers.

Swallowing and licking suddenly dry lips, Kedrigern said in a subdued voice, "Dyrax, I think it would be best if you blindfolded the horse and led him across. And keep to the path. Make sure you keep to the path and don't walk on the . . . the stubble."

Dyrax did as the wizard suggested, and asked no questions then or thereafter. He crossed the field without a glance to either side, his eyes fixed on the figure of Kedrigern riding before him.

Kedrigern, though he kept up a stalwart front, was dismayed. Those blackened nails and that peeling mottled fungoid flesh had given him a turn. A field of dead man's fingers—and dead women's and children's, too, judging by the size of some of them—was a thoroughly nasty piece of work. Bad enough to see them sticking up out of the ground at all, but that obscene wriggling, as if they were beckoning to him, exceeded all limits. Whatever power lay behind this enchantment was certain to be something very unpleasant, and not the sort of thing to encounter when one's magic is not at peak operating efficiency.

And yet he had to get out soon, for Princess's sake, and there was no sure way out but to track down the source of the enchantment and neutralize it. How he would do this he had no idea, and the more he thought of that field of rotting writhing fingers the less he desired a confrontation with its maker. He hoped that no more demoralizing sight awaited them.

Unfortunately, one did. They came upon it very soon after reentering the woods.

The path had widened, and they were riding side by side. Despite their proximity, they were silent. Kedrigern was dredging his memory for haemony lore, and Dyrax was wondering if he had really seen what he feared he had seen in that field and hoping that he had not, even though he grew ever more certain that he had. It was only a glimpse out of the corner of his eye, but it was unforgettable. He wanted a good rest, and soon. On a slight rise off to the side of the path a massive tree stood in the middle of a clearing, and Dyrax pointed to it.

"Master Kedrigern, this looks like a good place to stop for a while," he said.

"What? Oh, yes, a stop. All right. Under that big tree?"

"Yes. It looks clean, and we can see clearly in all directions."

"Very prudent thinking, Dyrax." Kedrigern studied the site, then asked, "What kind of tree is that, anyway?"

"Hard to say. It has the outline of . . . an oak, I'd say."

"But look at the fruit. What are they, apples?"

"That can't be an apple tree. The shape is all wrong. And the fruit is too big. Maybe it's . . ." Dyrax rode closer, then gave a horrified cry, sprang from his horse, and was spectacularly sick by the side of the path. "Oh, Master Kedrigern," he said feebly when he had recovered. "I never thought I'd see . . . It's . . . They're . . ."

Kedrigern reached down to give him a reassuring pat on the shoulder, then guided his steed closer. It was even worse than he had feared. Not fruit, but swollen heads hung from the branches, and their wide agonized eyes turned to follow his approach. Their mouths gaped and worked fitfully, but nothing came forth beyond a soft choked moaning. Kedrigern dropped his gaze. When he saw what lay on the ground beneath the branches he shut his eyes tightly, swallowed hard, and fought against the swift rising of his gorge. The curled russet slips that lay all about were not fallen leaves, they were tongues. His great black steed sniffed at them, snorted, and tossed his head with a flash of silver, drawing back out of the shadow of the tree.

"Can you tell me anything? I'll end this enchantment if I can, and set you free," Kedrigern called to the heads that swayed above him. They gave no answer, only a low and mournful wailing. He turned and rejoined Dyrax.

"I don't want any more of this, Master Kedrigern," the shaken youth confessed.

"Neither do I," Kedrigern replied.

"What shall we do?"

"Well, we can't stay here."

"No!" Dyrax said emphatically.

"So we go on."

"Where? It gets worse and worse. Think what might lie ahead!"

"I'm thinking about it, Dyrax. Believe me, I'm thinking about it. But we have no choice."

Dyrax glumly conceded that point. He remounted, and they went on. No further grisly sights lay on their way. They proceeded without incident until midday, when they stopped to eat and rest, and resumed their travels with spirits restored. They had gone only a short way when Kedrigern reined in his mount and turned to Dyrax.

"I feel a tingle in the air," he said excitedly.

"I feel nothing."

"Well, I do. It's unmistakable. My power is building up. The haemony is working."

"What will it be this time, a swamp of entrails?" Dyrax asked squeamishly.

"It feels more like a fairy spell. Nothing messy."

Dyrax nodded and said no more. They rode on, and in no time at all came to a hillside overlooking a spectacular castle, all spires and turrets and towers of gleaming white stone, rising from an island in a lake surrounded by tall trees. It was not an excessively large castle, nor was it formidable nor menacing, nor was it at all impregnable, for a broad bridge led from the opposite shore to the gate, and the drawbridge was down.

"Do you think we might find an ogre in there?" Dyrax asked. He sounded considerably perkier than he had since their entry into the enchanted wood.

"Hard to say," Kedrigern replied thoughtfully.

"How about a giant?"

"If there's a giant in there, he's awfully cramped," said the wizard, reaching into his tunic.

"I hope it's something I can confront blade to blade, and do a great feat," said the young man eagerly.

Kedrigern took out his medallion and sighted in on the castle through the Aperture of True Vision. He checked turrets, gate, and bridge, and gazed long at the statues, perhaps a hundred of them, that stood in niches in the wall and in grottoes here and there in the parkland. They were statues of men and women in postures of piety and reverence: clearly, of saints. Blinking and rubbing his eye, he turned to Dyrax with a broad smile. "I think you may have a chance to do your feat, my boy, and you won't even have to break a sweat."

"What do you mean, Master Kedrigern?"

"You'll see. Come on."

Kedrigern raced down the hillside, with Dyrax close behind. Their horses clattered over the stone bridge, thundered across the drawbridge, sent a host of hollow echoes flying about the gatehouse, and finally clopped to a halt in a courtyard. All was still. No one had attempted to stop them. They waited a few minutes, but no one appeared to greet them or challenge them. The silence was unbroken.

"A strange place, Master Kedrigern," said Dyrax, laying a hand on his swordhilt.

"Just an enchantment."

"What sort of enchantment? What kind of ogres or evildoers dwell herein, that dare not show their faces? It is I, Dyrax, son of Lutermine, who challenge you one and all!" the youth cried boldly. Echoes rang from wall to tower, dwindled and died, and still there was no sign of life.

Kedrigern dismounted and led his horse to the stables. Within lay horses and grooms and a pair of cats, sprawled in abandoned postures, unmoving.

"Foully slain!" Dyrax cried, drawing his sword.

"Dead men don't snore," Kedrigern pointed out. "Look at them. They're all breathing." As if to endorse his words, a groom shifted position and a cat twitched its paws and the tip of its tail in a dream pursuit. "It's a sleeping spell, that's all."

"Then you must disenchant them."

"No," said the wizard, shaking his head and smiling. "*You* must disenchant them."

"I? I am no wizard."

"These spells generally call for a handsome prince. Now, you're a prince, and you're a decent-looking lad, so you should be just what these people need."

"What feat must I do?"

"Somewhere in this castle there's certain to be a sleeping princess. When we find her, you kiss her, and that will end the enchantment."

"Is that all?" asked Dyrax, crestfallen.

"That's all. Nothing to it."

"Nothing, indeed, Master Kedrigern. To kiss a sleeping maid is no great feat."

"Believe me, she'll thank you for it. Let's get started. You take the upstairs and I'll look on this floor," said the wizard, entering the nearest open doorway, which led to the kitchen.

Dyrax went ahead in search of the staircase, but Kedrigern lingered to inspect the kitchen, for he was fascinated by what he saw. A fire was burning in the huge fireplace and a cauldron of water hung over it, simmering. How long the fire had burned and the cauldron had simmered, he could not guess, but the cauldron was still nearly brimful and the fire had scarcely darkened the topmost logs. It was a subtle touch.

Across the room was another sight to gladden his professional heart. A scullion had been pouring water from one bucket into another when the spell struck her. The water poured on in an unbroken ribbon, but the receiving bucket remained half-full, and the surrounding floor was dry. This spell was the work of an artist, and Kedrigern greatly admired it.

Leaving the kitchen, he entered the great hall. Finely dressed ladies and gentlemen with refined features lay inelegantly about where they had succumbed to the spell, snoring as loudly as any churl. A king and queen, a distinguished couple in appearance, were slumped in their thrones, heads propped on hands in almost identical positions. But there was no sign of a princess.

Kedrigern next looked in a small chamber set into the wall just off the great hall. Again he was struck by the tidiness and attention to detail of the enchanter, for a candle stood on a small table, burning steadily without consuming wax. Kedrigern smiled appreciatively, reflecting how seldom one saw spelling of this quality nowadays. It was certainly a far cry from the nastiness of the forest, and a welcome relief.

Sitting at the table, chin cupped in one hand while the other hand grasped a freshly inked quill pen, was an elderly scribe, spelled in mid-sentence. Kedrigern, always curious about what people considered worth setting down, leaned over to read his work. After scanning the opening words, he gave a little yelp of excitement, for he saw a familiar name. He traced back up the long sheet for the beginning of the passage, and read on from there.

Then did Vorvas, called the Vindictive, come to the castle Cent Saints to seek the Princess Blamarde her hand in marriage, who did surpass in beauty all the fairest of song and legend, for having heard of her and seen the image of her face and form by practice of his art, he was fain to possess her love and enjoy her beauty. And the king her father, having intelligence of

Vorvas his vindictiveness, was loath to say him nay
despite the displeasure of his wife and the shrieking of
the fair Blamarde and the weeping and lamentation of
all in the castle. And Blamarde, fearing herself lost, did
rise up before Vorvas and speak thusly: "Dirty old
wizard, thou stinkest like unto an oubliette, and sooner
would I die than be thy wife, maugre thy power and the
fear in which all men hold thee." And he replied:
"Then die thou shalt, and all herein shall die with
thee," and spoke a spell, and straightway the fair
Blamarde paled and fell in a faint and was carried to her
bed. Vorvas did darkly vanish, and a great fear came
over all in the castle Cent Saints. But the queen did then
recall the promise of the good fairy Zickoreena, who
had been invited to Blamarde's christening and given a
golden cup and spoon as presents, and tidbits from the
queen's own dish to eat, that she would come to the
princess's aid in her time of direst need; and she did
send messengers to seek Zickoreena and beg her presence at the castle. And the fairy did come, and hear the
account of Vorvas his mischief, and did say: "Fear not,
for Blamarde shall live. Though I have not the power to
break the spell of that evil man, yet can I soften it, and
so I shall. The fair Blamarde shall not die, but sleep for
an hundred years, and all herein shall sleep also. And at
the end of the appointed time a handsome prince shall
come to the castle Cent Saints, and with him shall be a
good wizard of much power, and counseled by the
wizard, the prince shall kiss the princess and set her and
all herein free of the spell. And from this day until that,
the castle shall be called castle Cent Sans Sens, for that
for an hundred years all herein shall be deep in sleep."
And having said these words of comfort, the fairy departed amid great thanks. And the king bid all to make
ready for a long sleep, and gave order

The account ended abruptly with a slightly crooked final
letter, presumably at the point where the sleeping spell had

overtaken the aged scribe. Kedrigern reread the lines with great satisfaction. He had sensed fairy magic, and here it was; his powers were returning rapidly. And if Vorvas had been involved, then Louise's kingdom might be very near. Things were looking up.

He emerged from the little chamber, and as he stood in the great hall, glancing about, deciding where to look next, he heard a cry. He ran toward the voice and when he reached the staircase, Dyrax appeared at the top, waving wildly to him and looking uncertain. "Master Kedrigern, I've found her!" he cried. "I've found the sleeping princess! Quickly, come this way!"

···⚜ *Ten* ⚜···

a king without a queen

AND MEANWHILE, as Princess and Kedrigern coped with various magics both good and evil, what of Hamarak? Truthfully, not much.

At his first glimpse of Berrian, Hamarak was deeply smitten. She was a pretty girl, and she seemed awed by him. This was something new to Hamarak, and he found it very pleasant. His prior experience with pretty girls had not been encouraging. He had not seen very many of them. The ones he had seen had either ignored him, teased him, or told him to go away. Berrian was not like the others.

In the back of Hamarak's mind was the vague feeling that if he intended to get seriously involved with any woman, she really ought to be a princess. He was, after all, a king, and kings were expected to marry princesses. If a king decided to marry a goose girl, or a baker's pretty daughter, it always turned out that the goose girl or the baker's daughter had been a princess all along, only in disguise. All the tales Hamarak had ever heard worked out that way. He had never been able to figure out the sense of it, but that was the way the tales went. It seemed unlikely to him that Berrian was a princess in disguise. Still, he preferred the prospect of marrying Berrian to that of marrying a princess.

Hamarak's experience with princesses was limited. He had not gotten to know Louise well, despite their travels together. Besides, Louise was a sword. Even a king was not expected to marry a sword. The only other princess he knew was a wizard and the wife of a wizard, the lady with the wings. She seemed nice enough, but she had the same way about her as Louise, a way of taking charge of things and arranging affairs the way she wanted them. The wizard hadn't seemed to notice it, but Hamarak could tell.

Berrian didn't seem like that at all.

Of course, there was the dowry to think of. A king always married a woman who brought him territories and castles and chests of gold, or caused everlasting treaties of peace and friendship to be signed. In Berrian's case, the dowry would probably be baked goods. They would be delicious, but bread, rolls, buns, cakes, and pies were really not the same thing as castles and provinces.

Actually, thought Hamarak, they were better. Pastry was sure to be a lot less trouble than land full of greedy nobles and unhappy peasants and robbers and enchantments and all sorts of things. Just running Dendorric was going to be difficult enough without adding more problems. Even chests of gold and jewels led to trouble, making people jealous and greedy and ending in raids and maybe even invasion. Pastry never hurt anyone.

Kingship was a lonely job, and the castle was a lonely place. Berrian would make everything nice. And what was the good of being a wizard-warrior-king if you couldn't have everything nice? Hamarak gave the question much thought.

···⅋ *Eleven* ⅋···

a sleep without a dream

"HER NAME is Blamarde. Lovely, isn't she?" said Kedrigern. He stood at Dyrax's side, gazing down on the sleeping princess.

Blamarde lay in the center of a broad, comfortable-looking bed. An exquisitely embroidered counterpane was drawn up almost to her shoulders. Her head was tilted to one side, her lips slightly parted. Long golden hair spread like an aureole over her pillow. One hand lay by her cheek, the fingers half closed in a charming childlike gesture.

"I found her lying just like this, Master Kedrigern. I have not touched her," Dyrax said nervously.

"It was good of you to wait for me, Dyrax. Well, go ahead. Kiss her. Break the spell. Get things moving around here," said the wizard.

Dyrax looked back and forth between the wizard and the princess. He moved from one foot to the other, but did not get any closer to Blamarde. At last he said, "I'll have to climb into her bed."

"It certainly looks that way."

"But if everyone wakes up, and they find me in the princess's bed, kissing her . . ." Dyrax shook his head uneasily and took a step away from the bed. "I have my honor to think of, Master Kedrigern."

144

"Then be honorable. Marry her."

"But I don't love her! I love another. I will always love the fair Kressimonda, always, always, Master Kedrigern!"

"Don't be obstinate. Blamarde is pretty, and this is a nice castle. They all seem like pleasant people. Besides, if you're an honorable prince, you have a duty to help a princess in distress."

Dyrax pondered that for a moment. He moved a step closer to the bed, looked at Blamarde, and said, "She's blonde. I like redheads. Kressimonda's hair is like an autumn sky at sunset."

"Blamarde's hair is like spun gold. Kiss her."

After further scrutiny, Dyrax turned to the wizard and frowned. "She's too thin."

"She's willowy, my boy. Svelte. Go on, kiss her."

Still Dyrax hesitated. He fidgeted aimlessly with his hands and finally began to fumble with the pommel of his sword. "Her skin is dry," he muttered.

"That's dust," said Kedrigern. He leaned toward the sleeping princess and blew softly on her face. A small cloud of dust particles whirled into the air. "See? Dust. She's been here a long time."

"Her nose is funny."

"It's a lovely nose."

"And she has freckles. Look at all those freckles."

"They're adorable. She's a charming lady, Dyrax. What's the matter with you? If I were a hundred and fifty years younger and a bold prince, and single, wild horses couldn't hold me back. Stop dawdling and kiss the lady."

In a desperate voice, Dyrax burst out, "If I kiss her and she wakes up, I'll be bound in honor to marry her, and I'm not ready for marriage! I haven't accomplished anything! Just kissing a sleeping princess is no great feat. I want to slay a dragon, or overcome an armed host, or something like that. Then I'll be ready to settle down."

"You overcame an armed host to make your way to Kressimonda's side, didn't you?"

"Yes, but look what happened: the woman I love told

me she would always be like a sister to me. That is hardly a great feat, under the circumstances, Master Kedrigern.''

''Waking a princess from an enchanted sleep and ending a hundred-year spell on a whole castleful of people *is* a great feat, Dyrax,'' the wizard pointed out.

Dyrax looked at him anxiously, doubt and hope mingled in his expression. ''Do you really think so? It seems so easy.''

''Easy?! You're the only one who can do it!'' Kedrigern cried. ''If you walk out of this bedroom, these people will have to sleep forever!''

''They will?''

''They certainly will. On the other hand,'' said the wizard in a friendly tone, smiling brightly, ''if you bring this off, I'll see to it that you're immortalized. I know a man who can make this into a legend. So go to it, Dyrax. Kiss that princess!''

Dyrax blinked rapidly several times and turned to face Blamarde. He unbuckled his sword belt and handed it to the wizard, then climbed into the bed and made his way on hands and knees to the princess's side. With one last glance at Kedrigern, who urged him on with a stern gesture, he leaned down and gave Blamarde a peck on the cheek.

For a moment, nothing happened. Then she sighed, shifted slightly, and began to snore in a delicate ladylike register. Dyrax looked at her for a time, then turned to Kedrigern, his expression desolated.

''I never had any luck with women,'' he said.

''It's no wonder, if that's the way you acted. You're not kissing your aged grandmother, you know,'' said the wizard irritably.

''How should I act?''

''Act like a normal handsome prince kissing a typical beautiful princess. Act natural, you dummy!'' Kedrigern snapped.

A look of recognition dawned on Dyrax's face. He nodded eagerly, and then he clasped Blamarde in his arms and began kissing her throat, her shoulders, and her lips. She stirred and blinked, raised one arm hesitantly, and then she flung both arms around Dyrax's neck and returned his embraces and kisses with enthusiasm.

"That's it, Dyrax. You've got it now," said the wizard. Dyrax continued his ministrations to Blamarde, who had entwined her fingers in his hair and begun to nibble at his ear. "I think she's awake now. You can have your sword back," said Kedrigern. Dyrax waved him off with one hand, holding Blamarde close with the other arm. Kedrigern heard sounds of life outside the room. "Everyone's coming in here, Dyrax. Get out of that bed!" he cried.

They both looked at him. Blamarde blinked and rubbed her eyes, into which Dyrax stared in wonderment. She turned to him and said, "Who are you, anyway? Do I know you?"

He seized her hand and kissed it loudly several times. "I am Dyrax, a prince from a faraway land. I have traveled here to free you from your vile enchantment."

She yawned and said, "You don't have anything to do with that dirty old wizard, do you? You're nice, but if you work for him, I'd rather go back to sleep."

Puzzled, Dyrax said, "Kedrigern is a very clean wizard."

"Who's Kedrigern?" asked Blamarde.

"He is," said Dyrax, pointing. Kedrigern nodded and waved.

"I don't mean him, I mean the one who smelled like the moat on a hot day. He wanted to marry me." She paused at the onrush of memory, then blurted, "He cursed me! He said I'd die!"

Raising a hand, Kedrigern said, "Fear not, Princess Blamarde. The curse was mitigated by a friendly fairy. You did not die, but slept for a hundred years."

Her eyes widened. "A hundred years?" she repeated in a shocked voice.

"It was an enchanted sleep. Very refreshing. You haven't aged a day," he assured her.

Dyrax was by this time at Kedrigern's side, adjusting

his sword belt and hastily smoothing down his rumpled hair. The sounds outside the room grew louder. Voices called out; footsteps echoed in the corridors; a door slammed; something fell with a loud clatter, followed by angry cries and then laughter. A head poked in the doorway, disappeared, then returned to gape. Another head joined the first. A woman entered, pointed to the bed, and cried, "She's awake! Princess Blamarde is awake! We're saved!"

People began to pour into the bedchamber, pointing to the princess and the strangers, whispering excitedly to one another, shouting the good news to those still outside. Kedrigern smiled graciously at the growing crowd, waving in a friendly way, while Dyrax edged to the bedside and took Blamarde's hand to help her up. A waiting woman dashed forward to fall at the princess's feet, weeping for joy, and then rose to assist her in donning a fur-trimmed robe. Others quickly placed slippers on her feet and a coronet on her brows, while still others plumped the pillows and smoothed the counterpane, raising clouds of dust that set off a wave of sneezing.

The crowd surged forward and then suddenly parted, to admit the crowned couple that Kedrigern had seen enthroned below. Their crowns were slightly askew, and their chins were reddened where they had rested for a century cupped in the heel of a hand, but they moved smoothly and showed great alertness.

Like a sudden ebb tide, the crowd all around dropped to their knees, and scores of hushed voices murmured, "Your Majesties," as heads bent. Kedrigern gave a deep bow, but no one seemed to notice.

"My baby! My little baby Blamarde!" cried the queen, running forward to take the princess in her arms and kiss her repeatedly, cooing endearments as she kissed and petted her. "You're alive! We're all alive! Oh, bless the good fairy Zickoreena, we're alive! And who's *this*?" she demanded with sudden sharpness in her voice, turning suspicious eyes on Dyrax.

"He woke me, Mama. Isn't he nice?" Blamarde said,

beaming a quick fond smile on the blushing Dyrax. "He kissed me and woke me up, and we're going to be married."

Dyrax gave a bit of a start and looked at Kedrigern, who smiled and shrugged his shoulders. Neither man spoke.

"Married?" repeated the queen.

"Yes, Mama. Right away."

"How long have you been awake?" the queen demanded, her eyes narrowing as she looked from Blamarde to Dyrax and back again. "Don't you lie to me, now."

"And who is this fellow? Looks like a commoner to me," said the king.

Dyrax released Blamarde's hand, took a step forward, and bowed deeply and gracefully, in the manner of one accustomed to such courtesies. "I am Prince Dyrax, eldest son of Lutermine, King of the Red Forest and the Marshes of Tadraxia. I seek the hand of your daughter in honorable marriage," he said with dignity.

"Well, at least he's a prince," the queen muttered.

"Lutermine? Who's Lutermine? Nemp rules in the Red Forest, and there are no marshes in Tadraxia. What's going on here, anyway?" the king demanded angrily.

"If Your Majesties will permit me," Kedrigern said politely. When they turned suspicious, hostile eyes on him, he explained, "You and your people have slept for a hundred years. Much has happened in that time. Nemp was overthrown by a—"

"A hundred years! That's what Zickoreena promised!" the queen blurted. "We wouldn't die, we'd only sleep for a hundred years. And then . . . yes, a prince would come here and wake Blamarde and all of us!"

"A prince and a good wizard," Kedrigern added by way of clarification.

Again came the suspicious glance, even more hostile this time, and the king asked, "Are you the wizard?"

"I am, Your Majesty. I am Kedrigern of Silent Thunder Mountain, master of counterspell and disenchantment."

"Are you in with that other wizard? The smelly one?" the queen cried, pointing an accusing finger at him.

Kedrigern raised a hand to his breast in an aggrieved gesture. "Indeed not, Your Majesty. I am in fact on a quest to undo another of his foul enchantments. I must ask you not to judge all wizards by the likes of Vorvas."

The king grunted noncommittally. He kept his eyes on Kedrigern for a time, then he turned to Dyrax and gruffly asked, "Is he all right, son? Tell me the truth, now."

"I can vouch for him, Your Majesty. On our travels together he has served me loyally and well," said Dyrax.

Kedrigern's eyebrows rose, but he said nothing. That's royalty for you, he thought. They'll use anyone, then spit him out like a cherrypit. Only people they're polite to are each other, and that ends pretty quickly when there's a chance to snip off a bit of territory and a few thousand tax-paying subjects. I should've expected this.

"I like you, son," said the king, laying a hand on Dyrax's shoulder. "You come right out and speak straight."

The queen frowned. "But can we be *sure* he's a prince?"

"I know a prince when I see one. Would our daughter want to marry a commoner? Be sensible. He's a prince." The king turned to face the crowd. Raising his voice to a tone of regal command, he said, "All right, now, everybody back to work. This place has been neglected for a hundred years, and there's a lot to be done. We'll be holding a grand ball here three nights hence, to celebrate our awakening and Blamarde's betrothal. I want to see this palace sparkle, do you hear? Hop to it!" As the room emptied, the crowd dispersing with markedly less buoyant spirits than they had displayed upon entering, the king took Dyrax's arm and said, "We have things to talk about, son. I want to know more about your family, and how you came here, and how well you can use that sword."

The queen took his other arm, saying, "It will be nice to see Blamarde settled down. Having a beautiful unmarried daughter can be an awful trial. You wouldn't *believe* the sort of people who come here seeking her hand, Dyrax dear."

As they left the room, arms cozily linked, the king was

asking Dyrax whether he had ever led an army. Blamarde and Kedrigern looked after them, then turned to one another.

"At least they get along," Blamarde said.

"Quite well, it appears."

"Are you really a good wizard, wizard?"

"I'm one of the best, especially at counterspells."

"No, I mean are you a *nice* wizard. You aren't going to make something awful happen to us on our wedding day, are you? Like changing Dyrax into a toad or something?"

"My dear princess Blamarde, I wouldn't dream of doing such a thing. You have my word on it," said Kedrigern with his most reassuring smile.

"Good. That other wizard was *nasty*. He hadn't changed his robe for about three hundred years. There were things moving around in his beard. And he was really mean, besides. *He* would've done something like that." Blamarde pouted fetchingly and gave a delicate shudder at the prospect of Vorvas's maleficence.

"I'm sure he would, but he can do such things no longer. Vorvas the Vindictive imprudently turned himself into Vorvas the Vole and was eaten by his familiar."

"Oh, that's nice," said the princess brightly.

"Can you tell me anything more about him?"

"I only saw him that one time, and I didn't look at him closely. He was too repulsive." Blamarde made a wry face and paused for a time, thinking, then added, "Quode might know something. He's a scribe. He lives in the castle someplace."

She excused the wizard willingly, being eager to dress and join her parents and Dyrax. Kedrigern hurried downstairs and went directly to the little chamber in the wall. The scribe sat where Kedrigern had left him, staring dazedly at the pen in his fingers.

"Are you Quode, the scribe?" Kedrigern asked.

"I am," said the aged man softly, with a touch of uncertainty in his voice. "You find me somewhat confused, sir. I seem to have dozed off in the middle of a sentence, something I have never done before."

"Actually, you've spent a hundred years in an enchanted sleep, just like everyone else in the castle."

Quode looked at him blankly, then set down his pen and rubbed his eyes. He blinked and said, "I see. Yes. I believe I do recall something about a spell."

"It's all there on the page you were writing."

"Ah. Yes. Yes," the scribe murmured, bending down to read the careful letters, punctuating his reading with little puffs of breath and *hmphing* sounds and such whispered interjections as "So!" and "Aha!" At the point where he had left off writing he looked to Kedrigern. "Has all turned out well, good sir?"

"Just as it was supposed to. But tell me, Quode, do you know anything more about Vorvas?"

"The malodorous necromancer?"

"That's Vorvas. I'm trying to break a spell he cast on a family from a neighboring kingdom about a hundred and . . . well, about thirty years before you all went to sleep. Can you help me? It's rather urgent."

The scribe's pale brow wrinkled in deep thought. "I do seem to recall . . . yes, there was mention . . . was a young lady turned into a sword, by any chance?"

"That's the spell, Quode! Princess Louise was her name. Her sister Alice became a golden crown, and their brother William—"

"Became a shield! Yes, of course. Why, that took place in our neighbor kingdom!"

"Is it close?"

"At moderate speed, one can ride there, enjoy a leisurely lunch, and be back here before sundown the same day. At least, so I have been told. I never travel, myself."

"You're a wise man, Quode. Which direction?"

"Turn left at the end of the bridge and go straight until you cross the Moaning River, then left again along the road to the Singing Wood. The castle is in the wood."

"Thank you, Quode. One thing more: there's an enchantment on the woods all around this castle. Is that Vorvas's doing, too?"

Again the old man frowned in deep concentration. At last he said, "Vorvas spoke of a partnership formed on his way here. I remember that distinctly. He gloated over it in a most offensive manner. The woods are in the power of his partner, but who the partner is, or what sort of partnership they formed, I know not, wizard."

Kedrigern sighed. "I had hoped that breaking the spell on Blamarde might have freed the wood from enchantment, too, but now it seems less likely to work out that way. Well, at least I'm prepared."

"Prepared for what?" Quode asked.

"Something very bad."

"I think you will find it. I wish you well."

"Thank you, Quode. And could you do me one favor?"

"Anything I can, good wizard."

"When things settle down, will you ask Dyrax to send a messenger back to King Ezrammis? He'll know what you mean."

"I will do so," promised the scribe.

Kedrigern left the castle through the kitchen door. He crossed the courtyard to the stables, where a crowd of grooms and stable boys and servants had gathered in a roomy ring around his great black steed. The horned horse was unfazed by the attention. He munched idly on the hay before him, raising his head now and then to roll his red eyes and give an unsettling toss of his silver horn, but he did not appear displeased. Kedrigern worked his way through the crowd to the horse's side, laid a gentle hand on the beast's muzzle, and fed it a few sprigs of haemony, which it ate with great pleasure.

"Is that your . . . your creature, sir?" a groom asked.

"It is. Thank you for feeding him."

"He found for himself, sir. There's not a man here who'd get within reach of that horn, and those hooves," said the groom, eliciting a general murmur of assent from the crowd.

"He's actually very gentle. Remarkably intelligent and

well behaved. Aren't you, old fellow?'' said Kedrigern fondly, stroking the velvety black muzzle.

"If you say so, sir. What's his name?''

Kedrigern turned to the questioner with an expression of disbelief. "Do you think I'd presume to give *him* a name? What if I picked out one he didn't like?''

The groom and the others looked at him, the horse, and at one another with wide astonished eyes, and all drew back a step. Kedrigern saddled and mounted, and they shrank back still farther, breaking the circle. With an amiable wave of his hand, Kedrigern urged the black steed forward. Silver hooves struck sparks from the stone of the courtyard and the horn gleamed like a bright blade in the light of early afternoon as they rode at a brisk gait to the bridge.

What lay ahead, Kedrigern could not imagine. The castle, freed now from Vorvas's enchantment, was a pleasant oasis, but he had no desire to stay there. Even if he had been smothered in thanks—as he deserved to be—and feted as an honored liberator, he would have been anxious to find Princess. He nibbled on a bit of sausage—remarkably tasty, considering its age—that he had appropriated while passing through the kitchen, and reviewed his knowledge of enchanted woods and forests. It was not an encouraging exercise. They were bad places all, with bad reputations.

He turned left at the end of the bridge and hoped for the best.

For nearly an hour, Kedrigern rode steadily on, with not a disquieting sight or sound or the slightest warning tingle. He relaxed without letting his guard down, and allowed himself the comforting thought that the enchantment was weakening, or at least diminishing in malignancy; or, best of all—though least likely—that he had somehow escaped the region of enchantment unawares.

He noticed, far ahead, what he took to be a post in the middle of the road. A few paces farther on, he saw a glint of gold. Curious now, he drew out his medallion and sighted in on the object. It was no post but a monk, clad in rough brown robes, his head bowed and concealed by his cowl, hands tucked into his sleeves. A golden staff rested against his chest and shoulders, clutched in one arm.

There was no sign of life anywhere around. The monk was obviously some kind of effigy—a warning, a signpost, a shrine, perhaps. But as Kedrigern came closer he felt eyes upon him, digging deep and seeing things no eyes can hope to see. And yet the air carried no warning.

He halted a dozen paces from the figure, and the monk's head went up. The cowl fell back, revealing a bleached skull. A bony hand rose to signal the wizard to a halt, and the great black steed obeyed with Kedrigern's direction. Kedrigern could feel the penetrating gaze of that eyeless thing and hear words coming from the lipless, tongueless mouth: "Bear this against the Enemy."

Kedrigern cleared his throat and asked politely, "What Enemy awaits me, good monk? And how shall I wield that staff against him?"

"Beware his promises. Fear his gifts."

"I will, I promise you. But who is the Enemy?"

The gaunt hands closed on the staff and held it out. "Take it, and ride on. The Enemy awaits."

Kedrigern dismounted and approached the grisly figure, halting a couple of paces before it. He reached out hesitantly. The monk gave the staff an urgent little shake, and Kedrigern took a step forward and reached out to grasp it. To his surprise it was not cold or clammy, but warm as living flesh.

"Confront the Enemy without fear. Resist his blandishments and you will vanquish him. We are with you," said the monk. He tucked his bony hands into his sleeves and bowed to Kedrigern, then turned and walked into the wood, striding resolutely over dry leaves and twigs without the slightest sound.

Kedrigern remounted and rode on deep in thought. One expected this sort of thing to happen in an enchanted wood, but one found it perplexing all the same. An Enemy lay in wait somewhere ahead; that much was clear, and hardly came as a surprise. And this staff would somehow help Kedrigern to overcome him. It was a good staff, a bit more than a tall man's height, capped with silver at both ends, with a broad ribbon of gold winding around it from top to bottom. In a bout at quarterstaves it would be a telling weapon. But why should a wizard bother with a quarterstaff at all? And was this Enemy the one who had caused the enchantment, or just another piece of it? And who was the monk? And why had there been no prickling of the air when he appeared? Here was a puzzle indeed.

Not until his mount gave a low snort and slackened his pace did Kedrigern look up and see that they had emerged from the wooded way into a circular clearing filled with stones of all sizes, most of them standing erect, some tilted at precarious angles, a few lying full-length on the ground. On one of the fallen stones sat a chubby, moon-faced man with bright red cheeks, dressed in the simplest and plainest of garments. He was alone in this dreary place, and yet his wave of welcome was cheerful and his voice merry as he called out, "Well met, traveler! Forgive an old man for not rising. These ways are rough and my feet are tender."

Kedrigern noticed then that the man's feet were calf-deep in a puddle of muddy water. There was no sign of a staff or any other weapon within reach; the fellow was not of a threatening appearance; this could hardly be the fearsome adversary he was to face; it might, in fact, be a helpless traveler in need of his protection. Kedrigern dismounted and joined the round little man on the fallen stone.

"That is a fine creature you ride upon," said the chubby man. "Very fine it is, indeed, sir."

"Yes, he's a good horse," said Kedrigern socially.

"Sir, you understate! A king could ask no nobler steed—an emperor would be honored to ride him! You must be very proud."

Kedrigern waved the compliment aside. "I'm grateful, but I don't have much call to be proud. I didn't make the creature, just came upon him. Sheer good fortune, that's all.''

The other man beamed. "You are humble, sir. A fine quality in a man of such obvious excellences as yourself. It would be fine, though, would it not, to have a stable of such horses? Nay, a herd! Ah, picture them, sir, decked in scarlet and gleaming gold and silver harness, set with rare gems . . . hooves and horns polished and gleaming . . . and astride each animal a magnificent warrior in armor, clad in your very own livery, ready to strike fear into the hearts of your enemies and bring the kingdoms of the world to worship at your feet! Think of it, my friend! Tempting, is it not?''

Kedrigern scratched his seat and replied, "Not really. I can't see any point in having the nations of the world worship at my feet, to be honest with you. Never get a moment to myself with that sort of thing going on.''

The chubby man laughed loudly, throwing his head back and growing even redder in his cheeks from mirth. "You're a practical man, sir. No nonsense, no fripperies for you. A meat-and-potatoes man, I can see. Speaking of which, sir, may I offer you a snack? A light repast would not be ill-timed, would it? If you would do me the favor, sir, of looking behind this rock . . .?''

Kedrigern did so, and found a basket packed tight with delicacies, and a small winebarrel. He placed them on the stone, and his companion began at once to rummage through the basket and pull out tempting morsels to place before him, muttering, "One must never travel without adequate provision, sir. There's enough food here to fill our bellies to a comfortable repletion, and wine to make the world seem a cozy and sensible place. And after dining, we can take a nice long nap, and wake and dine again, and drink some more. That's living for you, eh, sir? Eat and drink, and drink and eat, and sleep in between. A man's a fool to do more.'' He looked up, a wurst in one hand and a jampot in the other, leered at the wizard, and said, "Unless, of course, a pair of merry maids come skipping by.

Oh, then we'll be lively, will we not?'' He laughed heartily, put down the wurst and the jampot, and reached into the basket again.

"You needn't take out all this food. I'm really not the least bit hungry right now,'' Kedrigern protested mildly.

"Don't be a fool, sir. Eat all you can, whenever you can, and have all the wine you can hold. Eat, drink, and be merry, as the saying goes.''

"I'll just have a sip of water. If I eat heavily and then have a lot of wine—especially in the afternoon—I'm more likely to eat, drink, and be sleepy.''

"Your self-discipline is exemplary, sir. Truly exemplary,'' said the chubby man. He tore a chunk from a loaf of bread, stuffed it in his mouth, and followed it with a slab of pâté and a handful of grapes. Kedrigern sipped from his own water bottle as the other man thrust one bit of food after another into his mouth, chewing vigorously, swallowing loudly, and all the while keeping up the conversation in unintelligible syllables. Eventually he said, quite clearly, "Am I correct in assuming that you are a wizard, sir?''

"I am. I hope that doesn't make you nervous. Some people seem to feel uncomfortable around wizards.''

"Not I, sir, not I,'' said the other, filling a stone mug to the brim with blood-red wine. He drank off half of it, wiped his lips with the back of his hand, and repeated, "Not I. I'm a man who likes wizards, sir. You might say I collect wizards. May I ask your name, sir?''

"Kedrigern of Silent Thunder Mountain,'' said the wizard, rising. "I'm sorry I can't stay longer, but I really must dash. Someone may need my help, you see.''

"But my dear Kedrigern, you haven't taken even a nibble of this delicious food. Do stay and indulge yourself.''

Kedrigern made a little helpless gesture. "I finished a very spicy wurst only an hour or so ago, and I really couldn't eat another thing. All I needed was a drink of water.''

"Oh, come now, you can't go riding through these

woods with nothing in your stomach but water and a bit of
wurst. Have a taste of this pâté, and a chicken leg, and
some bread and cheese, and rabbit pie, and some grapes
and apples and pears, and a cherry tart or two, and a
cheering mug of good red wine.''

"Thank you, no. You're really most generous, but I
must go."

The chubby man pressed his hand to his brow and said,
"Kedrigern . . . let me think, now . . . I've heard that
name, I'm certain. Kedrigern . . ." He looked up excitedly and exclaimed, "Of course, Kedrigern! You were a
member of the Wizards' Guild!"

"A charter member, actually."

"A charter member! And yet . . . if memory serves me
. . . you were badly treated by your fellows. Most shame-
fully treated, if rumor is to be believed."

Kedrigern waved the remark off. "There was a misun-
derstanding. It's all resolved now."

"Yes, yes, it comes back to me. Some business with an
alchemist . . . Quintrindus, that was the fellow's name!
You saw through the rascal from the very start, but they
wouldn't listen. Practically drove you out for daring to
question their judgment, didn't they?"

"They didn't drive me out," said Kedrigern, who was
still rather sensitive on this topic. "I resigned of my own
volition."

"You did? Well, of course you would. Yes, certainly. I
heard it told differently, but these things do get garbled in
the retelling," said the other man soothingly. He shook his
head and made little clucking noises of sympathy. "It
must have been hard for you to see them strutting and
preening and calling themselves the greatest wizards of the
age and pocketing healthy fees for their work, and you
knowing all the time that they were dupes of a sneaking
alchemist. All that recognition and honor—not to mention
those fat fees—should have been yours. And all the fawn-
ing over Quintrindus, and the things they must have been
saying about you behind your back . . . nasty, malicious

things . . . lies, sir, shameless lies . . . it fairly makes your blood boil, doesn't it? Even a patient, easy-going soul like yourself must get furious at the thought,'' said the chubby man, looking up with concern on his round features.

"Well, when you put it that way . . .''

"Yes? Go ahead, sir, speak out.''

"I suppose . . . oh, but what's the point of dragging it all out again? It's over and done with. Forgive and forget, as they say.''

"Hard to forgive, impossible ever to forget, I'd say, sir. The best thing to do in these cases is speak out, get it all off your chest. Give vent to your righteous anger, sir! You can speak your mind freely in my presence, I assure you,'' said the other man with a generous sweep of his arms.

Kedrigern was about to speak when he felt the staff in his hand give a quick and almost imperceptible twitch, like the flick of a cat's ear, and the monk's words sounded in his mind: "Resist his blandishments and you will vanquish him.''

This cheerful, pudgy, smiling little man was the Enemy. Kedrigern closed his eyes, swallowed, and took a deep breath. He had come very close. But now he knew how to handle the situation. Turning his blandest smile on the man, he said, "Actually, I forgive them. I love them all, sir. Even Quintrindus. I *especially* like Quintrindus.''

The chubby man's sudden look of dismay turned in quick succession to anger and then to scorn. "If you can say that, sir, then you're not much of a wizard. Indeed, you scarce deserve the name.''

Meekly, Kedrigern said, "Perhaps not.''

"Is that all you can say? If so, sir, then you don't even deserve the name of a *man*! Do you hear me, sir? I'm insulting you!'' cried the other, red-faced.

"It's no more than I deserve. But let us not waste time talking about such a worthless wretch as myself. Tell me, if you will—''

"I will tell you nothing until you cease acting like a

worm and show some spirit. If you wish me to converse
with the likes of you, you must force me to do so by
violent means.''

"Those are the words of a man of true power,'' said
Kedrigern. "What a powerful fellow you must be, to
venture into these woods alone and unarmed!''

"I do not choose to speak of my power, worm,'' said
the other, scornfully, "but rather of your contemptible
weakness.''

"Ah, now *that's* the speech of a powerful man. Tell
me, sir, do you work spells? Do enchantments? Can you—''

"Shut up, you fool! You idiot! You meek, groveling,
forgiving, spineless, milk-blooded coward!'' roared the
man, shaking his pudgy fist in Kedrigern's face. "Aren't
you getting angry?''

"How could anyone be angry with such a splendid
fellow as yourself? I'm eager to learn of your great power,
your courage, your—''

"Oh, blast my power! To hell with my power!'' howled
the other. A sudden gust of wind swept over them, warm
and sulphurous, and he paled and turned horrified eyes on
Kedrigern. "No!'' he whispered. "I didn't mean that! I
didn't!''

"But you said it.'' Kedrigern reached out and tapped
him on the shoulder with the silver tip of the staff. He
vanished with a wail that echoed and re-echoed among the
stones like the cry of one falling down a bottomless well.
The puddle went up in a hiss of foul-smelling steam that
quickly dissipated. Baked in the mud at its bottom were
the prints of two broad hooves.

Kedrigern let out a deep shuddering sigh of relief and
set the staff against the rock, tucking his hands close
against his ribs to still their sudden trembling. To his
astonishment, the rocks in the clearing faded away, leaving in their places a group of men and women and horses
who gaped at one another, and at him, in astonishment.
The rock upon which Kedrigern had been sitting was now

a tall, well-armed knight, whom the wizard assisted to his feet.

"I thank you for your kindness," said the knight. His hair was shot with gray, as was his beard, and his face was lined with years and cares. He looked about, and his expression brightened when a woman of matronly mien, but still of great beauty, hurried to his side with eager arms opened to his own embrace. With one arm protectively around her waist, the knight asked, "Now, good fellow, can you say what has befallen us?"

"I think you've been under an enchantment—perhaps for as long as a hundred years."

"Indeed?! I recall very little. We stopped here for the night. A stranger joined us . . . a fat, friendly man . . ."

"He shared his provisions with us most generously," said the lady.

"So he did, my dear. A very friendly, generous man. But . . . there was a quarrel. I know not the cause, but tempers flared . . . swords were drawn. . . ." The knight shook his head, perplexed, and looked helplessly to his wife for help in remembering.

She exclaimed, "Hendso! He tried to make peace, but no one listened, not even to the exhortations of that holy man. And then something . . . something happened to him. Something terrible, I think. . . ."

"Was Hendso a monk?" Kedrigern asked.

"Yes. He was our household chaplain," the lady said.

Kedrigern told of his encounter with the grisly monk, and its outcome on this very spot. When he had finished, he took up the staff and handed it to them.

"We will honor Hendso's memory. He was a good man," said the lady.

With a sigh, the knight said, "He was indeed, but he was born into bad times. There has been nothing but unrest since the fall of the Kingdom of the Singing Forest."

"Is that where the princess was turned into a sword?" Kedrigern asked.

"One into a sword, another into a crown. And their

brother into a great iron shield! It all happened just across
the river," said the lady, gesturing in the direction Kedrigern
had been heading.

Gloomily, the knight said, "Nothing but accursed wizardry and enchantment everywhere these days. One cannot
even visit a cousin in safety. We were only an hour or so
from the castle of Cent Saints, where my cousin rules,
when this spell came upon us. Now, who can say what we
may find there?"

With a broad smile, Kedrigern said, "I've just come
from there. They, too, were in an enchanted sleep, but it's
over, and Blamarde is to marry in three days. You'll be in
plenty of time for the festivities."

He excused himself and slipped off to remount and be
on his way before anyone got a good look at his horse and
started asking questions. The enchantment on the woods
was broken now, and his way was clear.

A few hundred paces down the road he came upon the
packhorses grazing under a cluster of birches. They seemed
unaffected by their sojourn into enchantment; the only ill
effects Kedrigern could discern was the slight damage
done by the fieldmice that had gotten into the packs. He
tied the animals behind his mount and proceeded until he
came to a feeble trickle of water running between steep
banks. As he crossed he heard it whine and grumble; at
this time of year it was too low to moan in any satisfactory
way, but he knew it to be the Moaning River. Passing on,
he came to a forest where the air was filled with the far
faint sound of voices, like a children's choir heard at a
great distance. He glimpsed beyond the trees the outlines
of a castle half in ruins.

Emerging from the forest, he saw the horses tethered
before the castle gate. Princess's transparent mount shimmered faintly among them, apart from the rest. He rode
closer, and still saw no one. He dismounted to tie up the
packhorses, and just as he turned toward the castle a
brilliant burst of light blazed silently forth from gate and
windows, smokeholes and arrow slits, and every crack and

crevice in the massy walls. He stepped back, blinking, and when his vision cleared he saw men dressed all in black stagger from the gate, helplessly bedazzled by the light.

He sprang to the back of his black horse and rode into the castle over a narrow stone bridge that rocked beneath the great silver hooves and collapsed with a terrible roar behind him.

···⁍ Twelve ⁌···

a knight without a sword

PRINCESS AWOKE to a misty dawn. She felt a bit stiff in the neck and shoulders, but well rested and eager to be on her way. After the flight of the three weird sisters, the night had gone by without disturbance, clear and dry and comfortably mild.

Louise had passed the night as a staff, to avoid any possibility of rusting, and remained so through Princess's hasty morning ablutions and dreary breakfast. Disinclined to small talk at so early an hour, Princess did not summon her, and Louise did not, in fact, resume the sword mode until Princess found herself at a fork in the path with no indication of the proper way.

"Louise, I need directions," she said, giving the dark staff a gentle shake.

Once again the air resounded with the peal of struck metal, and the blade responded, "Directions, did you say?"

"Yes. We're at a fork. . . ."

"I see." Louise was silent for a time, struggling to remember, and then she cried, "To the left! It's only a short way to the river, Princess, and then we're practically home! We're almost there!"

"I do hope Kedrigern's waiting there for us. I'm very

165

concerned about him," said Princess, directing her horse to the left-hand path.

"I'm sure he's safe. If there's anyone who can deal properly with an enchanted wood, it's a wizard."

"If he were at full strength I wouldn't be concerned for a minute," said Princess earnestly, "but the Green Riddler cost him a lot of magic. And on top of everything else, he's probably worrying about me and not concentrating on his own predicament. He's like that, you know."

"It would seem that you two have a good marriage."

After a thoughtful pause, Princess said, "I believe we do. I don't mean to sound smug, but I really believe it. I only wish I knew more married couples, so I'd have some grounds for comparison."

"How many do you know?"

"Two. Three, counting toads. But we never see them, so I have no idea how they act toward one another. And I can't recall a thing about my own family," Princess confessed.

"Well, if it's any help to you, I remember my mother and father worrying about each other's well being and happiness all the time, and they seemed to have a very nice marriage."

"That's encouraging. Thank you, Louise."

"I do wish they'd passed along the secret, whatever it was," the sword went on, somewhat pettishly. "I couldn't imagine being happy with any of the princes who came to the castle seeking my hand. What a dismal lot they were!"

Princess nodded in knowing sympathy. "Handsome princes aren't all they're cracked up to be."

"Frequently they're not even handsome. There was one who resembled a wild boar: great big head, little piggy black eyes, hardly a trace of chin. He behaved like a boar, too. And another one looked exactly like a toad. He was the ugliest . . ." Louise stopped abruptly. In a chastened voice, she said, "Oh, my dear Princess, I *am* sorry. I didn't mean . . . He wasn't an actual enchanted toad, you understand. . . . Oh, I feel terrible."

With a comforting pat on Louise's pommel, Princess said, "I understand completely. Believe me, I do. I didn't feel the least bit attractive when I was a toad, and the other toads looked positively ugly to me."

"All the same, it was a thoughtless thing for me to say. I'm terribly embarrassed."

"No more of that, now, Louise. Let's forget it ever happened." They went a short way in awkward silence, and Princess suddenly said, "I wonder how Lalloree and Conrad look to each other. That never occurred to me before."

"Who?"

"Lalloree is that little princess who was turned into a toad by the magic mist. Conrad was caught in it, too. It seemed to bring them together."

"Was Conrad turned into a toad?"

"Yes. In a sense, it worked out conveniently for both of them. It's so difficult to meet someone suitable once you're enchanted like that."

"It isn't all that easy when you're *not* enchanted, believe me. If they're not . . . unattractive, they're like merchants. It's bargaining, not romance. I want nothing to do with it."

Princess said thoughtfully, "I suppose I was lucky to meet someone as I did."

"How is it, being married to a wizard? I don't mean to pry, but one so seldom meets a wizard's wife."

"It has its advantages, Louise. Marriage to a prince— even a handsome prince—can be dreadfully boring. Princes are always dashing off to slay something or do battle with giants or ogres or recreant knights. If they're not doing that, they're planning a war, or fighting one, or recovering from one."

"That sounds quite exciting," Louise observed.

"It's exciting for *them*, I suppose, but what's a wife to do while they're off somewhere hacking and smiting? They only come home to unload their booty and give their wounds time to heal and knock the dints out of their armor, and then they're off again. By the time they're thirty, they're all covered with scars and have bits and pieces missing. Your wizard, on the other hand, is basically a homebody." She paused, then went on, "Of course, *that* can be a problem, too. It's very difficult to get Kedrigern out of the house. He abhors travel. But it's never boring. Wizards have interesting friends, and the clients are sometimes interesting, too. There's generally something going on around the house. On the whole, it's a pleasant life, especially if you learn a bit of magic yourself."

The road began to dip, and when she noticed this, Louise lost all interest in the homelife of wizards and grew quite excited. She asked Princess to hold her as high as possible, so she might survey the area. After a brief look around, she shouted, "There it is! The Moaning River— it's just ahead!"

"Are you sure? I don't hear any moaning," Princess said cautiously.

"You won't at this time of year. The water is low. All you get is a kind of peevish muttering and a lot of sighing," Louise explained. "You have to listen carefully."

A few moments later Princess exclaimed, "I can hear it, Louise! It sounds like . . . like someone in the next room with a toothache."

"It does, doesn't it? You really ought to hear it after a good heavy spring rain. You'd think you were at a royal funeral."

The horse splashed through water that was scarcely deep enough to wet its hooves, then scrambled up the far bank onto the level path. They crossed a grassy field, and then the forest closed about them once again. As they rode ever deeper into the cool, shadowed wood, a wind rose, and the air filled with voices. The deep drone of basses rumbled from the trunks of ancient oaks, and thin tenors sang clear and sweet from the tops of the tall pines. They had reached the Singing Forest at last, and in safety, and the beauty of its song made words quite unnecessary. The voices surrounded them like an *a cappella* choir of angels, growing ever richer and finer, until they glimpsed a broken tower ahead, and a poignant melancholy note crept into the song. Louise gave a little stifled sob, then a sniffle, and then was bravely silent again until they emerged from the Singing Forest to the neglected grounds of a castle half in ruins.

At the sight of her home, Louise could hold back her feelings no longer. Walls had fallen; towers had crumbled; massive stones lay in a tumbled sprawl, like dominoes flung by an angry child. The wooden roof of the keep had collapsed in several places, and windows gaped to show the sky. The grass was high and thick, blanched by autumn to the pale hue of almonds; vines reached high up the ragged walls. Everywhere was neglect, abandonment, and the ravaging of time.

"Oh, Princess, it's all gone to pieces, and it used to be so lovely!" Louise wailed. "Beautiful crenellated walls, and round towers with painted timber hoardings . . . and fine smooth lists in front, for jousting and tourneys . . . and look at it now!"

"It's . . . picturesque," said Princess, trying her best.

"It's a ruin! A desolation! Oh, why did I return here? I should have known better! It's all madness and vanity!" cried Louise, her words coming between outbursts of tears.

"Be brave, Louise. We had to come here to seek cousin Hedvig's descendants. They're your only hope. It's too bad about the castle, but—"

"*Too bad*?! It's heartbreaking!"

"You can rebuild it once you're yourself again. First things first."

Louise took deep slow breaths to calm herself. "You're right. You're absolutely right," she said tautly. "I mustn't give way to my feelings. Let's have a good look around."

The gossamer steed picked its careful way among the rubble and the clinging grass in a slow circuit of the walls which, though fallen in many places, had nowhere been breached to the extent that a horse might enter. Coming at last to a dilapidated bridge that led to the gatehouse, the animal hesitated and pawed anxiously at the ground.

"I think it's nervous about crossing the bridge," Princess said.

"Silly beast! Even after all these years, that bridge will support an army. My father employed the finest workmen in seven kingdoms," said Louise indignantly.

"No sense in forcing the poor creature. I'll tie him out here and we'll walk across," Princess said, lightly dismounting.

She looped the reins over a fallen tree. The horse at once set contentedly to grazing, and Princess, with Louise resting on her shoulder, walked to the end of the bridge and set one tentative small foot on the stone. There was a faint grating, a groan, and the rattle of dried mortar and gravel cascading down the side of the ditch. Princess stepped back quickly.

"I think we'd better fly across," she said.

"Of course!" Louise cried excitedly. "I keep forgetting that you can fly! It will give us a much better view of things."

They lifted off and circled the walls once again, this time at tower height, looking down on the bailey. It was empty, save for the debris of fallen partitions and caved-in sheds, and the remains of what had probably been a well-house. The grass was tall in the places that received the most sun, and a few saplings had sprung up around the ruins of the well-house. It was a forlorn, depressing scene, and Louise maintained a gloomy silence.

Princess climbed higher, until she could look down on the keep. Charred beams were all that remained of the roof, and debris was strewn about the upper floor. The hoardings were burnt away, and several stones of the crenellated parapet had fallen, but the building seemed otherwise intact.

"Was there a battle, do you think?" Princess asked.

"No. Lightning, most likely. Or plain carelessness," Louise replied despondently.

"It must have happened recently. I can smell wood smoke."

"It doesn't look recent."

Princess came down daintily on one of the merlons and sniffed the air, eyes shut in concentration. "All the same, I smell wood smoke," she said.

With all the force of feelings too long held in check, Louise cried. "Oh, that wicked, evil, smelly old Vorvas! It's all his fault, all of this! We had such a beautiful, impregnable castle, and just look at it now!"

"Let's go inside. There may be something that will tell us where we'll find Hedwig's descendants," said Princess, lifting off.

Louise sighed. "They're probably all dead. Of shame. Or despair."

"It won't hurt to look. And it will be nice to get out of this cool air."

Princess swooped down and entered the keep by a window on the third level, where the great hall had been. She was startled by the sight of a small fire burning in the great fireplace, and a table drawn up nearby on which were a trencher and a flagon of wine.

"Someone's here, Louise," she said, zooming up to ceiling level and surveying the room carefully.

"We'll take care of any intruders, dear. And please remember: Panstygia."

Blade at the ready, Princess landed by the table. Taking up fighting stance, she announced in a loud clear voice, "I know you're here. Come out at once and explain yourself."

For a moment there was no response, and then a ragged, dirty youth with straw-colored hair and wide blue eyes crept from behind a moldy arras on the far wall and fell face down at Princess's feet. He was trembling.

"I believes, I believes, really I does!" he cried in a muffled voice. "I only never said so because nobody ever asked me! Nobody ever asks poor Shanzie anything, ever, nohow, but I believes in angels!"

"I'm not an angel," Princess said.

The huddled figure was still for a moment, absorbing

this news, and then he burst out afresh, "I believes in fairy godmothers, too! I believes, and I never meant no harm!"

"I'm not a fairy godmother, either."

Shanzie timidly raised his head, staring with pale eyes out of a pale face surrounded by a thicket of pale hair. He gaped at Princess for a silent interval, gave a little despairing cry, lowered his head, and moaned, "Then I believes in flying ladies with great black swords, whatever they be, and I never done anything, I swear it, and I never meant to, and I'll never do it again if you let me go this time, and besides, they made me do it, I never wanted to, not ever, nohow, I swear!"

"What exactly have you done?" Princess asked.

"Whatever you came to punish me for," Shanzie said in a muted, hopeless voice. He covered his head with his hands and awaited his fate. "Only I didn't do it."

"What do you think?" Princess whispered.

"Harmless," said the blade, adding, "Probably useless, too."

"Now, listen to me, Shanzie," Princess said in a firm but not unfriendly voice. "I'm going to ask you some questions. If you tell me the truth, I won't hurt you." Shanzie's only response was to moan and tremble, and Princess, with a touch of impatience, said, "Get up on your feet and stop making those ridiculous noises. Pay attention."

Shanzie climbed to his feet and stood before her, head bowed, cringing and wringing his hands. He was a pitiable sight. His clothing was an assortment of tatters, knotted and pinned in place with thorns. His face, hands, and rags were caked with dirt. He gave off an aroma rather like that of an old damp heap of straw in which several generations of small animals have lived untidy lives. Princess wrinkled up her nose and took a step back.

"What are you doing here?" she demanded.

"Just living here, your excellent ladyship, ma'am," he replied with a clumsy attempt at a bow.

"Do you know whose castle it is?"

"Yes, your worshipfulness! It belonged to a beautiful princess who was enchanted by a wicked sorcerer ever so long ago. So people say. And they say that the beautiful princess will return one day and take away all the evil magic that's been placed on the land."

"And so she has, and so she shall!" cried Louise in a call like the midnight clangor of brazen bells.

At the sound of the sword's voice, Shanzie dropped to the floor with a soft despairing whimper. He lay there, hands over his head, awaiting death, the devil, or whatever worse might befall.

"Oh, get up, Shanzie," Princess said.

"The sword, your greatness, ma'am—it talked to me!" Shanzie squeaked.

"Of course I talked. Do you think I am an ordinary sword? I am Panstygia, Mother of Darkness, the great black blade of the west, returned at last to my ancestral castle. I shall free the land from evil and restore my lost kingdom to its former glory. Is that clear?" the blade thundered.

Shanzie made a faint mewing sound. Whether or not he understood was uncertain, but he was not arguing.

"You need not fear. Serve me loyally and you will be well repaid," said the sword more mildly.

"Serve us *both* loyally," Princess added.

Shanzie looked up. Clambering to his feet, he eagerly blurted, "Oh, I will, I'll serve you faithfully, I will, I swear it! What must I do?"

"Well . . . there's nothing at the moment . . ." said Louise.

"Oh, yes, there is," said Princess. "Shanzie, get this place cleaned up. But first, clean up a private room with a good working fireplace, lay a fire in it, and bring me plenty of fresh evergreen branches to sleep on. What are you cooking over the fire here?"

"It's a rabbit, your supreme ladyship, ma'am. It's yours. Take it."

"Thank you, Shanzie. It should suffice. You may eat

after you've made up my room, but I want this entire floor spotless before you go to sleep. My husband will arrive shortly, and I don't want him seeing a mess. You can do the lower levels tomorrow, but I want this one done tonight."

"Yes, your magnificent excellence," said Shanzie, bowing.

"And please refer to me as 'my lady.' "

"I will, I will, your . . . my lady, ma'am."

"One thing more: I have a horse outside. He's transparent, so you may not see him at first, but he's tied up near the bridge. Feed and water him, and bring my saddle in. He'll he safe where he is, I think."

"Yes, my lady. Right away, my lady," Shanzie repeated, making his way to the door.

"That was a stroke of luck," said Princess when he was gone. She placed the sword on the table and took up the flagon. The wine was passable. The rabbit was nicely done by this time. She put it on the trencher and settled down to dine.

"He seems a bit dim to me," Louise observed.

"We don't need a philosopher, we need a servant. I'd rather have my own house-troll, but Shanzie will do."

"I hope you're right."

Licking her fingers, Princess said, "At least we'll have a clean warm place to wait for Kedrigern to arrive. And food while we're waiting."

"Must we wait? Can't *you* do something?"

Princess shook her head decisively. "He does the counterspells and disenchantments. He knows exactly what to look for."

As Princess dined, Louise gave occasional deep sighs and at last said, "Maybe it's no use at all. Maybe there's nothing to be found. The castle is in ruins. Our story is forgotten. It's all over. I'll be a sword forever."

Her mouth full of rabbit, Princess could only frown and shake her head. Swallowing, she said quickly, "You mustn't talk that way. Shanzie remembered the whole story, didn't he?''

"He did not. He didn't know about William and Alice, and he didn't even know that I'd been turned into a sword. He was very inaccurate."

"He had the general idea. And apparently people do expect you to come back."

"I *have* come back, and look what I've found! Dirt, cobwebs, ruination . . . not a sign of Hedvig or her descendants . . . no archives, or annals, or cryptic messages . . . nothing!"

"Cheer up, Louise. When Keddie gets here, things will start looking up. Meanwhile, let's relax."

Relax they did. Shanzie dutifully cleared a pleasant little room off the great hall. He built up a good fire and brought in armfuls of soft fragrant evergreen branches which Princess arranged into a comfortable mattress. A simple spell kept the spiders, mice, beetles, and other small creatures at a proper distance; another sealed the rickety door and kept out the noise and dust of Shanzie's sweeping and swabbing. Princess slept soundly, undisturbed from sunset to dawn, and lay cozily woolgathering until full light.

Noise from below indicated that Shanzie was already at work. She breakfasted lightly from her own stores, then went to check on his progress. He had made the upper level look, if not exactly tidy, at least much more respectable than it had upon her arrival.

Shanzie was less apprehensive this morning. He seemed to have accepted the fact that he now worked for a winged lady who carried a talking sword and traveled on a horse that one could see through, and having settled that in his mind, he concentrated on doing his work well. Around midday, he brought a wild fowl to Princess and spitted it over the fire. When it was done, she told him that he might take his meal with her. Squatting on the floor beside her chair, he ate rapidly and noisily, appetite overcoming any lingering misgivings about his new mistress. When he

finished eating and wiping his greasy fingers on his rags,
he rose to go, but Princess detained him.

"Shanzie, are there any old books in the castle?" she
asked.

"I don't know, my lady. What's *books*?"

"Oh, dear. A book is . . . it's about so big and so
thick," she said, accompanying her words with illustrative
manual gesture, "but books can be bigger or smaller, or
thicker or thinner. Inside, they're all full of thin sheets
covered with marks. Sometimes they have pictures, too."

"They sounds like grand things, my lady. I never saw
one of those."

"Is there anything in the castle that's been here since
the time the princess was enchanted?"

"Only the big chest that no one can open and no one
can move, my lady."

Princess bounced eagerly to her feet. "Lead me to it at
once, Shanzie," she ordered, taking up the black sword
and saying to it in a confidential undertone, "Did you hear
that?"

Louise sighed and said, "He's probably talking about
the dustbin. It's hopeless, Princess. I appreciate your efforts, but I can see that it's all hopeless. I'll be a sword
forever. Except when I'm a stick."

"Now, now. Mustn't give up," Princess said with a
reassuring squeeze of Louise's hilt. Louise sighed deeply
and sank into a despondent silence.

They descended to the lowest level, a dank and muddy
place once used for the storing of food and prisoners. The
big chest, it turned out, was not only too heavy to be
dragged off by looters, it was too heavy for rotting floorboards to support; some years ago it had crashed down
from the floor above and half buried itself in the dirt.

In the light of Shanzie's torch, the iron chest looked like
the coffin of a giant, rescued in the act of desecration by
graverobbers. It was sunk in the floor almost to the level
of its elaborate triple locks, which showed the scars of

violent efforts, but were intact, and now rusted almost to solidity.

"What about this?" Princess asked, holding the sword up for a close look.

"I remember this chest. I was standing just before it when that evil old wizard enchanted me. But there's nothing of any importance in it. We used to store arrases and worn-out state robes in it," said Louise dully.

"It won't hurt to look inside."

"It won't *help*."

"Well, we don't know what might have been put in it after you were all enchanted, do we?" Princess pointed out. When Louise made no reply, she turned back her sleeves and said, "So let's have a look."

She laid her hand on the rough cold lockplate, center of the three, closed her eyes tightly, and frowned in deep concentration. After a time her lips began to move, but no sound came forth. She stopped and took a step back, blinking and breathing deeply, as after strenuous physical exertion. From within the lockplate came a reluctant creak, as rusted metal moved after a century's idleness. The sound rose to an ear-piercing screech, then ended in a sudden clang. With a bright smile, Princess said, "So much for *that*. Get the lid back, Shanzie, and let's see what's inside."

Awed, Shanzie thrust the base of his torch in the soft dirt and gripped the edge of the lid with both hands. Still more squealing of rustbound metal followed as he urged the heavy lid up and up until it left his hands and tilted backwards from its own weight, rocking the entire chest and sending Shanzie skipping quickly aside in fright. He took up the torch and raised it high. He and Princess inched forward to peek into the chest.

"Just a lot of old clothes, my lady," Shanzie announced.

"I told you that's all you'd find," said Louise.

"It's not a total loss. Shanzie, find yourself a new outfit. Anything's bound to be better than those filthy rags you've got on."

"Yes, my lady. Thank you, my lady!"

Shanzie groped about, found a fine embroidered jerkin, and pulled it forth. He studied it with delight, turning it this way and that, to make the golden threads and crystal buttons and scarlet silk glitter in the torchlight. With a grateful glance at Princess, he draped the jerkin over the lid and rummaged deeper. As he dragged aside a heavy arras, a beam of light shot up from the depths of the chest. Shanzie sprang away, startled. The arras fell back, and the light was gone.

"Hold that torch high, Shanzie," Princess ordered, stepping up to the chest and digging in.

She pushed aside a cloak and a huge fur-trimmed hat, seized the arras, and tugged. The light shone forth again, and Princess, with a triumphant shout, reached for the source. She straightened and turned. In her hand was a slender wand, gold and ivory, with a glowing crystal star at its top.

"Wanda!" Louise cried.

"Are you sure?"

"Yes! I'd know her anywhere. Oh, Wanda, poor dear innocent! It's all my fault for making that foul old man angry! Wanda, can you forgive me? Say you forgive me!" Louise wailed.

The wand was silent. Princess spoke to it softly, even shook it, very gently, but it did not respond.

"She's been in there for a long time. You can hardly expect her to come around right away," said Princess.

Eagerly Louise said, "Yes, of course. We must be patient. She'll be all right, I'm sure. We just have to . . . let's get her someplace airy and bright. That's sure to help, isn't it?"

"We'll do that," said Princess soothingly.

"The chest! Maybe they're all in there!" Louise cried. "Oh, please, Princess, search for them!"

Tucking the wand in her girdle, Princess returned to the chest, and with Shanzie's help emptied it to the bottom. They found no crown, nor any shield, although Shanzie came out of the operation with the makings of a splendid outfit.

"I'm sorry, Louise," said Princess, taking up the sword.

"Never mind, Princess. I didn't really expect to find them. I'm happy to have found Wanda. Let's get her upstairs."

With a curt nod to Louise, Princess turned to Shanzie. "Take what you need, and put the rest back in the chest. And be sure you take a bath before you put the new things on," she directed him.

"A bath, my lady? Is that like a book?" he asked, mystified.

She sighed. "No, Shanzie. A bath is taking off all your rags and getting into water and scrubbing yourself until you're clean."

"I never did that, my lady," he said guardedly.

"I can tell. Do it before you put those clothes on."

Leaving the apprehensive Shanzie, Princess and Louise returned to their chamber. Princess laid Wanda gently on her bed of pine boughs, placing her so the sun shone full on her.

"Nothing to do now but wait," she said.

"I do hope Wanda comes around soon," said Louise, sounding worried. "I hope she's all right. She's so still. So quiet . . ."

"The poor thing's been in that chest for a hundred years, Louise. You can't expect her to be chatty and bright."

"That's true, I suppose. And she was always a shy girl."

They waited. Midday came, and Princess lunched lightly, and there was still no activity on Wanda's part. As the afternoon wore on, Louise became so anxious that Princess cradled the wand in her arms like a baby, and walked about the great hall crooning to it. This made her feel foolish. She stopped and sat by the fireplace, and as she rested, Shanzie burst in. He looked quite different with a good wash and elegant clothes on, all scarlet and green and gold, with ruffles and ribbon, slashes and sashes, and a great plumed bonnet, but his manner was unchanged. He was beside himself with fear.

"My lady, my lady! Horsemen! Ever so many of them! Here!" he burbled.

"Horsemen? How many?"

"Ever so many, my lady, and they're all big and angry-looking, and all of them dressed in black! They're coming to the castle, my lady! We must flee!"

"No need to fret," said Louise coolly. "Just leave everything to me. And remember: I'm Panstygia."

Princess tucked the wand away, rose, took a couple of practice swings with Panstygia, and then strode to the center of the room. With the sword in her hands, its point resting on the floorboards, and the wand safe in her girdle, she waited.

The first thing she heard was the voices, as men shouted commands back and forth. Soon she heard footsteps below, then ascending the stone steps. One by one, men in black issued from the stairwell. They stared at her, but said nothing, either in threat or greeting. Princess counted twenty, and they kept coming. "Can you handle this many?" she whispered.

"Easily," the sword assured her.

There were thirty of them now, perhaps more. They spread out to encircle Princess, still without speaking a word. One last man joined them, bigger than the rest. He, too, was in black. A slender gold band ringed his right arm. Slung behind him was a round iron shield. In his right hand he clasped an iron mace. The black scabbard at his side was empty.

"Who are you, and what do you mean by bursting in here like this?" Princess asked with icy dignity.

"Insolent woman! Wretched usurper! Thief!" the man in black responded.

"You'd better watch your language," Princess said.

"Villainess!" he snarled. Baring his teeth in a ferocious grimace, he raised his mace and sprang for her.

··· ❧ *Thirteen* ❧ ···

a dragon without a hoard

THE MACE CAME up and around. At the top of the mace's arc, the black blade seemed to spring to life, darting up as if of its own volition to shear the spiked head free. It spun through the air, narrowly missing two of the encircling men, and bounded across the floor, leaving a trail of splinters. The attacker staggered off balance, freezing into immobility when the point of the blade pricked the skin of his throat.

"Answer my question, fellow," said Princess, unruffled. "Who are you, and what is the meaning of this attack?"

Before the man could speak, the sword cried, "How dare you attack a lady? How dare you insult a princess, and call her names?"

"I seek the great sword Panstygia," said the man hoarsely.

"You do, do you? Well, you're about to find it—hilt-deep in your sweetbreads, you vicious brute! You coward! Know, ruffian, that I am Panstygia, Mother of Darkness, and my only business with the likes of you is—"

"No, wait!" shouted three voices simultaneously, followed at once by a babble of "Louise, it's Alice! It's William, dear sister! Great-great-aunt Louise, have mercy!

181

Don't you recognize us? Stay your blow, sister! Hold! A miracle!'' until Princess called imperiously for silence.

When all was still, she said to the man in black, "For now, I want *you* to do the talking. Is that gold band on your arm Alice, the crown?"

"It is, my lady," he said, relieved at her intercession.

"And that great heavy shield—is it William?"

"It is indeed. But he's not heavy, he's her brother," said the man in black, with a slight nod of his head and a downward shift of his eyes to indicate the black blade still touching his Adam's apple.

"And who, then, are you?"

"My lady, the blade . . . if you would . . ."

Princess withdrew Louise. Bowing deeply, the man in black said, "I am Rokkmund, fourth of that name, known to the world as the Knight of the Empty Scabbard. I am the great-great-grandson of Elsa, younger sister of Hedvig, second cousin to Louise, Alice, and William, who once ruled in the Kingdom of the Singing Forest, and I am now the sole and rightful heir to that Kingdom."

"He's telling the truth, Louise," said a deep resounding voice from behind the man's shoulder.

"William? Is that really you?" asked the sword.

"It is, dear sister."

"And I'm Alice!" cried a joyous voice from Rokkmund's right arm. "I'm too small to fit his head, but I make a lovely armband."

"And you, Louise, true to your courageous nature, have become the great black blade of the west," said Rokkmund. Smiling, he held out his hand. "Come, my great-great-aunt, and join us. Together, we will rebuild the Kingdom of the Singing Forest and overcome our enemies. We will be invincible!"

"I've had quite enough of being invincible, thank you," said Louise.

"It is your duty, great-great-aunt. Enemies must be smashed."

"What enemies? All our enemies are dead by now."

Setting his grim features even more grimly, Rokkmund said, "There are always enemies. Our kingdom has been overrun and divided among neighbors who took advantage of our family's misfortunes. We must wring it from their thieving grasp!"

"I don't want to wring anything from anyone's grasp, Rokkmund. I only want to be myself again. I'm thoroughly sick of being a sword."

"It's no use, Louise," said William. "Being a shield is no fun, believe me, but there's no way out. Vorvas is dead, and no one can lift the spell."

"That isn't so, William. The spell can be lifted if we can find out the exact words Vorvas used. Princess and I have been searching high and low for any archives, or annals, or chronicles, or anything at all that might tell us what Vorvas said that day."

"But you found nothing," said Rokkmund.

"Not yet. But what about you? What do you know about Vorvas's spell?"

"Alas, nothing. Great-great aunt Hedvig was devastated by the spectacle of your transformation. She entered a convent that very day, and never spoke another word. Her secrets all died with her."

"Then . . . there's no hope for us at all," said Louise faintly.

"None whatsoever. Accept your destiny. Be my blade, and lead us to glory!"

"Just a minute, Louise," said Princess. "I don't think you should make any decisions until you've had a chance to speak to Kedrigern."

"But there's no hope for us. He can do nothing without knowing the spell," said Louise, her voice leaden.

"He may think of something. Despelling is his specialty."

"If I may ask, my lady, who is this person Kedrigern?" Rokkmund inquired politely.

"He is my husband, a wizard of great skill."

Smiling sardonically, Rokkmund folded his arms and looked down on her. 'So, a wizard? And are my great-

great-aunts and my great-great-uncle, after all their suffering at the hands of the evil wizard Vorvas, to submit themselves to another wizard in some vain hope of deliverance? I think you mock us, my lady.''

"Kedrigern isn't like Vorvas. He's very clean," Louise said.

Princess looked Rokkmund in the eye and said, "Kedrigern is a great wizard who knows everything there is to know about despellings and disenchantments. If anyone can help your family, he can, and he will.''

"But no one can help them, and you know that well.''

"Kedrigern just might.''

"And if he fails? Think of the consequences, my lady. If great-great-uncle William becomes a chafing-dish instead of a shield, will he be happier? And if great-great-aunt Alice finds herself turned into an embroidery hoop, will her lot be improved? If Panstygia, black blade of the west, is transformed into a bodkin, will—"

"Oh, my goodness! I just realized . . . the mace! Was it a relative of ours?'' cried Louise in sudden horror.

"It was no one at all. A simple mace, and no more,'' Rokkmund assured her. She gave a deep sigh of relief, and he went on, "Why dawdle? Why waste time waiting for a wizard who can do nothing to help you and who may, without intending it, do you harm? Come, join your brother and sister. Ride at my side, to battle, to victory, to glory!''

Princess felt the blade twitching. Pulling Louise close in a protective gesture, she said, "Leave her alone, Rokkmund. It's not fair, pressing her like this. She needs time to talk with William and Alice.''

"My lady, I offer her a lifetime of close union with them.''

"But Louise is unhappy being a sword. We've discussed it many times.''

With an expression of sweet reasonableness, Rokkmund spread his arms wide, palms open generously, and said, "Of course she was in the past, dear lady. What sword would not be unhapppy buried in a tree, or wielded clumsily by non-swordspersons and mean wretches of low ambition? But I offer her fulfillment—the chance to flash in battle—to carve a path to glorious victory! Together, we will conquer an empire!''

"That's very thoughtful of you, Rokkmund, and I appreciate it," said Louise warmly. "I'd just like to think about it, and talk it over with Kedrigern."

"I understand, dear great-great-aunt. Perhaps . . . perhaps while we wait, you would like to try my scabbard. It has been empty, at my side, awaiting you."

"Do try it, sister," said William. "He had it made especially for you. It looks very comfortable."

"Go ahead, Louise. You always did look good in black," Alice urged.

Hesitantly, Louise said, "Princess . . . do you think . . .?"

"It's entirely your decision."

"Well . . . I don't suppose it would hurt to try it on."

Rokkmund extended his large hand. Princess gave him the sword, not without misgivings, for she did not like his looks nor his manners, and doubted his motives. But he was Louise's relation (though not, as far as Princess could calculate, a true great-great-nephew unless one allowed a very flexible use of the term) and had the better claim. Louise was free to choose, and she had chosen.

Rokkmund raised the sword high and brandished it proudly. With a fierce, clenched-teeth smile and a low laugh that Princess heard with deep foreboding, he slid it home in the black scabbard. There followed a moment of expectant silence, which Rokkmund broke.

"Well?"

"It's very comfortable," Louise said, her voice muffled.

"Made expressly for you, my dear Panstygia."

"I never had a scabbard of my very own."

"This is only the beginning. We will go on to greatness, the three of you and I. You will be immortal. In ages to come, when men speak with awe and envy of the empire of Rokkmund, Panstygia, Mother of Darkness, will be ranked with Balisarda and Joyeuse, with Durendal and

Sanglamore . . . with Excalibur itself! They will also mention my shield and my crown, of course,'' he quickly added.

"It's a very nice scabbard, and it was thoughtful of you to have it made for me, Rokkmund—"

"—A pleasure, dear great-great-aunt—"

"—But I'd still rather be a princess."

"Unfortunately, I have no need of a princess. I need Panstygia, Mother of Darkness, the great black blade of the west. And now I have her,'' said Rokkmund, smiling and laying a large possessive hand on Louise's pommel.

"That's just what Mergith said! You're all alike!'' cried the sword in a muted voice of outrage. "And I'll tell you what I told him—I'll never serve you! I'll stick in my scabbard! I'll give you painful calluses! I'll lose my edge!"

"You will do none of these things, Panstygia, because I am your only living descendant and you cannot let me come to harm. So you will do my bidding—my exact bidding—as your brother and sister have learned to do it,'' Rokkmund said confidently, looking amused by this exchange.

"He's right, Louise. We have no choice,'' said William in a dull, hopeless voice.

"At least we'll be together,'' said Alice, trying to be brave.

Rokkmund favored Princess with a low bow and a courtly flourish. Still smiling, he said, "Now, good lady, I leave you to this pile of rubble, to make what you will of it. I go to forge an empire!"

"No, you don't. I won't have you leaving this place until Kedrigern arrives, and we see what he can do for your relatives. And I won't have you carrying Louise off with you if she doesn't want to go. Or Alice or William, either, for that matter,'' said Princess.

"You are fiery, my lady—but your fire will do you little good. When you wielded Panstygia, I had good reason to be wary of you. Now you are powerless. Rant if you will. Threaten if you like. You can do nothing more.''

"I can do a great deal more, Rokkmund."

"You bet she can," came the muted voice from the scabbard.

Rokkmund's brows rose. "Are you a sorceress, then? Or a witch?"

"A wizard," Princess corrected him.

He laughed a soft mocking laugh. "But not enough of a wizard to assist my great-great-aunt. I think I have little to fear from you, my lady."

"My husband is the one who specializes in despellings and disenchantments. I do other things. And if you try to leave here, I will do them to you and your men, and do them gleefully."

Rokkmund looked down on her for a moment, thoughtfully scratching his chin with one large hand. Princess did her best to look forbidding as she searched her memory for a quick effective spell to suit the situation. Rokkmund left off scratching, gave a curt, decisive nod, and murmuring, "Only one thing to do, then," swiftly drew Panstygia and cocked his arm back for a neck-high stroke. Panstygia screamed, but could do nothing to prevent him. Taken completely by surprise, Princess had no time for a spell. She snatched the wand from her girdle and stuck it out before her. The black blade came swiftly around and met the white wand. There was a silent burst of dazzling light, as if the sun had exploded in their midst, and a shock that left her dazed and helpless. She heard sudden cries of pain and alarm, hurried footsteps, the crash of men colliding with one another and with articles of furniture, the clang of weapons dropped or thrown aside in panic, and then she sank to the floor, unconscious.

She awoke to the sound of a familiar voice, and opened her eyes to see Kedrigern's anxious face looking down on her. He raised her to a sitting position and held a flagon to her lips.

"Drink this, my dear. Slowly, now. You've had a bit of a shock, I imagine," he said.

"Oh, Keddie, it was terrible!" She swallowed some of the wine, then quickly went on, "Rokkmund tried to cut my head off with Louise, and she couldn't do a thing about it. I held up Wanda. . . ."

"You found Wanda, then?"

"Yes. She was in a big iron chest, poor thing. And Rokkmund had found William and Alice. I don't think he was very nice to them. I do hope you can help them, Keddie."

"My help is no longer required, my dear. It looks as though you've taken care of everything," Kedrigern said proudly, assisting her to her feet and gesturing dramatically to the floor nearby. She blinked and rubbed her eyes, before which dots and particles of blackness still swam, and looked at the spectacle in amazement.

Three women and a man, all complete strangers to her, were in a tangled heap on the floor where she and Rokkmund had clashed. They looked like victims of a violent but noninjurious accident. One dark-haired woman dressed all in black, broad-shouldered and formidable of chin and bosom, attractive in a vigorous, outdoorsy way, sat clutching her side and grimacing as if she had received a painful blow in the ribs. Behind her, leaning back-to-back in mutual support, a young man with the same sturdy shoulders and determined jawline was patting his arms, legs, trunk, and head in delighted disbelief. A woman with deep yellow hair, in appearance a younger sister of the other two, was staring at them in astonishment. And a slender, delicate girl in a milkwhite gown, with hair of the palest gold and skin like cream, lay supine at her side.

"William! Louise! I'm disenchanted!" the yellow-haired woman exclaimed, flinging her arms joyously wide, then hugging herself tightly.

"Well, I'm disenchanted, too. We're all disenchanted," said the woman in black, rubbing her side. She looked around, saw Princess, and cried, "Princess! You're safe! And Kedrigern's come at last!" She climbed gingerly to her feet and embraced Princess, wincing slightly. Stepping back, she asked, "What happened?"

"I held up Wanda. There was this terrible flash. . . ." said Princess vaguely. She appeared perplexed.

"A very clever move it was, too, my dear," Kedrigern said. "With all the enchantees in close proximity like that, the contact forced the magic back in on itself, and . . . well, here you all are."

"Yes, here we are. I'd like you to meet my sister Alice and my brother William. These are my friends Princess and Kedrigern. Wizards, both of them. They've been absolutely wonderful," said Louise, beaming, as they exchanged greetings and embraces with one another.

"Am I correct in assuming that the lady on the floor is cousin Wanda?" Kedrigern asked, pointing to the motionless figure.

"Poor Wanda. She never could take roughhousing. I imagine she'll be out for days," Alice said.

"And she'll have a bad bruise on her ribs, too," Louise observed, holding her own side. "Rokkmund had a powerful swing."

"Where is he? He was right at the center of . . ." William began, and then they noticed the toad sitting stupefied near Wanda.

It was a large toad, almost the size of a cat, and of a green so dark that it was nearly black. It took one unsteady bound toward them, landing clumsily and nearly falling. It turned its gaze full on the group and loudly croaked, "*Grugump!*"

"How wonderfully appropriate!" Alice said, clapping her hands. "Oh, thank you, Princess!"

"Nicely done, my lady. It shows excellent judgment," said William, taking her hand and raising it to his lips.

Princess acknowledged the compliments with a secretive smile. Louise squeezed her hand in appreciation. Kedrigern caught her eye and winked, and she quickly averted her gaze.

"Where is Shanzie?" Louise suddenly demanded. "We'll

need someone to prepare meals and fix up our chambers
and get this place into shape. There's lots to be done.
Whatever became of the lad?''

"I'm sure he ran off when he saw Rokkmund and his
men coming," Princess said. Turning to Kedrigern, she
asked, "Did you happen to pass a little boy, very color-
fully dressed?''

"No, but there's no need to worry. You'll have no
trouble finding all the help you'll require. Rokkmund's
men will be looking for employment, and I'm sure they'll
behave themselves after seeing what happened to their
master.''

The toad seemed to understand. With one last defiant
grugump, he turned and hopped it for the stairs.

"We're well rid of him. He was beastly to us," said
Alice with a shudder.

William nodded grimly. "He certainly was. He threatened to pound me into foil if I didn't go along with him."

"William, you never mentioned that!"

He laid a comforting hand on Alice's. "I didn't want to
upset you. I was afraid even to think of what he might
threaten to do to you."

"The swine! The absolute swine!" Alice hissed.

"Absolute toad, actually," Kedrigern corrected her. "And
I think Rokkmund is literally just that. Considering the
amount of concentrated magic that went off here, he's
certain to be a toad forever, absolute and unchanging."

Pleased smiles were exchanged all around at this professional opinion, with which Princess concurred. "Reassuring news indeed," said William. "And now, if you will
excuse me, I will see about offering a place in our service
to such of Rokkmund's men as I find suitable."

"Look for one who can cook. We all need a good
dinner," said Louise.

They enjoyed good dinners that night and the next.
Princess and Kedrigern took their leave on the third day.
They were well attended during their stay. Rokkmund's

men, upon learning the full story, were quick to swear allegiance to Louise, Alice, and William, and they took up their duties energetically. There was much hard work to be done, but none of it was of a violent nature. Where Rokkmund had been profligate of his followers' lives and limbs, these new masters were interested in workmanship and willing to reward it. No one regretted Rokkmund's downfall.

When all the gratitude had been expressed, rewards promised, and eternal friendships sworn, Princess and Kedrigern mounted the great black steed and waved a last farewell. They emerged from the gatehouse into a crowd of men, who shrank back at sight of the silver-horned, red-eyed beast. From a cautious distance, their leader waved and hallooed for attention.

"Master Kedrigern! My lady! You can't get across this way," he cried. "We haven't repaired the bridge."

Smiling and returning the wave, Kedrigern said privately, "Shall we make a dramatic exit, my dear?"

"What exactly do you have in mind?"

"I think this noble steed of mine could easily jump twice the distance over the bridge."

"Are you sure? I've got my wings, but you and he might hurt yourselves."

"I have every confidence, my dear. Trust me." Cupping his hands, he called to the workmen, "Stand clear, please. We're going across."

"You'll never make it! It's too—" a man started to say, but he fell mute at a glare from the horse's red eye and a menacing flick of his horn.

Kedrigern leaned forward over the glossy black neck and the mane thick as midnight and said softly, "What do you think, my friend? Can we make it?"

The great beast tossed his head and gave a snort that echoed loudly in the gatehouse. The snort had a distinctly affirmative note. Backing up a few steps, he lowered his head, pawed the ground, and shot forward, launching himself over the edge of the fallen bridge and landing lightly as a leaf a good six paces beyond the farther rim. He reared up, silver hooves and horn resplendent in the morning sunlight, and snorted flame from his nostrils. A loud, wholehearted cheer went up from the awed workmen.

"They'll never forget that moment," said Kedrigern.

"Neither will I," said Princess when she caught her breath. "He's quite a horse."

"Indeed he is. Now let's find yours and start home."

Princess's translucent stallion had been regularly fed and watered. They found him at the center of a ring of ordinary workhorses and their own packhorses. Soft whinnying, subdued neighing, and amused snorting ceased as they drew near, and the group broke up and moved off with a few guilty sidelong glances at the humans and the black steed.

"He's a great raconteur, that horse of yours," Kedrigern observed.

"He does seem popular with the other horses. I often wonder what kind of stories he tells them."

"Probably shameless gossip about us. But he's a good horse. He got you through that enchanted wood safely."

"Yes, he did. And he doesn't seem to be afraid of anything. And he's fast."

"It's his speed that interests me now. Silent Thunder Mountain is a long way off, and the days are getting shorter and cooler. The nights have been positively chilly. We'll have to make good time if we're to be home before the first snow."

"Can't we stop anywhere?" asked Princess, dismayed.

"I promised Dyrax that I'd pass along the news of his great feat to Zorilon and have it made into folklore. And I suppose we ought to stop in Dendorric and see how Hamarak is managing. But that's really all the time we can spare."

The morning's ride was pleasant and relaxed. The woods, freed now from their long enchantment and not yet filled up with bandits and outcasts, seemed to charge every breeze with the sweet scent of liberation. Saplings bowed and gnarled old ancients dipped their branches to Kedrigern as he passed, in token of gratitude. He acknowledged these gestures with a gracious wave or a nod, which Princess seconded with a sweet smile.

"It's nice of them to show their appreciation," she said as they came to a clearing.

"Trees are much better than people at such things, I've noticed," said Kedrigern with a world-weary sigh.

Neither of them spoke for a time, riding on in meditative silence until they came to a brook that bisected an open field and the wizard suggested that they rest and refresh themselves here. He unrolled a blanket, Princess laid out bread, cheese, and wine from their provisions, and they partook of a leisurely light meal. Kedrigern lay back comfortably, face up to the sun, and Princess snuggled close to him, her head on his shoulder.

"I hope you're not too terribly disappointed, my dear," he said without opening his eyes.

She raised her head and looked at him curiously. "Disappointed? Why?"

"Well, the whole point of our journey was to find you a wand, and we're no nearer to that than we were on the day we left. Farther from it, actually, with Wanda back in human form—that makes one wand fewer in the world."

"I don't mind. Think of all the good we did. The curse is off these woods, and the Green Riddler is no longer a threat to travelers, and Blamarde and all her kingdom are awake . . . and Pensimer and Ezrammis are free of that ridiculous curse. . . ."

"And Louise and her family are people again," he added.

"Except Rokkmund," Princess corrected him.

"Ah, yes. Rokkmund. Tell me, my dear, did you really mean to turn him into a toad?"

"It was in the back of my mind, but I didn't really *try* to do it. All I intended to do was avoid having my head cut off."

"You acted instinctively, and everything worked out.

That shows that you've got the makings of a first-rate wizard. I'm really impressed with what you've done," he said, hugging her close.

She returned the hug. "You taught me everything I know."

"Yes, but one needs a good pupil to be a good teacher. You're an excellent pupil. Most important of all, you've got the right instincts. An ordinary person would have ducked, or screamed, or tried to run—you held up your wand."

"It seemed the right thing to do."

"And it was. Knowing that is the mark of a wizard."

She sighed contentedly. They lay in cozy silence for a time, and then Princess sat up and said, "I don't really want a wand at all. What's the point? I've had my chance to use one, and I'll never top what I did back at the castle."

Kedrigern propped himself on an elbow. Thoughtfully, he said, "That's very sensible, my dear. One problem remains, though."

"What's that?"

"Finding you a proper anniversary present."

She laughed and rose, tugging him to his feet. "Let's see if there are any berries left on those bushes," she said.

Hand-in-hand they walked toward the brook, where thick bushes lined the banks. A shadow passed over them as they walked, and they looked up to see a formidable shape circling overhead. The sun flashed off scales of gold and scarlet, gleamed on crystal claws. Broad wings of translucent green stretched on either side of the slender, glittering trunk and dartlike head and tail. The horses looked up, whickered softly to one another, and resumed their browsing.

"Is it anyone we know?" Princess asked.

Kedrigern drew out his medallion, sighted through the Aperture of True Vision, and shaking his head in perplexity said, "I don't recognize it, but it seems to know us."

"Look! It's waving!"

"Did you meet any dragons while we were separated, my dear?"

"I met no one at all . . . except for poor Shanzie."

"I heard the name mentioned. Who is he?"

"A funny little boy who was living in the ruins of Louise's castle. He was dreadfully dirty and ragged, but good-hearted. I found him some clothing in the chest where Wanda was kept. It was probably the first decent outfit he had ever worn. He looked very nice all cleaned up, in a lovely scarlet jerkin trimmed with gold, and a shirt with green sleeves, and crystal. . . . Oh, my, do you think . . .?" she asked, turning to him with wide anxious eyes.

"It's very likely, my dear. Law of Conservation of Magic, you know."

They both waved at the dragon, who zoomed low, pulled up sharply, and went into a series of slow barrel rolls while circling the clearing. He was a very skillful flier.

"What's the Law of Conservation of Magic?"

"Magic doesn't just disappear. All that heavy-duty enchantment on Louise and her family had to go somewhere, and turning Rokkmund into a toad doesn't account for more than a fraction of it."

"I feel terrible, Keddie. The poor boy!" said Princess, clasping her hands ruefully.

"Shanzie seems quite pleased with the change, judging from the way he's cavorting about up there. You may have done him a great favor," Kedrigern said, putting his arm around her shoulder.

At once the dragon ceased his acrobatics and dove directly at the pair, coming to earth heavily a short distance before them. Rearing up, raising his golden head, he roared, "You leave that lady be, you nasty villain, or I'll rend you!"

"Shanzie, is it you?" Princess called to the creature.

"Yes, my lady. Have no fear. I'll save you," he said, claws flashing wickedly as he flexed them.

"No, Shanzie! This is my husband!"

"Your husband?"

"I told you he'd be coming, remember? Well, he did, and now we're on our way home again." Princess paused, then asked, "And how is everything with you, Shanzie?"

"It's wonderful, my lady! I never felt so strong—and I can fly! Did you see me fly?"

"Indeed I did, Shanzie. You're very good."

"It's easy! It's as easy as walking! I used to look at birds and wish I could fly, but I never thought I'd be able to do it. Oh, I'm so happy, my lady!" Shanzie burbled in a deep rumbling voice oddly suited to his boyish enthusiasm. Puffs of white smoke accompanied his words.

"We're very glad for you. And you have only Princess to thank," said Kedrigern, gesturing to his blushing wife with a dramatic flourish.

The dragon looked from one to the other, his innocent blue eyes widening in astonishment. "Is it true, my lady? Did you do this for me?"

Reddening steadily, Princess said, "Oh, really now, Shanzie . . . it was . . . I only raised Wanda, and there was this flash. . . ." She looked uncomfortably down at her feet and gave a little gesture with one hand.

"Oh, my lady, thank you! Thank you!"

"Not only that, Shanzie—in the same instant, she turned one man into a toad and disenchanted four people who had been under a powerful spell for over a hundred years. Now, that's what I call wizardry," said Kedrigern proudly.

Shanzie breathed out a slim ribbon of flame and shook his head in astonished silence.

"Well, someone had to do something," Princess said.

"You certainly took the bit between your teeth, my dear."

Princess patted Kedrigern's hand, smiled, and turned to the dragon. "What do you plan to do now, Shanzie? Will you be staying on at the castle?"

"Oh, no, my lady. There's no place for Shanzie at the castle," the dragon said fearfully. "First time I showed my face, a bunch of men threw spears at me and shouted,

'Slay the dragon! Destroy the foul dragon!' I don't want to stay where I'm not wanted.''

"No, certainly not. Especially when people throw spears.''

"How about guarding a gold-hoard? That seems to be the primary occupation of dragons in this part of the world,'' Kedrigern observed.

"I don't know where to look, my lord. I don't suppose there's that many gold-hoards around.''

"A good point,'' the wizard conceded, adding, "Please don't call me 'my lord.' 'Master Kedrigern' will do.''

"Yes, Master Kedrigern,'' Shanzie said, attempting a salute with his gleaming foreclaw.

"Keddie, what about that mountain of gold Buroc showed us? We never got around to doing anything with it, and it's just lying there. Shanzie could guard that, couldn't he?'' Princess suggested.

"Perfectly all right with me, my dear.''

They turned to the dragon, who looked at them nervously and emitted a few tentative wisps of smoke before he said, "It's very kind of you, my lady and Master Kedrigern, but I was thinking . . . well, now that I'm a dragon and can fly and all . . . I was thinking how nice it would be to travel a bit and see something of the world. I'm just not ready to settle down.''

With a comforting maternal pat on his foreclaw, Princess said, "Then you ought to go traveling, Shanzie, by all means. We'll keep the gold-hoard for you until you're ready. Where did you plan to travel?''

Shanzie hesitated for a long time before blurting, "With you!''

"With us?'' Princess repeated.

"Just for a time, my lady. I won't be any bother. I can guide you, and I'll protect you from all danger. I can light you a nice fire every evening, and catch lovely fresh dinners for you. Please let me come with you!''

"Keddie . . .?'' she asked softly.

"It's entirely up to you, my dear. He seems attached to you."

"He was very helpful at the castle. A good hard worker, and dependable. He'd save us a bit of magic on the way home. And I suppose I owe him something. After all, if it weren't for me, he'd still be human."

"Yes. He'd still be a poor human boy, slaving away at Louise's castle, instead of a golden dragon free to fly wherever he chooses. I don't think you have anything to feel guilty about, my dear."

"Not guilty, exactly. Responsible. I can't just tell him to go away," she said.

"Then invite him along."

Princess turned to the expectant dragon. "All right, Shanzie. You may come with us. You'll be my anniversary present."

Shanzie spread his green wings with the sound of a sudden wind bellying limp sails into taut plumpness. He soared high, then did a series of loops over the clearing, trailing smoke in a curling ribbon. Princess looked on like a proud parent, and applauded when he alit before them and bowed as well as his saurian configuration permitted.

"Lovely work. Much better than a wand," said Kedrigern.

···⁑ *Fourteen* ⁑···

return to dendorric

SHANZIE WAS a great help; there was no question about
that. He kept them on the trail, cleared fallen trees with a
swipe of his claw, dried up boggy patches with a scorching
exhalation, and had a lovely fire waiting for them at the
end of each day's ride, with a choice cut of fresh meat
spitted over the flames, timed to reach medium-rare done-
ness when the night's shelter had been erected and the
blankets laid out. He took his own meals at a polite
distance, leaving the wizards to dine in privacy, joining
them for a brief postprandial visit before removing himself
to a vantage point for sentry duty.

With no demands on his magic, and with the help of a
hot cup of haemony broth each morning, Kedrigern was
soon himself again. And being himself, he naturally began
to brood over the fact that in the shrinking days of late
autumn he was on horseback, far from home, with duties
still to discharge before he could settle in comfort before
his own fireplace with a chronicle or a good book of
spells, a beaker of Vosconu's choicest vintage at his side
and faithful Spot ready to minister to his every wish. And
not only was he traveling, he had a dragon for a traveling
companion. Shanzie was a very obliging dragon, to be
sure; a good sort, even-tempered, serviceable, deferential,

and eager to please; but a dragon all the same, and devoted to Princess. How long he might linger on once they
were home, and with what effect on their mode of life,
Kedrigern contemplated with great misgivings. Would
Shanzie and Spot get along? How many clients would
Shanzie frighten off? Would he attract other dragons? Was
the comfortable, remote cottage on Silent Thunder Mountain to become a hangout for idle dragons? And if such a
thing threatened, how did one get a dragon to move on
without the expenditure of considerable magic and the
ever-present risk of conflagration? It was a bad business,
rapidly worsening; and all the result of traveling. Travel
never did anyone any good. Look at Odysseus. Consider
the Ancient Mariner. Travel meant nothing but fuss, discomfort, and annoying complications in one's life.

"You're very pensive today," Princess observed as he
rode along thus preoccupied.

"Thinking of home, my dear. Wondering how long it
will be before we finally get there."

"You're always thinking of home. It does you good to
get away," she said. His only response was a lugubrious
grunt, and she went on, "This is the best time of year to
be traveling. Just smell the air!"

He sniffed and made a queasy face. "Dank. Very dank."

"And look at the foliage!" she exclaimed with a sweeping gesture that encompassed the boughs overhead and the
woods around. "Have you ever seen such color? Aren't
they brilliant?"

"Dying leaves," he said sadly.

"Don't be morbid. Perk up. The air is brisk and
invigorating."

"It chills one to the bone. I want a nice fire—indoors,
in a fireplace, with a soft chair I can pull up close."

"You'll have that when we get to Zorilon's house."

"When will that be? I thought we'd be there by now."

"Shanzie's looking for it. He'll let us know as soon—
there he is now!" Princess cried, waving at the dragon as
he came into sight through a break in the gaudy forest

canopy. "I don't think he sees us. I'll just fly up and see what he's found."

"Be careful, my dear. Don't get too close. One swipe of those wings and you'd be knocked out of the sky."

"Shanzie would never do anything to hurt me."

"Not intentionally, but dragons can be clumsy. He's still new at this, you must remember."

"I'll be careful," she said, rising smoothly from the saddle and making her way through the branches to the open sky.

He looked after her, and returned her wave with a cheery smile. She had become a skillful flier. And she was rapidly becoming a considerable wizard. Granted, luck had been on her side at Louise's castle, but she had made all the right moves, and made them instinctively. What was luck, after all, but the proper match of instincts to opportunity? Any number of people could be in the right place at the right time, but only those who sensed the rightness could turn it to advantage.

Kedrigern allowed himself a few moments to be proud of Princess and her accomplishments, then returned to his glum ruminations on the discomforts of travel. He had scarcely worked himself up to sulkiness when Princess swooped past him, laughing merrily, and landed lightly on her saddle with an announcement that lifted his spirits.

"Shanzie sighted Zorilon's cottage. We'll be there before dark. You'll have your comfortable chair and your fire this very evening," she said.

"And a bed to sleep in," he added happily. Then his face fell and he added in a subdued undertone, "And more of Zorilon's tales to listen to."

"He may have profited from our criticism," Princess pointed out.

"I sincerely hope so. I promised Dyrax that I'd have him made into a legend and immortalized. If Zorilon hasn't learned how to tell a tale properly, there's not much immortality in store for Dyrax, I'm afraid."

"That's not your fault, Keddie."

"No, I suppose it isn't, said the wizard thoughtfully. They continued on their way and he suddenly turned to Princess in alarm. "Did Shanzie fly over the cottage? Was he seen?"

"No. He told me he was very careful to stay out of sight. He remembers how the men at Louise's castle reacted."

Kedrigern nodded and gave a low, whistling sigh of relief. "That's good. I think it would be best for Shanzie to stay out of sight until we've prepared Zorilon to meet him."

Princess looked puzzled. "But wouldn't Zorilon, of all people, be likely to *want* to meet a genuine dragon?"

"Yes. But not by surprise."

Princess thought that over for a moment, then nodded. "You have a point. I'll tell him to stay hidden until we call him."

Kedrigern's precaution turned out to be wise. Zorilon had undergone rough usage at the hands of Rokkmund and his men, and was not in a suitable frame of mind for an unanticipated encounter with a dragon.

"It was most unpleasant," he said as they warmed themselves before the fire. "This big fellow who called himself the Knight of the Empty Scabbard kept threatening to do bad things to me, and his men cuffed me about and overturned the furniture and swore great oaths, and all to find out where you were going with your enchanted sword. You hadn't asked me to keep it secret, so I told them, but they kept right on threatening and thumping me and tossing the chairs and tables about."

"Their sort think it's expected of them. They didn't hurt you, did they?" Kedrigern asked.

"Just a bruise here and there. Nothing serious. And it gave me some good material. I learned a lot about miscreant knights."

"Still writing fairy tales, then?" Princess asked.

"Oh, yes, my lady. I've been working steadily on

revisions since your stay here—with that one interruption
by Rokkmund and his men. You were both very helpful. I
have nearly two hundred tales completed, and they're
good. Full of conflict and struggle and fearsome obstacles
to happiness which lovely princesses and handsome princes
manage to surmount, but only after much hardship.''

"Do they get to live happily ever after?"

"Every time," Zorilon said confidently.

With a sharp snap of his fingers that brought the dozing
Rumpelstiltskin to instant alertness, Kedrigern said, "That
reminds me: I have a story for you. I promised this prince
that I'd tell you of his deed so you could make him
immortal. The fellow's name is Dyrax. He kissed a beautiful princess and woke her, her whole household, and the
entire kingdom—every single person—from an enchanted
sleep of a hundred years. I was on hand for the whole
thing, so I can give you all the details."

Zorilon frowned slightly. "Were there any unusual features to the story? Was Dyrax grotesquely ugly, for
instance?"

"No. He's a fairly good-looking lad. He was in disguise, if that's any help."

Zorilon nodded knowingly. "As a huntsman? Woodsman?"

"A humble guardsman."

"That would have been my third guess. I suppose he
was looking for some heroic feat to do in order to win
back his lost love."

"As a matter of fact, he was. How did you know?"

"We authors know these things. I do appreciate your
thinking of me, Master Kedrigern, but actually, this story
does not suit my present needs. I'm badly overstocked
with handsome-prince-kisses-beautiful-sleeping-princess stories at this time. I've done four, and I wouldn't want to do
another unless it had a clever variation on the theme. For
example, if the prince kissed the princess and *she* woke up
and *he* went to sleep, that would be a nice twist. Or if they
both turned into something nasty."

"But that's not the way it happened," Kedrigern said plaintively.

"We authors can't allow ourselves to be limited by facts. We're talking fairy tales, not chronicles. Artistic truth is what we're after, not mere recording of events."

"I did promise Dyrax. . . . Look, if you've already used this plot, couldn't you just change the names of the characters in your story? That would make Dyrax happy, and it wouldn't present any problems, would it?"

Zorilon pondered a moment, then said weightily, "Not a *major* problem, but I have to think about it. We authors don't name our characters arbitrarily, you know. A lot of work goes into the proper naming of characters."

"We understand," said Princess. " 'Larry the little man' must have been a great creative effort."

"Give it a try. 'Dyrax' and 'Blamarde' are pretty good names for a prince and princess," Kedrigern added.

"They're not bad," Zorilon conceded. "Not bad at all. Maybe I could change 'Prince Gluddbuttz' and 'Princess Blomblooglefutzer' to 'Prince Dyrax' and 'Princess Blamarde' without really hurting the story. They're in my story 'The Clean Little Thimble,' about the handsome prince disguised as a woodsman who kisses a sleeping beauty and wakes up everyone in her kingdom."

"Why don't you call that story 'Sleeping Beauty'?" Princess asked.

Zorilon's eyebrows flew up nearly to his hairline. His eyes sparkled. "That's it! That's a perfect title! Thank you, my lady," he said with great enthusiasm. "It's not easy, coming up with catchy titles time after time."

"I've noticed that," said Princess with a polite smile.

"People seem to think that a maker of fairy tales does nothing but sit all day in a comfortable chair, dreaming up stories of princesses and little men and irate fairies and enchantments and ogres. Nothing could be further from the truth, believe me. It's just work, work, work, drudge, drudge, drudge, day after day. I never have a minute to relax. Always busy, busy, busy."

"Why don't you come along with us to Dendorric?" Kedrigern suggested. "You could try your stories out on a whole new audience. You might pick up some new material, too."

"I'd be honored to travel in your company, Master Kedrigern, but I simply can't tear myself away. I'm stuck in the middle of a new tale and I have to work out a few details before I can complete it. I need information."

Princess turned to her host. "What sort of information, Zorilon? Perhaps we can help."

Zorilon smiled tolerantly. "I doubt that, my lady. I'm writing about a dragon, and the plot requires information concerning the personal habits of dragons."

"Why not ask a dragon?" Princess suggested with an airy gesture.

"Well, what I'm after is rather intimate information. A dragon wouldn't pass it on casually to a stranger. And besides, where am I going to meet a dragon? I can't just wait for one to land in the dooryard. And if I do manage to meet a dragon, how does one talk to a dragon without considerable peril? It's a dilemma, my lady."

Kedrigern rose and stretched. He winked at Princess, then said to Zorilon, "Would you excuse me for a minute? I'd like to step outside."

Princess returned his wink, and he nodded surreptitiously. Rumpelstiltskin looked up lazily, heaved a loud sigh, yawned, and resettled himself before the fire. Kedrigern left the room. At Princess's urging, Zorilon began drawing up a list of questions to be addressed to any cooperative dragon he might chance to meet. He was awkward and uncomfortable about the process at first, since—as he had mentioned—some of the questions were of an intimate personal nature; but Princess promised that she would not peek. Thus reassured, Zorilon set to work with a will. He had come to the end of his list, and was reading over the questions with apparent satisfaction, when from outside the door there came a great whooshing wind and a thump that set every loose object in the cottage to shaking. Rumpelstiltskin sprang to his feet and began to bark. Zorilon looked up in alarm.

"What was that?" he asked anxiously.

Unruffled, Princess said, "I imagine Kedrigern is back."

"Does he always return so . . . so dramatically?"

"It depends," said Princess, delicately covering a yawn.

Kedrigern entered, sniffing and rubbing his hands together after his turn in the chill evening air. "I'm back," he called. "I hope I didn't startle anyone. I brought someone with me."

"Oh? Who?" Princess asked innocently.

"A friend of ours, name of Shanzie."

"Where is this Shanzie?" Zorilon asked.

"He's out in the dooryard."

"If he's a friend of yours, Master Kedrigern, he's welcome to come in."

"Shanzie's a shy type. He'd feel better if you went out and spoke to him. I think you'll like him, Zorilon. He can be very helpful."

"Well . . ."

"Go on out," said Princess, urging her host toward the door with gestures and reassuring smiles.

Zorilon put down his pen and stood. He moved a step from his writing desk, then hastily returned to it and took up the list of questions, glancing at Princess and reddening slightly as he did so. He rolled up the list and thrust it inside his tunic, and walked out, muttering apologies. Princess covered her face and turned away, bursting with stifled laughter. Rumpelstiltskin scooted for the door, to follow his master, but Kedrigern swept him up *en passant* and held him tightly.

"You'd only complicate things," said the wizard, scratching him behind the ears.

A startled cry came from beyond the door, then a shout of joy, and sounds of laughter—both Zorilon's, and a much deeper, rumbling kind, equally merry. Princess joined in the laughter until tears came to her eyes. Kedrigern settled himself at her side, and Rumpelstiltskin obligingly stretched out on his lap.

"They seem to be getting on nicely," the wizard observed.

Princess burst into fresh laughter. "Zorilon brought his list . . . all his questions . . . too embarrassing to be left!" she said between fits.

"We'd better make ourselves comfortable, then. They may be at it for quite some time."

With Shanzie's assistance, Zorilon completed his dragon tale that very night and made the suggested revisions in "The Clean Little Thimble," which he also retitled. The next day was given over to getting his papers in order, and on the second morning following, just as the sun was rising, they all set out for Dendorric.

The wood was silent, and their journey was uneventful until the day Shanzie flew back to his companions, arrow-swift, at treetop level, to alert them to signs of an encampment not far ahead. Some forty or fifty men had bivouacked on the spot a few days earlier, and proceeded in the direction of Dendorric.

Zorilon, visibly shaken, urged instant retreat. Kedrigern pointed out that he was unlikely to find traveling companions who would provide better protection. Zorilon acknowledged the truth of this observation, but looked no less shaken. After Shanzie's discovery they were cautious, and Shanzie scouted the way conscientiously. They came upon other, larger campsites, suggesting to them that a great force was gathering in the wood and making its way to Dendorric, and they began to feel serious concern for Hamarak and his subjects.

Then, on the northward slope of the last hill before the river, the track of the force divided, half heading upriver, half heading down. There were signs indicating that at least five hundred men had gathered here. Not a single footprint went in the direction of the bridge.

"This is very strange," said Kedrigern, brushing dust and bits of leaf from his knees after a close examination of the ground. "They traveled for days, directly for Dendorric, and just as it was almost in sight, they turned aside."

"Maybe they didn't intend to go to Dendorric in the first place," Zorilon suggested hopefully.

"Or maybe they heard about Hamarak and changed their minds," Princess said.

"It doesn't make sense," said the wizard, shaking his head. "They didn't scatter, they divided about equally, into two large forces. This road leads to a swamp in one direction and a waterfall in the other."

"Then maybe they plan to cross the swamp and the waterfall and sneak up on Dendorric from the rear," Zorilon said.

Kedrigern looked unconvinced. "It's possible, but they'd have their work cut out for them. The waterfall is called 'The Cascade Impassable,' and the swamp is 'The Morass Impenetrable'. There may be an element of exaggeration in those names, but they certainly don't suggest easy going. And even if they do get across, there's no way to sneak up on Dendorric. The land is all flat and open. They'd be seen from the castle, and the defenses would be prepared."

"Then they've got some kind of trick up their sleeves. That ought to be obvious," said Princess. "Five hundred men don't assemble in the woods just to march off to a swamp, do they? Or to look at a waterfall? They're up to something, and we'd better warn Hamarak."

"You're probably right, my dear," the wizard conceded. He looked up at the overcast sky and said, "It's getting dark. We may as well stay here tonight. We can be in Dendorric early in the morning."

"Here? A night here, when we could all be safe in town?" cried Zorilon in disbelief.

"We're safe here. The invaders have all gone off."

"There may be stragglers. A *lot* of stragglers. Or deserters. Desperate, violent men. We could be murdered in our sleep," Zorilon said. His pallor was noticeable even in the fading light.

"Nobody will sneak up on us with Shanzie nearby."

"Even dragons have to sleep sometime."

Princess, in her most comforting voice, said, "Don't be afraid, Zorilon. Remember, you're traveling with wizards. We'll put a nice spell around the campsite."

"What if there are wizards among the stragglers?"

Princess and Kedrigern exchanged a long, thoughtful glance. She raised a dark eyebrow. He rubbed his chin and nodded. At last he said, "It isn't completely dark. I suppose we could find our way through the woods."

"There'll be a light in the guardhouse on the bridge, and lights in the castle," Princess added.

"I will fly ahead and point out the way," Shanzie said, flexing his wings.

"Let's go, then!" Zorilon whimpered.

Kedrigern raised his hands and said sharply, "Wait a minute!" Laying a hand on the dragon's neck, he said, "I think it would be best if you stayed with us, Shanzie. The people of Dendorric are a nervous lot. If they caught sight of you, there's no telling how they'd react."

A quick jet of golden flame spurted from Shanzie's nostrils. His blue eyes narrowed. In a voice of unaccustomed hardness, he rumbled, "I am a dragon. I do not fear their puny slings and arrows."

"It's not a question of your fearing them, Shanzie," Princess said gently. "I'm sure the fear will all be on their side. We just don't want to make an unfortunate first impression."

"Dragons do not worry about first impressions."

"Wizards do. Remember, Shanzie, when we agreed to let you travel with us, you promised to behave," Princess reminded him.

Shanzie rumbled unhappily, emitting some dark smoke, and finally said, "I will do as my lady wishes."

"Good. Let's get started," said Kedrigern.

By the time they reached the hilltop, full dark was upon them. Dendorric lay below, a handful of scattered points of faint light on the farther shore of a great sea of blackness. Not a star shone, and no hint of moonlight broke the encompassing night. They made their slow way down the trail, guided by the light from the guardhouse at the far end of the bridge, and at last emerged from the wood and started across. Kedrigern led the way, followed by Princess, then Zorilon, and at a longer interval, Shanzie.

A sleepy pikeman stumbled from the guardhouse at Kedrigern's approach, straightening his helmet and waving his pikestaff about maladroitly. Luckily for all parties, it was too dark to afford the guard a clear view of Kedrigern's horse. "Here, now, what's this? Who are you, and what do you want on our bridge at this hour?" the guard demanded querulously.

"I am Kedrigern of Silent Thunder Mountain, a wizard of great renown."

"A wizard, are you?" said the guard.

"What's that? A wizard?" asked a second guard, who had just popped out of the guardhouse.

"Two wizards," said Princess, drawing up at Kedrigern's side.

"Two? Is that all of you?" the first guard asked, his manner more polite then before.

"There are others with us, but we're the only wizards. We've come to see Hamarak the Invincible. Take us to the castle," said Kedrigern.

"What do you want to go to the castle for?" the guards asked.

"To see Hamarak."

"You won't find my lord Hamarak at the castle. Won't find nobody at the castle these days, not since it collapsed," said the first guard.

"Collapsed? Is Hamarak all right?" Princess cried.

"Course he is, my lady. Invincible, isn't he? He's living over the bakery shop, him and Queen Berrian."

"How soon will the castle be repaired?" asked Kedrigern.

The guard shrugged carelessly. "No need for it anymore, is there? We don't need castles in Dendorric. Don't even need guards, really. We've got Hamarak the Invincible to protect us with his magic sword.''

Kedrigern bowed his head and covered his eyes with his hand. Princess laid a comforting hand on his arm. In the silence Zorilon rode up behind them and stopped. As the travelers and guards stood, a steady thumping tread came from the bridge, drawing near. The guards studied the three arrivals, glanced uneasily at each other, and then peered around the horses for a glimpse of the fourth member of the party.

''Heavy, whoever he is,'' said one.

''Taking his time, too,'' said the second.

''Look at the size of that horse! It's as big as a . . . as a . . .''

''Dragon!'' shrieked the second guard. He sprang back, colliding with the other. Both dropped their pikestaves, raced for the guardhouse, and bolted the door behind them. Muttering impatiently, Kedrigern dismounted and went to the door.

''It's all right. He's with us,'' he said loudly.

''It's a dragon! That's a dragon you've got out there!'' said a hushed, fearful voice.

''He's a friend. There's nothing to be afraid of.''

''There's a *dragon* to be afraid of.''

''Oh, all right, all right. I'll send him away.'' Kedrigern went to Shanzie, who was sitting by the end of the bridge.

''They fear me, do they not?'' the dragon rumbled.

''I think they're just startled. I didn't prepare them.''

''They fear me,'' Shanzie repeated with evident satisfaction. ''It is right and proper for men to fear dragons.''

''Be that as it may, we're here to help these people, not frighten them out of their wits. Remember that.''

Shanzie gave a low rumble of reluctant affirmation. ''I have promised my lady,'' he said.

''What you must do now,'' the wizard continued, ''is fly up to the hilltop, to the ruined castle, and keep watch over the plain. I'll come up tomorrow. Fly as quietly as you can, and stay out of sight until I tell you to come out.''

''Is this my lady's will?''

''It is, Shanzie,'' Princess called to him.

Grumbling, the dragon spread his wings. He sprang up without a sound and sped into the darkness. Kedrigern looked after him until he vanished, then returned to the guardhouse and rapped heavily on the door, saying, ''You can come out now. The dragon's gone.''

The door opened a crack. A strained whisper asked, ''Is it *really* gone?''

''It's really gone,'' Kedrigern assured them.

The guards inched forth, circumspect, holding torches aloft and keeping their backs to the wall. When they were satisfied that the dragon had indeed departed, they retrieved their pikestaves and stood about looking sheepish.

''Never saw a dragon before,'' one of them muttered, eyes downcast.

''Well, now you've seen one,'' said Kedrigern, remounting. ''And when you've recovered, we're ready to see Hamarak. Lead on.''

···⚜ *Fifteen* ⚜···

dendorric preserv'd; a plot discovered

PRECEDED BY one guard and followed by the other, the
three travelers made their way up a narrow staircase at the
rear of the bakery and entered the state chamber and
throneroom of Dendorric, a garret redolent of fresh-baked
bread. Hamarak was seated near the fire in a sturdy, high-
backed wooden chair, with his feet up on a cushioned
stool. Papers lay on his lap and were strewn all around him
on the floor, and he was staring unhappily at the far wall.

Berrian, who was seated opposite him at a tub of steam-
ing water, scrubbing a pot, jumped up and said, "Company! Company's come, Hammie!"

Hamarak turned, sending papers cascading to the floor,
and climbed to his feet with a glad shout. "You're back!
You're safe! How is Louise? Did you help her?" he asked
as he pumped their hands vigorously in welcome.

"Louise is back in human form, and so are Alice and
William. They send their regards," said Princess.

"This is Zorilon," Kedrigern said, pushing their young
companion forward. "He makes up fairy tales and legends.
He'd like to do one about you while he's in Dendorric.
The dog's name is Rumpelstiltskin. It's a family name."

The two shook hands and Hamarak asked, "How long
do you plan to stay in Dendorric?"

"As long as Your Majesty permits," Zorilon replied with a bow.

"Can you read?"

"I read and write with great skill, Your Highness," said Zorilon with a second, even more graceful, bow. Rumpelstiltskin wagged his tale amiably.

"He does. We've seen him," Princess added.

"Do you want to work for me?" Hamarak asked. "People keep sending me papers, and I don't know what to do about them. They've started piling up," he said, gesturing toward the litter around his chair, and little piles in the corners, and on and under tables.

"The throne room's a mess," said Berrian, pushing a few of the papers under the chair with one foot. "It's been difficult managing things since the castle collapsed. Fortunately, my old room was empty, so we moved in here. It's only temporary."

"It smells nicer than the castle," Hamarak said.

"I love your curtains. And the cushions look very comfortable," Princess said.

"I made them myself. The bedclothes, too."

"They're lovely," said Princess, and the men murmured approvingly.

Berrian smiled, then sighed. "I don't look forward to doing them for a whole castle, but I suppose we'll have to, eventually. You can't run a kingdom effectively out of one room over a bakery."

"You can't run it if you don't know what's going on, either. Will you take the job?" Hamarak asked Zorilon.

Bowing once again, Zorilon said, "It would be an honor, Your Highness."

"Good. I never realized how much paperwork there is to being a king. I thought it was going to be exciting."

"It may be more exciting than you like in a very short time. Can we confer in private?" Kedrigern asked.

Hamarak looked around the room, then turned to the wizard, shaking his head. "I don't think so. It's awfully crowded in here."

"Let's give it a try, Hamarak. This is important. Send the guards to the inn to reserve us a room, and tell Zorilon to start putting your papers in order. Princess and Berrian are quite preoccupied with their own conversation."

When Hamarak had complied with the wizard's suggestions, they wedged themselves behind the washstand, and Kedrigern, in rapid muted phrases, related what he, Princess, and Zorilon had seen in the woods, their suspicions of an impending invasion, and Shanzie's vigil in the ruins of the castle. When he finished, Hamarak looked at him blankly for a moment, then sighed and said, "Well, that's the end of Dendorric."

"You mustn't give up so easily," Kedrigern said.

"There's no hope. Even with the real Panstygia, I couldn't fight off five hundred men. My arms would get tired. And I don't have the real Panstygia, only an imitation."

"It's a very good imitation."

"Oh, it is, and I'm grateful, wizard. But it's still an imitation."

"The invaders don't know that."

"They'll find out pretty quickly once they start fighting with me," said Hamarak glumly. Then, brightening in an instant, he cried, "Unless you have a spell to make me the world's greatest swordsman! That would do it. It wouldn't have to be permanent; just for a day or two. I wouldn't have to be the world's greatest, either. If I could be the best swordsman in the kingdom for a few days, Dendorric would be saved."

"That kind of spell is out of my line, Hamarak. I'd have to go back to my study and look it up, and we can't spare the time."

"Could you make me invulnerable?"

"Yes . . . I could do that," the wizard said in a slow, hesitant voice, rubbing his chin thoughtfully.

"Then do it!"

"Don't be hasty. Invulnerability spells are very tricky. One has to approach them with great care, and work them very precisely, or they're worse than useless. Look at Achilles and Siegfried.''

"Who are they?''

"Two men who were supposed to be invulnerable, and they're both dead.''

Hamarak's face fell. "I'm sorry. Were they friends of yours?''

"No, no, no. I'm just using them as illustrations.''

"Of what?''

"Of how invulnerability spells don't necessarily make you invulnerable. You see, if I get very specific, and protect you against swords, daggers, spears, arrows, and so forth—carefully naming each weapon—someone could still knock your brains out with a ladle, or stab you with a pitchfork. And if I try to get around that by using a universal spell encompassing all possible weapons, I have to spread the magic out so thin that it's easily countered. So what I'd like to do is find some other way of protecting you and Dendorric.''

"What other way?'' Hamarak asked eagerly.

"I haven't decided yet. Let me sleep on it. We have a few days before the invaders arrive, and I'll come up with something by then.''

"Are you sure?''

"Of course, Hamarak. Trust me,'' said Kedrigern with a confident smile.

Zorilon stayed behind, at a small and somewhat doughy table in a warm corner of the bakery, to press forward in his work on the state papers. Since most of them were petitions, he was proceeding rapidly.

As they made their way through the dark narrow streets of Dendorric to the inn, Kedrigern said to Princess, "You and Berrian were having quite a chat back there. Surely you weren't talking about curtains and cushions all that time.''

"Oh, no. She told me about the collapse of the castle. It seems that once the workmen started carting away the rubbish, everything started to sag. The rubbish was all that had been holding things together," Princess said.

"Why didn't they just leave the rubbish where it was?"

"My very question. Somehow a rumor started and spread among the workmen that vast amounts of treasure were buried somewhere deep below the castle. No one wanted to stop digging, even when walls were collapsing and floors were caving in. Berrian said it was a miracle no one was killed."

Kedrigern shook his head. "Greed is a terrible thing."

"So is rubbish," said Princess emphatically. "At least now they'll have the chance to build something modern, and in a nicer setting."

"You're very optimistic, my dear. An army of five hundred desperate ruffians is marching on the city, the castle is in ruins, Hamarak has an imitation enchanted sword which he barely knows how to hold in his hands, the guardsmen are terrified of their own shadows—and you're wondering where they'll build the new castle."

"I'm not being an optimist, Keddie, you're being a pessimist. Surely you can turn back an army of ruffians. Look at what you did to the Green Riddler and his men."

"And remember what happened, my dear: I was weak as a baby for days afterward. If I hadn't come upon that haemony I'd still be nearly helpless. We have some hard traveling to do before we get home, and I don't like to be on the road when my magic is low."

"You still have plenty of haemony," Princess pointed out.

"It's not such a vast amount. What if the invaders have a wizard or two of their own with them? We can't overlook the possibility."

"You've already overlooked something," said Princess, and her voice was chilly. "You overlook the fact that I, too, am a wizard, and perfectly capable of seeing us home safely even if all *your* power is drained."

"My dear, I haven't overlooked your powers at all.

Quite the contrary, I counted on having you at my side to face the invaders—if it comes to that.''

"You did?"

"Of course. That's why I'm worried. If we both have to use every bit of magic we've got, we may save Dendorric but we'll be helpless for weeks, even with regular doses of haemony."

Princess thought that over for a while, then suggested, "Maybe we could turn a few into fieldmice, or crickets, or something like that, and the rest would get the idea."

"Maybe. But it would be best for Dendorric to have some defense of its own. We can't come dashing over here every time some mob of brutes take it into their heads to invade Dendorric."

"Oh, no, that would never do. Can't you just put a spell on Hamarak?"

"We've discussed that. I really can't do anything until I know what we're up against. I'd look pretty foolish if I made him invulnerable to all edged weapons and then found that the invaders carried clubs."

"Quite right. That would never do."

"And there's always the possibility that we'll face magic."

"Do you really think so?"

"It's the only thing that makes sense to me, my dear. After Hamarak's feat at the bridge, any band of ordinary brigands is going to stay clear of Dendorric unless they know they have a chance to defeat Hamarak and his magic sword—and that means magic of their own. Brigands are stupid, but they're not *that* stupid."

Princess was silent for a time, and then she said, "I'm not so sure about that. I think they're even stupider than you suspect."

"You do?"

"Well, consider Rokkmund. He was your typical brutal warrior swordsman bully, and he was very casual about enchantment. I warned him, but he attacked me with an enchanted sword. I think they're all that way."

Kedrigern grunted thoughtfully. After a long pause, he said, "You have a point there, my dear."

"And Buroc. Remember Buroc."

"I remember him well."

"Brutal people always depend on brute strength, Keddie. Fifty men couldn't defeat Hamarak, so they rounded up five hundred and they're going to try to sneak up on him. That's exactly what Rokkmund would do. Now, if there were only a handful of them, and they were coming openly, I'd be worried about enchantment. But an army of five hundred is sure to be a mob of browless, neckless, club-waving brutes," said Princess with calm confidence.

"A convincing argument. Most convincing. Now, if only we can work out a way to make Dendorric independent of our help . . ."

"We'll think of something," said Princess, no less confidently. They turned a corner and saw a man standing in a lighted doorway. A boy stood near him, holding a lantern. Both were attentive. "There's the inn. I hope we can get something to eat. I'm famished," she said, waving to the innkeeper.

"I imagine we'll be able to get anything we want. After all, my dear, we're friends of Hamarak the Invincible," said Kedrigern, adding a cheerful wave of his own.

They were treated very well indeed. Their horses were led to the stables by smiling hostlers, no longer apprehensive at the sight of the creatures. The innkeeper settled them in his finest room with his personal oath that it was free of fleas and that the mice were so small and so light of foot that they were scarcely noticeable. His wife produced a haunch of venison, some smoked trout, a basket of ripe fruit, two loaves of fresh bread, half a roast fowl, and a pitcher of quite decent ale. They seated themselves before the fire and dug in.

When they retired to their room, they found the bed-clothes warmed and pleasantly scented. Their baggage was neatly stacked against the wall and a fire burned cozily in the grate. When they turned down the bed, they found, to their amazement, that the linen was clean.

Princess was in bed and sound asleep before Kedrigern had time to remove his boots. Tired as he was, he sat up, staring into the fire, wringing his memory for the one proper spell, the one right charm, the one exact enchantment, to solve Hamarak's problem and preserve Dendorric from these and all future assaults. He yawned and nodded off and jerked awake and rubbed his burning eyes and found no solution. Finally he crept into bed beside Princess, yawned one final yawn, and was asleep before he could console himself with the thought that a new day would bring a new outlook and fresh ideas.

When he awoke, Kedrigern found that the new day had dawned on the old day's problems and brought no solution. He dragged himself from the warm comfort of the bed, muttering softly and peevishly to himself as he dressed.

"Keddie? You're up early," said Princess in a muffled, sleepy voice.

"I have to see Shanzie. Then I'll talk to Hamarak."

"Do you have any ideas?"

"None that I didn't have last night."

"Oh. I'll see you at the bakery, then. I imagine Berrian could use some cheering up."

"She's not the only one," said the wizard gloomily.

The castle was a scene of utter devastation. Walls and towers had collapsed inward, leaving a low barrier of ragged stone enclosing a jumble of rubble on the hilltop. Kedrigern circled the ruins twice, calling out Shazie's name, and received no response. Dismounting, he gathered a heap of stones and began to throw them over the broken wall, pausing after every few throws to shout Shanzie's name again.

After a score of throws he heard a grating sound from within, as of shifting gravel under a heavy, slow-moving body. Three more throws and a shout, and he heard a deep ominous rumble, followed by a gout of flame and a spurt of thick black smoke that plumed upward and slowly dissipated on the morning breeze. He paused, hefting a stone, ready to throw, and a low angry voice reverberated around the crumbled walls, "Who dares disturb a dragon's rest?"

"It's Kedrigern, Shanzie," the wizard shouted.

Again the deep discontented rumbling came from within, and the sound of a large body moving over the loose stones, and then Shanzie's head, like a burnished golden dart, appeared above the wall and fixed narrowed eyes on the wizard. The head lowered, chin reclining on the top of the wall. Thin streamers of pale smoke rose from the nostrils.

"Why do you fling stones at me?" Shanzie hissed.

"You didn't answer when I called your name."

"I was resting. I am comfortable in these ruins."

"Resting? You're supposed to be watching for invaders!"

Shanzie's head reared up, and he snorted flame. "I fear no invaders! Woe to him who intrudes upon my ruins!" he roared.

"Maybe the invaders don't worry you, Shanzie, but they worry Princess and me and our friends. You promised to protect us, remember? You don't protect us by sleeping."

The head sank. The eyes glazed in thought, and after a time Shanzie said, "It was right to sleep. I felt at home."

"What's come over you, Shanzie? You haven't been yourself for the past few days."

Again the golden head reared, and Shanzie cried in a great voice, "I am becoming my true self, wizard! I am a dragon, and I must live a dragon's life in a dragon's way! I brought you safe to Dendorric, and now I do no more for you. These ruins call me. I must stay."

Eyes gleaming, the golden head withdrew from sight. There was silence, then the crunch of Shanzie's heavy tread over the rubble, retreating to the heart of the ruins.

It all came clear to Kedrigern in a flash: treasure actually did lie under these ruins, and Shanzie, as his dragonhood grew daily stronger, was drawn ever more irresistibly to it.

The fact that Shanzie had not been told of the treasure meant nothing. He was a dragon, and he sensed it in his own way.

"Shanzie! *Shanzie!*" Kedrigern shouted. When no answer came, he stooped and took up a rock in either hand, but before he threw he heard the footsteps approaching within the broken walls. Shanzie's head reappeared, and the wizard cried, "Shanzie, would you take one flight to see if the invaders are coming? Just one high circle around the city?"

"No," the dragon thundered.

"Shanzie, we must know! Please!"

"No need for flying, wizard. I can see them from here. A force coming from the west, another from the east. Many men, heading this way."

With a fervent whispered "Oh dear me," Kedrigern scrambled to the top of the wall and made his way to the highest point. It was as Shanzie had said. The invaders were making their way swiftly over the open ground. They would be in Dendorric by midday.

"Shanzie, help us! You promised you would, and now we need you. Swoop down on them and breathe a little flame. That's all we need. Just one swoop on each band," the wizard pleaded.

"I cannot, wizard," said the dragon in a strained voice. He backed off, halted, and with a visible effort, blurted, "This place commands me, I must not say no. Something holds me here. I must stay."

Kedrigern conceded a lost cause. "It's treasure, Shanzie. The royal treasury of Dendorric is buried under these ruins. I didn't know that when I sent you here."

"A treasure! Ruins!" Shanzie threw his head back and shot forth a long tongue of joyous golden flame. "I will work my way down to the deepest vaults, and there recline on the heaps of gold, the jeweled cups and goblets, the necklaces and arm-rings, the mighty swords and gleaming banners and crested helmets, to protect them from all who would lay thieving hands on them!" Rearing up on his hind legs, he gave another burst of flame, then crashed down heavily on his forelegs and cast a triumphant glance at the wizard. "None shall touch my hoard. It will be safe from all, forever!"

"It mustn't be safe from *all*, Shanzie. It's the royal treasury. You have to let the king take something from time to time," Kedrigern reminded him.

"All treasure is loot, wizard, and all loot is stolen. I will guard my hoard against every intruder, be he king or beggar."

Kedrigern shrugged. He saw no sense in debating the issue. Right now, Dendorric had a more pressing problem than access to the royal treasury.

His great black steed brought him swiftly to the bakery, where Princess was already deep in conversation with Berrian while Hamarak was patiently listening to Zorilon explain the contents of the more significant state papers. He called for their attention and explained the situation in a few sentences. Zorilon turned pale; Berrian frowned and furrowed her brow; Hamarak looked at him innocently and asked, "What should I do, wizard?"

"Get your sword and come with me," snapped Kedrigern.

"But it's not—" Hamarak began, clamping shut his mouth abruptly at a glare and silencing gesture from the wizard.

"I know it's not what we planned," Kedrigern said quickly, "but they've arrived sooner than we expected. We'll meet them under a flag of truce, just the three of us."

"The three of us?" Zorilon repeated in a shaky voice, looking around wildly.

Princess laid a gentle hand on his forearm. "The three of *us*—Hamarak, Kedrigern, and me," she said.

"Oh. The . . . three of you. I see." Zorilon swallowed and drew a deep breath. "In that case, my lord Hamarak, since I've organized all your state papers, I may as well be on my way," he said, grinning in feigned good spirits and backing toward the door, nodding at each of them in turn.

"You can't leave now, Zorilon," said Kedrigern.

"Oh, but I must. Hate to run, but I absolutely must. Pressure of work, you know."

"But you're Lord Chamberlain of Dendorric!" said the wizard, nudging Hamarak. "Haven't you been told? Hasn't my lord Hamarak made it official yet?" he said loudly, nudging again, harder.

"Oh, yes! Yes, you're my Lord Chamberlain," Hamarak said. "I forgot to mention it before. And Rumpelstiltskin is Official State Dog."

Zorilon stopped backing away. A look of interest replaced his ghastly grin. "I am? What are my duties?"

Hamarak looked desperately at Kedrigern, who quickly said, "Hamarak rules Dendorric and defends it. Your duty is to see that his rule is untroubled and that he's required to defend it as infrequently as possible."

"Is that all?"

"You'll read all state papers and arrange all ceremonies. Nice easy work, Zorilon. You'll have plenty of time to work on your fairy tales."

"Will I be able to read them to the people at state ceremonies?"

Hamarak smiled and said, "That's a nice idea. I like fairy tales."

"And will I get a fur-trimmed robe and a big medallion to wear around my neck? And a generous stipend? And a fancy collar for Rumpie?"

"Once this fuss with the invaders is attended to, we can work out all the details. I think you can trust Hamarak to treat you fairly," said the wizard.

"Yes, I'm sure I can. Well, in that case . . . I'd better get busy planning the victory celebration," said Zorilon decisively. "There *will* be a victory celebration, won't there, my lord Hamarak?"

"Oh, yes. Bread for everyone!"

"And dancing in the streets!" Berrian added, explaining, "There was going to be dancing in the streets at our wedding, but it rained."

"And fairy tales. Lots of fairy tales. I'll make all the arrangements," said the Lord Chamberlain solemnly.

"While you're doing that, we'll go and meet the invaders," said Kedrigern, taking Hamarak and Princess by the arm and drawing them toward the door.

Princess waved to Berrian and smiled reassuringly. "We'll be back in time for dinner," she said.

Kedrigern was silent as they waited for Hamarak's horse to be saddled. He seemed preoccupied, and mumbled to himself, frowning and shaking his head from time to time. Things were coming to a head much too quickly. He had no certain plan for handling the invaders, and while he anticipated nothing out of the ordinary (Princess having convinced him that his fears of wizardry were baseless), nevertheless he liked to be prepared. An army of five hundred desperate men, even without wizardly support, was not to be taken lightly and dismissed with a casual spur-of-the-moment enchantment.

Shanzie's help would have been much appreciated, but that appeared to be out of the question now. Shanzie had dragonized quickly and completely, and for the next few centuries he would care for nothing but his hoard. Sprawling in some dark underground vault on a heap of treasure seemed a boring and rather uncomfortable life for a robust young dragon, but Kedrigern knew from experience that many of them were hopelessly addicted to it. He tried to understand, but could not. One probably had to be a dragon to appreciate such things.

A fierce and dedicated band of guardsmen would have been helpful, if only to suggest to the invaders that the sack of Dendorric would be no easy task. But if one was to judge by the pair at the bridge, Dendorric was very short on both ferocity and dedication. Perhaps it was best to have no guardsmen accompany them; their terror and probable flight would only encourage the invaders.

Clearly it was going to come down to magic, his and perhaps Princess's, against muscle. Exactly what magic, and how much, he still did not know, and the uncertainty troubled him. He sighed and went on thinking as Princess and Hamarak drew up on either side of his great black steed.

"Where shall we meet them, wizard?" Hamarak asked.

"I've been going over a few spells," said Princess.

"Are you going to make me a master swordsman?"

"I was thinking that a small natural upheaval might suffice."

"Would it be better just to make me invulnerable and let them wear themselves out?"

"A great wind would be good against an army, wouldn't it? I was going to suggest a horde of gnats, but it's probably too late in the season for gnats."

"You couldn't turn my imitation Panstygia into a real enchanted sword, could you?"

"How about an earthquake?"

"Could you summon up a magic army?"

"Or bolts of lightning, and terrible thunder! Oh, that would do it, Keddie, I'm sure it would! Keddie?"

"Is there a way of making all their weapons disappear? Are you listening, wizard?"

Under the barrage of questions, Kedrigern had lowered his head and covered his face with his hands. Now he looked up, and his eyes were bright. He smiled wisely and benignly and said, "We will meet them by the ruins of the castle. And we will do nothing."

"Nothing?" they said simultaneously.

"Nothing. Unless we absolutely must."

"But who will make them go away?" Hamarak asked in utter bafflement.

"They'll bring it on themselves, if my plan works."

"What if your plan doesn't work?" Princess asked.

Patiently, Kedrigern said, "Then we'll do something."

He would say no more. They rode up the hillside in silence and drew up three abreast before the ruined walls of the castle. The invaders were plainly visible, little more than half a mile off. Both forces had joined, and now they flowed over the open plain like an army of mice homing in on a granary. The flashing of sunlight on metal indicated that they were well armed, and many of them wore helmets and breastplates. Kedrigern smiled contentedly, and even pointed out their armament to his companions. It was all to the good, as far as his plan was concerned.

The ground sloped away before them. About fifty feet down it leveled out to a broad crescent-shaped field and then sloped more gently the rest of the distance to the plain. Hamarak dismounted and walked to the edge of the slope, where he hunkered down and remained for a few minutes deep in thought.

"Studying the enemy formation?" Princess called to him.

He jerked around, startled, and rose to his feet. "No, my lady. I was looking at that level space. I never noticed it before."

"What about it, Hamarak?"

"It looks like a good building plot for the new castle. It's sheltered from the north wind and it commands the plain. We can use the stone from the old castle and save time."

"I wouldn't plan on doing that, Hamarak," Kedrigern said without taking his eyes off the approaching invaders. "You'd be wise to leave these ruins alone."

"Why, wizard?"

"You'll see very soon." Kedrigern leaned forward, squinting, and then groped wildly for his medallion. He looked through the Aperture of True Vision and let out an angry howl. "*Him*! It's impossible! What's he doing here?"

"Who is it, dear?" Princess asked.

"The Green Riddler." He turned to her, looking deeply injured. "I turned him into a fieldmouse, him and all his men, and now he's here with twenty times as many men as he had before. I don't understand."

"Did you use a temporary spell?"

"I used a very permanent spell, and I know it worked. I can't imagine how he got out of it."

"Well, apparently he did. What do we do now?"

"Not much we can do but wait. When I tell you, Hamarak, wave the flag of truce. I want to parley with them up here."

The first invaders soon appeared on the level space below, but they climbed no higher; instead, they waited for their leader to join them. When he saw the Green Riddler, Kedrigern gave word to Hamarak, who began to swing the white flag back and forth. The figures on the level below milled about for a time, then settled down, and to his delight Kedrigern saw the Green Riddler and two armed men emerge from the mob, raise a white flag of their own—a very dirty one—and begin to make their way up the slope.

"They've accepted the offer to parley. Everything is going to work out just right, my dear," Kedrigern said.

"It is?" she replied in surprise.

"Oh, yes. Maybe even better than I had hoped. The Riddler has a good loud voice."

Princess and Hamarak exchanged a mystified glance. The wizard waited patiently, silent, his eyes on the approaching trio. When the Green Riddler stood before them, looking very green, very large, and very menacing, Kedrigern said pleasantly, "Well, now, fancy this. I didn't expect to see you again."

"You won't sneak-spell me this time, Kedrigern. I'm ready for you," the Riddler growled in his deep booming voice.

"I give you my word, I'll use no magic unless you attack. I only want to talk to you."

"Plead for mercy, eh?" the Green Riddler said, chuckling in a sinister way. He leered down on his companions, who may have returned the leer—it was impossible to tell, because their faces were concealed behind elaborate helmets trimmed with gold wire and set with garnets and lapis lazuli—and all three laughed nastily.

"Actually I only wanted to ask you how you got out of my spell."

After another, nastier laugh, the giant said, "Your spell was worthless. A weakling's spell. A *woman's* spell."

"Now, just a minute, you big ugly—" Princess began, reddening, but Kedrigern quickly said, "He doesn't know any better, my dear. Mustn't lose our tempers. We're under a flag of truce."

"I'll show him a woman's spell," Princess muttered. "Just let him try something."

"Your puny little spell only lasted a few days. I fell asleep one afternoon, and when I woke up, at evening, I was my old self."

Kedrigern furrowed his brow thoughtfully, then beamed and raised a hand in a triumphant gesture. "You woke up in a field of little yellow flowers, didn't you?"

"What if I did?" snapped the Riddler.

Turning to Princess, Kedrigern said, "Haemony, my dear. I should have guessed. It must be all over in those woods."

"He'll need more than haemony. . . ." said Princess softly, through clenched teeth.

Quickly, Kedrigern asked the giant, "And what brings you to Dendorric?"

"Plunder, rapine, and destruction. And now, revenge."

"I see. But what's to plunder here?"

"The royal treasury of Dendorric, that's what!" cried the Green Riddler.

Kedrigern leaned forward, cupping his ear. "What was that? I didn't catch what you said."

Flinging his brawny green arms wide, the Riddler boomed, "I come to carry off the royal treasury of Dendorric, every single bit of it, and no man can stop me."

"You're probably right. Would you mind repeating that once more, just a bit louder?" the wizard asked politely.

The green giant inhaled deeply and roared forth his intention in a voice that echoed about the ruined walls of the castle. From within those walls came a grating, rasping, crunching noise, as of a large object stirring amid the heaped mass of broken stone.

"How about a riddle, Riddler?" Kedrigern asked, smiling expectantly.

"No more riddles! I'm ready for your magic this time, wizard. You won't surprise me again."

"Oh, come on. One last riddle before we get down to business. It's an easy one. Listen carefully, now:

> I dwell in ruins far from human ken;
> My bed is booty and my breath is flame.
> I guard my gold against the greed of men;
> If you can guess my secret, speak my name!"

The Green Riddler laughed loudly and pointed at the wizard in a mocking, contemptuous gesture. "It's a dragon, you fool!" he cried.

"A what? Would you mind saying that again?"

"A dragon! A dragon!" the Green Riddler roared, his voice growing louder with each successive word.

"You're absolutely right," Kedrigern said with a broad smile.

The sounds of motion within the castle walls resumed. A deep reverberating rumble drowned out all other noise, and was in turn drowned out by a voice like a deep slow drum demanding, "Who speaks? Who calls?"

"What was that?" the Green Riddler asked.

"The treasurer. He'll be right out," Kedrigern assured him.

"He'll hurry, if he knows what's good . . ." The Riddler's voice trailed off into silence as Shanzie rose from the ruins and came heavily to earth at Kedrigern's side.

"Who comes?" the dragon demanded ominously.

"This is the Green Riddler, Shanzie. He's come here with five hundred men to take away the royal treasury of Dendorric. Every bit of it, Shanzie." Smiling innocently, Kedrigern turned to the giant. "This is Shanzie. He guards the treasure of Dendorric."

"Well, he won't have to worry about it after today. Do

you hear that, worm? I'm taking your hoard, and my men and I—''

A rolling ribbon of golden flame burst from Shanzie's mouth with a hollow fluttering roar, like wind in a high chimney. When it ceased, and the dark oily smoke cleared, nothing remained of the Green Riddler but a charred spot in the grass, extending to the edge of the slope in a narrow elongated black oval. His henchmen took one horrified look, threw down their swords, tore off their helmets, and dove over the edge, rolling headlong to the plateau.

Shanzie, in a silence more terrifying than any roar, stepped to the side and spread his wings. He hurled himself forward, climbing to a considerable height, and circled the invading army, which was rapidly disintegrating into a frenzied mob. After three leisurely circuits to herd them into a manageable mass, he plunged down and set methodically to work. In less than ten minutes, nothing remained of the five hundred invaders but a few dozen patches of smoldering grass, scattered bits and pieces of brigand, and an armory of abandoned weapons. Shanzie returned to the hill, panting a bit from his exertions. A score of arrows and two javelins dangled loosely from his sides and tail, and he began to tug at the nearest with his teeth.

''Let me help you, Shanzie. You won't be able to reach them all,'' said Kedrigern, dismounting and rolling back his sleeves.

''Thank you, wizard,'' said the dragon wearily.

''I haven't removed them yet.''

''I thank you for warning me of these marauders, and for bringing me new treasure for my hoard.''

''I didn't know they'd brought any with them,'' Kedrigern confessed.

''As I flew over the field I saw wave-patterned blades, and helmets richly worked with gold wire and bright stones; supple shirts of fine ring-mail I saw, and spears of the straight ash with gleaming points, and cloak-pins, buckles, collars, and arm-rings of gold worked in intricate patterns.

You have helped me to add much to my hoard, good wizard.''

"I daresay you'll put it to no worse use than the Riddler's men would have done. You're welcome to your spoils, Shanzie. And since I've been so good to you, I'd like you to do something for me."

The dragon tensed and looked at him with eyes narrowed to suspicious slits. "What do you ask of me?"

"In return for all the new treasure, and for removing these troublesome arrows and things, I want you to promise to protect Dendorric and its people from all harm."

After a thoughtful pause, the reply came. "It is not the custom for dragons to protect humans."

"You're a new breed of dragon, Shanzie. You can't allow yourself to be bound by outdated customs. I'm talking about enlightened self-interest. Your hoard is the royal treasury of Dendorric, so whatever threatens Dendorric threatens your hoard. That's just common sense. Defend Dendorric, and you're defending your hoard."

"Wizards are clever with words. I would not be deceived."

"I'm not trying to deceive you, Shanzie. I'm offering a mutually beneficial arrangement," said Kedrigern as he tugged an arrow from its lodgment low on the dragon's back. Tossing the arrow under Shanzie's chin, he went on, "You could never have reached that arrow yourself, but a human can pluck it out for you easily. And think of how helpful humans can be today, to gather up all the stuff down there on the plain, and separate the good from the bad, and the broken from the sound, and clean everything up, and polish it, and carry it up here. That's no work for a dragon, Shanzie. You belong on your hoard, guarding it, not running errands. Hold still—this one is in deep," said the wizard, taking a firm grip on a second arrow.

Shanzie gave a little *whoompf* of steam as the arrow

came free, then said, "Your advice is sound, wizard. I will defend Dendorric and its people."

"You'll never regret it," said Kedrigern heartily, patting the dragon's scaly haunch. "I'll leave the details to you and Hamarak while I see to the rest of these arrows."

···⚓ Sixteen ⚓···

semi-sweet revenge

THEY LEFT Dendorric at mid-morning the next day. Kedrigern had hoped for an early start, but the dancing in the streets had gone on all night long, loud and merry and uninterrupted, much of it in the street that passed directly beneath the windows of the inn. The revelry had not abated to a level permitting sleep until nearly dawn, by which time he and Princess had abandoned all hope of rest and begun, half-comatose, to pack for their departure.

The day was clear and cold, the sky unspotted blue through the naked branches. They rode long without speaking, bundled in their cloaks, eyes fixed ahead in sleepy gaze, content in spite of their weariness. Dendorric was safe, now and for a long time to come; Shanzie had a hoard of his own; Berrian and Hamarak had a pleasant plot on which to erect the new castle. It had been a productive few weeks' journey, Kedrigern had to admit; but all travel, productive or not, was a dreary ordeal compared to the comforts of home and hearth, and he was cheered by the knowledge that the cottage on Silent Thunder Mountain was only ten days' ride from here, providing the weather held.

Princess's voice stirred him from his meditations, but her words were indistinct. He pushed back the hood of his traveling-cloak and turned to her.

"You spoke, my dear? I couldn't make it out."

"I just wanted to point out that I was right after all: brutal people *are* stupid, just as I said."

"I can't argue with that. But you also said that we'd have no wizards to contend with," Kedrigern reminded her.

"The Green Riddler wasn't much of a wizard," she said with a dismissive gesture.

"No, he wasn't," Kedrigern conceded. "Wasn't much of a riddler, either, poor chap."

"Don't waste pity on the Green Riddler, Keddie. He ate Ashan, and he would have done the same to us. Or worse."

"I'm sure you're right, my dear. He was better off as a fieldmouse. Too bad he blundered into the haemony."

"We just have to accept things as they are," said Princess firmly. "I'm sure there are those who'd say that Shanzie was better off as a boy, but I'm glad he's a dragon. He seems much more mature, and his appearance is greatly improved, too."

"And Dendorric is certainly much safer . . . only . . . ."

"Yes?"

Reluctantly, Kedrigern said, "Well, I hope Hamarak won't have any difficulty getting access to the royal treasury. Dragons can be very possessive about their hoards."

With a light, merry laugh, Princess said, "That will be no problem at all. Hamarak already *has* the royal treasury, such as it is. He keeps it in the royal mattress."

"Then what kind of hoard is Shanzie guarding?"

"According to Berrian, the lower levels of the castle are full of all sorts of junk—old bent swords and rusty mail shirts and dented shields and such, all heaped up every which way. She and Hamarak explored the whole palace pretty thoroughly, looking for some decent furniture, and all they found was rubbish like that. Apparently dragons can't get enough of such stuff, but it's not much use as a treasury. She found the real treasury behind a loose stone in the fireplace while she was dusting. It's only a bag of gold pieces and a few jewels, but it should pay for the new castle and leave a bit for emergencies.''

"That makes me feel much better. I would have hated to hear of a quarrel between Shanzie and Hamarak.''

They reflected upon the state of affairs in Dendorric for a time, and then Princess exclaimed, "And we did it all without using a bit of magic!''

"That's true, my dear. It's been days since either of us had to use any magic. As a matter of fact, I feel stronger than I did the day we left. It must be the haemony. Have you been taking it?''

Princess made a wry face. "I tried. It tastes awful.''

"You must force yourself. It's very good for you.''

"I feel stronger, too, even without haemony. I think some of the magic rubbed off on me at Louise's castle.''

"That's possible. All the same, you should try a dose of haemony now and then. Once we're home, I'll dry it out properly and we can use it as a seasoning. Just a pinch of it in stews and sauces, and you'll get all the good and no nasty taste.'' Kedrigern smiled and repeated the word, savoring it. "Home. I can't wait to get back.''

"Didn't you mention a shortcut when we were on our way to Dendorric?''

"I may have. I didn't want to take it then, when everything was still in full leaf. It's a gloomy ride. But it would save us two days, at least. Maybe three.''

"Let's try it, then.''

"It has a bad reputation. Strange sights and sounds, at least one ogre, and rumors of abominations and monstrosities. I'd like to save the time, but . . . well, it could be risky.''

"We've got our magic to protect us. We're not likely to encounter anything we can't handle between us, are we?''

Kedrigern thought for a moment, trying to recall the tales of horror recounted by travelers along that dismal route, and said, "No.''

"Let's take it, then. It's no fun sleeping outdoors in this weather.''

They came to a fork in the road later that day, and turned off to follow the shortcut. Except for scattered evergreens and the few tenacious holdouts on the oaks, the leaves had all fallen, and the deep gloom of the woods was slightly alleviated. But the ambience remained funereal and foreboding. The sky was a uniform gray. Dankness hung in the air; darkened branches dripped and lichenous trunks oozed moisture; the way was often plashy and clinging, and even the firmest ground felt unpleasantly spongy. From time to time, unusual sounds issued from the dark depths beyond the path: strange shrieks, and shrill twittering, and once something that began as a baby's cry and grew to a grunting roar that shook the ground beneath them. At night, secure behind a spell, they saw unpleasant shapes blot out the stars in their crossings, and lurid lights flare and dance and suddenly vanish. But though these disquieting phenomena persisted, and became more frequent as they pressed on, they encountered no one until the chill and drizzly morning of their fourth day.

They had finished breakfast after a night filled with varicolored lights and considerable overhead traffic, and just before dawn, a lugubrious moaning and whimpering that came from all sides, even from the ground beneath their blankets, and brought with it a sweet reek of decay. Having little taste for food, they broke camp quickly and were on the trail by dawn. They rode steadily, at a good pace, until midmorning, when they paused by the edge of a misted, murky bog to take some bread and cheese, and a sip of wine to give them cheer.

"I'll be glad to get through this place," said Princess with a shudder of mixed distaste and chill, drawing her cloak closer around her against the thin persistent rain.

"We've passed the halfway point."

"It's so dismal," said Princess forlornly. "It's as though everything is *working* at being dismal."

"Actually, this is a branch of the Dismal Bog—where we first met, my dear. Do you remember?"

"I do, Keddie, but I can't work up any sentiment. I'm

sorry, but I'm soaked through and chilled to the bone, and I feel miserable. I can't wait to get home and sit in front of a fire.''

"It won't be long. Just a few more days, and—what was that?"

"Oh, wizards, kindly wizards, good wizards, help me!" wailed a faint tiny voice.

"It came from the bog," said Princess, drawing closer to him.

"A woman's voice, or a child's."

"Imploring us to help."

They peered into the moist grayness that lay like a mantle over the black waters. Nothing moved but slow swirls of mist curling around dead trunks upthrust like splintered bones. No sound came from the depths.

"Wizards, unspell me, I beg you! With my last strength, I plead, I beseech, I supplicate!" said the wee voice suddenly, desperately.

"It sounds weaker," said Princess.

"We can't ignore it. I'm going to go a little way into the bog."

"Keddie, be careful. There's no telling what might lurk beneath the surface, waiting to drag you down to its foul lair."

He hesitated and looked at her thoughtfully. "Thank you, my dear. I hadn't thought of that. Perhaps if I took a good long stick and poked around, I'd—there! Look, over there, by that rock!"

A huge rock, blackened and slick with moisture and dappled with patches of gray-green lichen, loomed at the margin of the bog. Near it, just under the surface of the water, something glowed faintly. The light flickered and faded, and the voice gasped, "Alas, my strength is gone. . . . I am lost!" It sighed, and the light went out.

Heedless of danger, Kedrigern splashed into the black water and the clinging muck. He groped where the light had been, and his hand touched something smooth and warm. He dredged it up and turned to display to Princess a dripping globe of crystal which, warmed by his hands, gave off a feeble glimmer. Wrapping his cloak around it, for greater warmth, he slogged ashore, where he and Princess inspected their find.

Within the crystal globe a tiny figure no bigger than a medium-sized peapod lay huddled in the posture of a fearful child. Her hair was like white gold, her robe seemed woven of spiders' webs, and on her feet were tiny slippers of deep dark red, fashioned each from a single rose petal. Her wings were glittering opalescent ovals the size of a thumbnail.

"What a lovely little creature!" Princess exclaimed, laying her hands on the globe to add their warmth to Kedrigern's.

"It's a tooth fairy," said the wizard.

"How can you tell?"

"She's wearing a little porcelain crown."

"It's a strange place to find a tooth fairy. I wonder what happened to her."

"She's obviously been spelled. A cruel spell, too. She won't last long inside this globe."

"Then let's get her out."

"We shall do so forthwith. I think it's best if you keep the globe, my dear. Just hold it in front of you," said the wizard, relinquishing his hold and drying his fingers on a corner of his cloak.

"You're not going to smash it, are you?"

"Certainly not. Just make it vanish."

Standing before Princess, he placed two fingers on the top of the globe and began to recite the appropriate counterspell. At the last word he gave the globe a sharp tap with his index finger. It disappeared without a sound and the tooth fairy, blinking in surprise, lay in Princess's hands.

"Good wizards, you have saved me!" she cried.

With a bow Kedrigern said, "The tooth fairies were generous to me when I was young. It's a pleasure to be of service. Tell us, who did this cruel thing to you?"

"It was Bertha the Bog-fairy who imprisoned me. She is a cruel and wicked fairy, a disgrace to the rest of us. Do you know her?"

"I know her well," said Princess coldly.

"My wife spent some time as a toad because of a spell cast by Bertha," Kedrigern explained.

"Somehow, Bertha was overlooked when the invitations to my christening were sent out. Instead of writing a note, or complaining to my father, she placed an enchantment on me so that on my eighteenth birthday I turned into a toad. I didn't even have a piece of birthday cake," said Princess with growing anger.

The fairy patted Princess's thumb in a comforting gesture. "That is Bertha's way. She gets nastier and nastier. She demanded that I give the toothache to a prince who had somehow offended her, and when I refused she enclosed me in that awful globe and cast me into the bog."

"You're fortunate Bertha has a poor throwing arm."

"I am indeed, wizard. Fortunate, too, that you came this way and I sensed your presence while strength remained in me. But come, let us flee this place before Bertha learns of your kind deed. She detests kind deeds."

Even as the tooth fairy spoke, Kedrigern and Princess felt a chill added to the chill of the air, and the cold malice of a pair of hate-filled eyes upon them. They looked up, and atop the gray rock they saw someone who could only be Bertha the Bog-fairy. She was no mite, but a full-grown woman. Like all fairies, she was bright and resplendent, delicate in limb and feature; but there was an alarming coldness in her emerald eyes, and a threatening edge to her sweet voice.

"And who is this who interferes with my spell?" she demanded.

With a flourish and a sweeping bow, the wizard said, "I am Kedrigern of Silent Thunder Mountain."

"The name is not unknown to me. You are a wizard, are you not?"

"I am."

"And that baggage with you—is she your servant, or some trollop you found at the last inn?"

"Trollop?! Listen, you malevolent crone—" Princess began.

"Mind your tongue, wench!"

"Mind your own, hag!"

"Now, ladies, no need to get upset," said Kedrigern in a calm, friendly voice, raising his hands in a pacific gesture, smiling upon both.

"I'm not the least bit upset, Keddie. Who'd be upset by this old bag of wrinkles with her worn-out spells?" said Princess coolly. "And I'm sure she's not upset. After all, at her age . . ."

Bertha drew a wand from the sleeve of her shining gown. "It will be a great pleasure to turn you into a toad, you saucy jade," she said.

Princess's smile was sweet and solicitous. "You've already tried that, and it didn't stick. Don't you remember, you poor old thing? Or is your memory as weak as your throwing arm?"

"I do not clutter my memory with trifles, drab. But since you have already been a toad, I will not make you one again. *You* shall become a toad," said Bertha, pointing her wand at Kedrigern, "and your black-haired slattern will become . . . a grub. Yes, a grub will do nicely."

She gave the wand a slight flick. A shower of light burst about the wizard, faded, and left him standing with arms folded, smiling good-naturedly.

"It won't work, Bertha. We're safe from your magic."

"Do you think so, wizard? Do you really think a protective spell can save you from my anger?"

"I know some pretty good protective spells, Bertha."

"You forget that this is *my* bog. The waters obey me, and the muck obeys me, and all the creatures that dwell herein do my bidding. The winds blow where I direct them, wizard, and the waters rise and fall, and the mud sucks down. A thousand hungry mouths wait at my command," said Bertha, her voice rising. "Do you think you can withstand them all? Better for you if you had been turned into a toad, for now you will be annihilated!'' She raised her arms. The wand flashed, and the still black waters began to churn; the ground squirmed beneath their feet; the mist seethed and curled and congealed into grisly shapes that flowed toward them, groping with vaporous spidery fingers.

Kedrigern reached out for Princess's hand. ''This is going to take everything we've got,'' he whispered.

''Will it be enough?''

He hesitated. An honest answer would surely dampen Princess's self-confidence in this moment of crisis, and yet he felt obliged to tell her the full extent of their danger: notoriously cruel as she was, Bertha's power far exceeded her cruelty. Here in the heart of her domain, where all things were subject to her will, she would be at the height of her power. They were in for a bad time.

''Well, will it?'' Princess pressed.

He drew a deep breath, and was about to reply with the bleak and disheartening truth, when Bertha let out a wild howl and clapped her hands to her cheeks. She lost her balance and toppled over backwards, still howling, to land with a murky *sploosh* in the bog. Her wand flew through the air and landed at Kedrigern's feet. All around them became as before, and a deep silence settled on the bog, broken only by an occasional groan from the far side of the big gray rock.

''Of course it will, my dear,'' Kedrigern said casually.

As he squeezed Princess's hand and smiled reassurance, the tooth fairy circled their heads, laughing and clapping her tiny hands in childlike glee. She perched on Kedrigern's shoulder and tugged at his earlobe.

''I got all her back molars at once!'' she announced proudly.

''Your timing was perfect,'' Kedrigern said.

Bertha, soaked from head to foot and smeared with black muck, splashed around the rock and began groping wildly in the water. She paused only to shake her fist and bare her teeth in a snarl, then bent to resume her task. Kedrigern stooped, picked up her wand, and held it before him.

"Looking for this?" he asked.

"Yes! That's mine, you thief! Give it to me!" Bertha shrieked.

"Not on your life, old girl."

"I want it! I want my wand! I want my power! I demand it!"

"Demand away, Bertha. It's all up with you."

Bertha waved her fists, sending spray and droplets of muck in a wide circle. "I'll get even! My revenge will be terrible!"

"I wouldn't raise the subject of revenge if I were in your position, Bertha. It might give people ideas."

She looked at the wizard closely. For the first time, her voice softened, and the baleful glint of her green eyes was replaced by a look of uncertainty. "Ideas? What kind of ideas? What do you mean, wizard?"

"Well, if Princess were a vindictive person, she might decide to turn you into . . . oh, into a . . ."

"Into a toad," Princess said to complete the thought. "A fat, ugly toad, with nothing to look forward to but the next fly."

"Do it, do it! Make her a toad!" cried the tooth fairy, clapping her hands and flickering brilliantly in her enthusiasm.

Bertha's eyes widened. She staggered backward and came up hard against the rock. In a low, frightened voice she said, "No. Not a toad. I don't want to be a toad!"

"*Nobody* wants to be a toad," said Princess, her voice the voice of doom.

"She deserves it! Make her a toad, quick!" the tooth fairy urged.

Princess raised her hand and pointed at the cowering bog-fairy. Bertha paled and shrank back against the unyielding rock. Princess's hand wavered and drooped. Slowly shaking her head, she turned to the wizard. "I can't do it,

Keddie. She *does* deserve it! She deserves it so much it
gives me a headache just to think about it, but I can't make
myself be as nasty as she is, no matter how much she
deserves it!'' Her eyes were bright with tears of sheer
frustration.

"My wife is merciful. You're very lucky, Bertha,'' said
the wizard.

"What will I do without my wand?''

"I would suggest either a complete change of heart or
an immediate change of address. Once the news gets
about, others may not be so compassionate.''

"I'm not compassionate,'' the tooth fairy announced.
"I'm furious. It was awful in that globe. I'm bringing her
up before the next High Tribunal. Queen Mab will fix
her.''

"Mab? Do you think you'll drag me before Mab?''
Bertha laughed scornfully. "You're nothing but an insig-
nificant little tooth fairy. What makes you think that you
can—'' Bertha straightened up, covered her mouth, and
emitted a muffled groan of pain.

"Move along, you big clumsy muck-sprite! We're going
to Queen Mab right now! Come on, hop it!'' barked the
tooth fairy. She flew from Kedrigern's shoulder, gave a
wave of farewell, and faded to a dot of light receding
down the path at the back of the wailing Bertha.

Kedrigern turned to Princess and extended the wand.
"Happy anniversary, my dear,'' he said.

"How sweet! And exactly the right size, too. It's almost
as if . . . but you couldn't possibly have planned. . . .
Tell the truth now: did you?''

He gestured carelessly, gave a little enigmatic smile,
and looked up at the sky. "The drizzle has stopped, and
the sky is clearing. We'll have good traveling weather the
rest of the way.''

"Don't be evasive.''

"My dear, I'm being modest. Shall we ride?''

*   *   *

The remaining days of travel under a clear bright sky were pleasant but uneventful, and they returned home one afternoon to an exuberant welcome from Spot. The little house-troll prepared a lavish dinner, which they accompanied with Vosconu's finest wines. The first snow began to fall just as Spot cleared away, and they looked out at the fat slow flakes from the coziness of their table, smiling contentedly at one another and on all the world.

Seated before the fire that evening, a chronicle open in his lap, Kedrigern felt a great sense of peace. Princess sat at the other side of the fire, studying an introduction to wand-wielding. A tankard of good wine stood on the table at the wizard's side. The fire muttered and crackled, giving off exactly the right amount of heat for perfect comfort.

His travels were over, and it would be long before anyone or anything got him off silent Thunder Mountain again. One could accomplish a bit of good here and there while traveling and do a worthy deed now and then, it was true; but on the whole, one could accomplish a great deal more in the quiet comfort of one's own study, and avoid the muck and murk and mist and mire of the road as well. There were no brigands, or wicked fairies, or cranky dragons, or riddling giants, or selfish princesses, or any other such hazards of the wayfaring life in a study, except those safely confined between the covers of a book. There were in a study no foods of uncertain provenance, unhealthy color, and unpalatable taste; no thieving innkeepers overcharging for beds filled with tiny hungry life and stuffed with sharp-edged gravel and covered with grimy bristly linen; no pallid, grease-scummed, throat-searing wine; no fleas, flies, mites, or midges; in short, none of the pains of peregrination or the torments of travel. The study was for the civilized, the road for the barbaric. He thought of the pleasant hours ahead, sighed with contentment, and reached for his tankard.

"You sound quite pleased, Keddie," Princess observed.

"I am, my dear. It's good to be home."

"It certainly is. Especially with the snow falling."

He murmured agreement and sipped his wine. Princess turned a page. The fire rustled softly and settled, glowing sudden red.

"A cozy house, a good fire, pleasant company, fine wine . . . and you have your wand. We've got everything anyone could wish," Kedrigern said.

"We're very lucky," Princess said absently.

"Extremely lucky. Why, there's no need for us to stir from here ever again. What could we possibly desire?"

Princess shut her book and hitched herself up in her chair as if she had been given a long-awaited cue. She held up her hand, and ticking off a finger at each new item, she began, "For one thing, a wishing ring. A claock of invisibility would be useful, too, especially a good warm one. And I'd love one of those magic cloths that you only have to spread on a table and it's all set with the finest dishes and crystal and silverware, and superbly prepared delicacies and wines to suit the most demanding palate, and then when you're all done it cleans everything up and tidies the room. That would make it so easy to entertain." She paused, then turned down a fourth finger, saying, "One of those purses you can never empty, the ones that always have a gold piece in them no matter how many you spend, would be very useful when we travel."

"But, my dear . . . travel?"

"Well, not in this snowstorm. Maybe not until spring. But surely you don't want to spend the rest of your life on Silent Thunder Mountain."

"Actually . . . ," he began, but curbed his tongue. Princess's question had clearly been rhetorical; and in any event, it was not one to which he could give an honest answer without placing a strain on the tranquility of the evening.

Princess seemed not to have heard his curtailed response. Turning down her little finger, she proceeded. "A magic spinning wheel and loom and scissors and needle would come in very handy. That chest of clothing your friend left for me is quite tasteful and stylish, and I do

appreciate it, but I'd like something new . . . after all,
it's been nearly three years since I've had a new outfit.''

"You always look lovely," Kedrigern said hopefully.

"Thank you, Keddie. A woman does want a change
now and then, though. Oh, and of course you could get us
each a pair of seven-league boots. They'd save us ever so
much time when we travel. We both know how you dislike
travel, and the boots would make things much nicer. And
a comb that turns into a forest when you throw it on the
ground—to foil pursuers, you know—and a mirror that
turns into a glass mountain, and . . . oh, lots of things,
Keddie.''

"Yes, I see," he replied faintly. "Funny . . . I thought
the only thing you wanted was a wand.''

"It was. But now I *have* a wand.''

"Yes. So you do.''

"And there'll be all those future anniversaries. Now
you'll know what to get. You can surprise me, year after
year.''

He looked into the fire and nodded. Wishing rings and
magic tablecloths. Cloaks of invisibility. Enchanted furniture and utensils. Seven-league boots. Clearly, she wanted
to turn him into a nomad, a wanderer, constantly flitting
back and forth over the earth, never spending more than a
few hours in his study before dashing off on some new
escapade. He shuddered at the prospect.

"My dear, have you thought how useful a nice pair of
knitted wing-covers would be?" he asked.

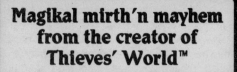